"A magnificent novel, one of those novels that is so good that I wish I hadn't read it yet, but still had it left to discover." —*Sydsvenskan* (Sweden)

"A dazzlingly well-turned book . . . With her new novel, Linn Ullmann shows that she has a piercing eye for present-day family life in the Nordic countries like few other contemporary writers."
—Kathrine Lilleør, *Berlingske* (Denmark)

"Although her language sparkles and shines, although she has a ruthless eye for human failings, although she succeeds in imparting something vital to the vilest of relationships, I would still claim that Linn Ullmann's strength lies in her structural command . . . Her distinctive quality as a writer is quite simply—grace. And there is nothing simple about that."
—Jan Arnald, *Dagens Nyheter* (Sweden)

"A novel that makes you want to drop everything else. A highlight of the spring season." —RBB Kulturradio (Germany)

"Magnificently told by flashing back and forward in time, the novel is bleak, sad, emotional, and highly exciting."
—*Berliner Morgenpost* (Germany)

"Some authors simply write well. Some characters just come to life. Some forms of discomfort, lies, and deception are given just the right distance and protection by two hard covers to be able to confront them. Linn Ullmann's precise and distinctive prose is the stuff that makes a novel come alive."
—Andreas Wiese, *Dagbladet*, Best Books of the Year 2011 (Norway)

"*The Cold Song* is fascinating, dense, profound."
—Maria Laura Giovagnini, *Io Donna* (Italy)

"Psychologically sophisticated, captivating entertainment."

—*Elle* (Germany)

"Reading *The Cold Song* was an unforgettable experience. The novel is a remarkably composed puzzle, where the fragmented structure is not an experiment in deconstructing the traditional novel form. *The Cold Song* is an ingenious game with structural elements. The characters . . . are real human beings and the depiction of their pain and sorrow serve as . . . an attempt at a healing process."

—ekultura.hu (Hungary)

"*The Cold Song* is an intense and unsettling read."

—Kultblog.hu (Hungary)

"Linn Ullmann condenses soft sounds, small gestures, and poetry into a splendid novel about the abyss of normality."

—*Petra* (Germany)

"Compellingly told and thoroughly composed down to the most detailed ramifications."

—*Schweiz am Sonntag* (Germany)

"Compelling. All the way to the last page."

—Constanze Alt, *Ostthüringer Zeitung* (Germany)

"A skillfully constructed, exciting book about all that is kept secret in a family."

—*Westdeutsche Allgemeine Zeitung* (Germany)

"A magnificent, psychologically profound family novel that shows how minor lapses, secrets, and repressed desires can cause a major tragedy."

—*Annabelle* (Switzerland)

"Ullmann writes about human relationships with near psychological X-ray vision . . . Sentences are often gossamer light, but just as often bitingly acerbic and filled with complex emotions. Her choice of words take the reader by surprise . . . *The Cold Song* is a complex novel that shows how quickly things can disintegrate when one doesn't pay attention . . . No matter how unpleasant the book may be to read (and it frequently is), one wishes to be part of Ullmann's universe. Perhaps because she describes us all too well . . . Ullmann is compassionate and empathic, with a big heart for all of her characters. She scrutinizes the most wretched and painful sides of our existence, holding them up to the light and pressing our tender spots with her gentle touch."

—Ellen Sofie Lauritzen, *Dagsavisen*, Best Books of the Year 2011 (Norway)

"The poignant and powerful story of a family . . . *The Cold Song* is the story of a dysfunctional family stumbling on, day by day . . . Shrouded in mystery, furtive, enigmatic. I, at least, found it difficult to put the book down . . . left tears in my eyes. Ullmann penetrates the vile, painful, and raw problems and challenges of human relations, and she does it with expertise. Pitch-black humor is one of her devices, and it is blacker in this novel than ever before."

—Bjarne Tveiten, *Fedrelandsvennen*, Best Books of the Year 2011 (Norway)

"*The Cold Song* shows novelist Linn Ullmann at her very best."

—Geir Vestad, *Hamar Arbeiderblad*, Best Books of the Year 2011 (Norway)

"Linn Ullmann has written a great and insightful novel . . . Every character is described with empathy and blindsiding psychological perception, with a story that is skillfully composed."

—Johannes H. Christensen, *Jyllands-Posten* (Denmark)

"Linn Ullmann is a master at letting people and events hover and tremble between reality and something else . . . Has Linn Ullmann ever been so viciously funny as she is here? . . . *The Cold Song* has breadth, but also a compelling Nordic gravity."   —Lise Garsdal, *Politiken* (Denmark)

"Masterfully written about fragile love, deception, and guilt, and about the difficult art of protecting what is most precious."

—*Uppsala Nya Tidning* (Sweden)

"[Ullmann] is a skillful writer . . . If one were to perceive traces of a literary inheritance, contemporaries such as Siri Hustvedt and Joyce Carol Oates, or classic authors such as Virginia Woolf, would immediately come to mind."   —*Västerbottens-Kuriren* (Sweden)

"A terrifying novel that is difficult to put down . . . Ullmann combines keen everyday observations with an obscure crime, but the dialogues also pose a number of recurring philosophical questions. Where is the border between a lie and a narrative? . . . an alternately riveting, humorous, and thought-provoking novel that captivates."

—Bjørn Gabrielsen, *Dagens Næringsliv* (Norway)

"Like a detective story, the young girl's fate is slowly revealed and the intensity increases. Not one word or phrase seems redundant, the words flow easily between the pages with exceptional precision. Almost understated, with bizarre and humorous undertones, we are drawn into an Ullmannesque universe that we don't want to leave."

—Anja Rålm, *VG,* six out of six points (Norway)

"Linn Ullmann casts a wonderfully caustic eye on human flaws . . . With elegant circular movements Ullmann writes her way into all that one cannot talk about in a family . . . Grief is rude and defiant in *The Cold Song*, giving the story a uniquely odious power. The novel also presents delightful reprises in which Ullmann revisits scenes, formulations, and memories, lending rhythm to the text and showing that there is no definitive ending to the story of a life . . . [Ullmann] stands more in the tradition of the great bourgeois novel (Balzac, Stendhal, Lagerlöf) . . . A trace of Virginia Woolf can be heard in *The Cold Song* . . . easy and compelling, [Ullmann] dissects human weakness, grief, and pain."

—Margunn Vikingstad, *Dag og Tid* (Norway)

"In this book, Ullmann brilliantly exploits the full spectrum of possibilities offered by the polyphonic novel . . . *The Cold Song* is a poignant novel about silence, ingeniously composed with open spaces."

—Gro Jørstad Nilsen, *Bergens Tidend* (Norway)

"The story of a family, in a class of its own."

—Sølvi Wærhaug, *VG,* Best Books of the Year 2011 (Norway)

"Linn Ullmann's *The Cold Song* is a sophisticated psychological thriller."

—*Göteborgs-Posten* (Sweden)

Praise for *A Blessed Child*

"With a light touch and tremendous empathy, Ullmann ranges among the perspectives of the three daughters . . . Ullmann's sentences . . . are a pleasure to read and her deft modern sensibility is winning."   —*New York Times*

"Linn Ullmann's *A Blessed Child* is a like a fine, long evening of light. There are all sorts of colors on the horizon, and even when the darkness becomes visible, there is still a place to turn to. This is a book for fathers and daughters, and for anyone who's beguiled by the country of family. The language is clear and runs deep. The story is profound and touching. Together, they announce another great storytelling feat by Linn Ullmann. She reminds me of Berger, of Aciman, of Tóibín: no greater praise."
                    —Colum McCann, author of *Let the Great World Spin*

"Ullmann excels just as much as a satirist as a psychologist . . . passages here carry faint echoes of Virginia Woolf's *To the Lighthouse* on the Baltic breeze . . . First affecting, then alarming, sometimes acerbically comic, *A Blessed Child* has an exhilarating candor and clarity in its grasp of family, period, and place."
                    —Boyd Tonkin, literary editor, *Independent on Sunday* (UK)

Praise for *Grace*

"Ullmann's mesmerizing, spare novel is a robust yet delicate account of that most prosaic, mysterious event of all. Comparable to Philip Roth's magisterial Everyman, the humor is drier, the poignancy more overt, yet it is equally, quietly impressive."   —Cathrine Taylor, *The Guardian*

"A delicate, haunting portrait of a fainthearted man trying his best to meet the end of life—and love—with a modicum of dignity and, yes, grace."   —Bruce Bawer, *New York Times Book Review*

Praise for *Stella Descending*

"Exquisitely written . . . As hallucinatory as August heat."
                                —*Washington Post*

"[Ullman]'s gift is for weaving the banal details of love, career, and family with the mystic world of dreams and ghosts into one seamless fabric . . . The hypnotic allure of the story adds to the reader's eagerness to return to Stella and share the enigma of her final flight."

—*New York Times Book Review*

"Weird and wonderful . . . Ullmann has effortlessly established a distinct literary voice." —*Elle*

"Magical in its imagery . . . Extraordinary." —*Boston Globe*

"Surrealistic . . . in the original 1920s sense: as a work of art that blurs the borders between mundane reality and the reality of fantasies and dreams . . . Where Ullmann differs is in her humor . . . her snappy prose and cheeky attitude." —*Los Angeles Times Book Review*

"Exquisite . . . The atmosphere and taut pacing make this an icily swift read, one whose chill lingers longer than a Scandinavian winter."

—*Entertainment Weekly*

Praise for *Before You Sleep*

"A perceptive and sparkling new creation."

—*New York Times Book Review*

"The gift Ullmann gives her readers is her intelligence and wisdom about desire, love, and motherhood, and scene after scene of poignant, prickly prose." —*Boston Globe Sunday*

"Her storytelling skills and sheer joy in performance shine on every page."

—*Vogue*

"Strikingly original . . . Reading this indelibly etched portrait of a family in crisis should keep many a reader awake, trying to finish it in one sitting before falling into their own restless sleep." —*Seattle Times*

THE
COLD
SONG

THE
COLD
SONG

LINN ULLMANN

TRANSLATED FROM THE NORWEGIAN
BY BARBARA J. HAVELAND

OTHER PRESS
New York

Production Editor: Yvonne E. Cárdenas
Text Designer: Chris Welch and Andreas Gurewich
Illustrations by Andreas G and Gary R
This book was set in 11.5 pt Granjon by
Alpha Design & Composition of Pittsfield, NH.

1 3 5 7 9 10 8 6 4 2

LIBRARY OF CONGRESS CATALOGING-IN-PUBLICATION DATA

Ullmann, Linn, 1966–
[Dyrebare. English]
The cold song : a novel / by Linn Ullmann ; translated from the Norwegian
by Barbara J. Haveland.
pages cm
"Originally published in Norwegian as Det dyrebare by Forlaget Oktober, Oslo, in 2011."
ISBN 978-1-59051-667-6 (pbk.) — ISBN 978-1-59051-668-3 (e-book)
1. Young women—Crimes against—Fiction.   2. Murder—Fiction.   3. Families—
Fiction.   4. Norway—Fiction.   5. Psychological fiction. I. Haveland, Barbara,
translator. II. Title.
PT8951.31.L56D9713 2014
839.82'374—dc23
2013025382

For Niels

'Tis Love that has warm'd us?

—JOHN DRYDEN

JENNY BRODAL HAD not had a drink in nearly twenty years. She opened a bottle of Cabernet and poured herself a large glass. She had imagined the warmth filtering down into her stomach, the tingling in her fingertips, but there was none of that, no warmth, no tingling, nothing, so she drained the glass and waited. Surely there would be something. Jenny looked at the open bottle on her bedside table. She had never said never! She had taken one day at a time, *one day at a time*, and never, *never*, said never.

She was in her bedroom, sitting on the edge of her large four-poster bed, almost done now. She'd put on her makeup, she'd put on a dress. She still had on thick, gray woolly socks, the ones that Irma had knitted. She looked at her feet. They looked twice as big in those socks and they were still cold, despite the socks. There was also the lump on the side of her right big toe, she could feel it, sometimes red, sometimes purple, sometimes blue, and she dreaded taking off the socks and thrusting her feet into her slender, high-heeled sandals.

She looked at the shoes, paired up like well-behaved children on the floor by her bed. Such pretty shoes, the color of nectarines, from the sixties, she remembered the store where she had bought them. Jenny poured herself another glass. The trick was to get the wine right down to her feet. She had never said never. She had said one day at a time.

For one, she would have to give a speech. There were other things too. Jenny recalled a list of very good reasons she had given for not wanting to go through with this celebration, which was the word everyone kept insisting on using, and then she tried to remember why nobody had listened to her.

Jenny stood up; twirled in front of the mirror on the wall. The black dress fit beautifully over her breasts. Yes. And her cheeks flushed rather nicely. And everything was ready. Soon, after one more glass, she would take off her socks and put on the sandals.

It was the fifteenth of July 2008 and Jenny's seventy-fifth birthday. Mailund, the big white mansion-like house where she had grown up after the war, was filled with flowers. She had lived in this house almost all her life, in good times and bad, and now forty-seven guests dressed in their summer finery were on their way here to salute her.

I

THE
TREASURE

MILLA, OR WHAT was left of her, was found by Simen and two of his friends when they were digging for buried treasure in the woods. They didn't know what it was they had found. But they knew it wasn't the treasure. It was the opposite of treasure. Later, when asked to explain to the police and their parents why they had been in the woods, Simen found this hard to do. Why had they started digging in that *particular* clearing? Under that *particular* tree? And what exactly had they been looking for?

Two years earlier, in July 2008, everyone had been out searching for Milla. Far and wide, over land and sea, in ditches and trenches, in the sand hills out on the point and all around the forbidding cliffs, in the pile of rubble behind the old school and in the empty, tumbledown houses at the end of Brage Road where grass grew out of the windows and no child was allowed to go. Simen remembered scouring every inch of town, thinking she might just be hiding somewhere waiting to be found, and that maybe if he looked really hard, he'd be the one to find her.

Everyone had searched for Milla, even the boy known as K.B., the one who was later arrested and charged with her murder, searched for her, and for two years she had lain buried under that tree in the woods, unfound, covered by dirt and grass and moss and twigs and stones until she had almost turned to dirt herself, all except for her skull and bits of bones and her teeth and the long dark hair, which was no longer long and dark, but wispy and withered, as if it had been yanked up out of the ditch, roots and all.

That summer when she went missing, Simen thought he saw her everywhere: She was the face in the shopwindow, the head bobbing in the waves, the long dark hair of some unknown woman fluttering in the breeze. Once Milla had looked at him and laughed, she had been real, like him, like his bike, but then she was a veil of night and frost that sometimes slipped through him and swept happiness away.

He never forgot her. In the two years she lay buried, he'd think about her when he couldn't sleep or when autumn was coming and the air smelled of cordite, damp and withered leaves, but at some point he had stopped looking for her and no longer believed that he would be the one to find her.

Simen was the youngest of the three boys. The other two were Gunnar and Christian. It was a Saturday at the end of October 2010 and the three friends were spending one last weekend together. The time had come to close down the summer houses for the winter and for their little seaside town a couple of hours south of Oslo to curl in on its own darkness. It was afternoon, not quite five o'clock, the light was already beginning to fade, and the boys had decided to locate and dig up a treasure they had buried some months earlier.

Gunnar and Christian couldn't see the point in leaving it in the ground forever. Simen didn't agree. As far as he was concerned that was *exactly* the point—that was what made it treasure. It was concealed from everyone except them and was a thousand times more valuable *in* the ground than *above* the ground. He couldn't explain why, he just knew that's how it was.

But neither Gunnar nor Christian even tried to understand what Simen was talking about. They just thought he was being a fool, they wanted their stuff back, *their* contributions, *their* part of the treasure, they really didn't give a shit about the treasure as treasure, so eventually Simen said it was fine by him, why didn't they just go out there in the forest right now and dig it up, he didn't care.

The story of the treasure had begun some months earlier, in August 2010, when Gunnar, the eldest of the three friends, suggested that they become blood brothers. The light was warm and red, and everything in that small town was lusher than ever on this particular evening, as things tend to be when summer is almost over. Soon they would be going their separate ways, back to the city where they lived far apart and called other boys their friends.

Gunnar had taken a deep breath and said, "Mixing blood is a symbol of eternal friendship."

The other two boys had balked at this, the thought of slashing the skin of your palm with a piece of glass from a broken Coca-Cola bottle was not something you would want to do, not even in the interest of eternal friendship; and even if you were mainly given to kicking a soccer ball about and using your legs, you did actually need your hands too—Simen tried to say this, but couldn't find the right words—needed them for all sorts of things, without bloody cuts and scratches, but how did you tell Gunnar without ruining everything, without being accused of being a coward?

They were sitting on the deck outside their secret cottage in the woods, the one they had built the previous summer. They had lit a fire and grilled hot dogs, eaten chips, and had some Coke; they were all Liverpool fans, so they had plenty to talk about; they sang songs too, because there was no one there to hear them, *Walk on, walk on, with hope in your heart*, and Simen had thought to himself that when you sang that song you felt like your life really was about to begin. But then Gunnar— and this was typical Gunnar—had started talking about how just because they spent their summers together that didn't necessarily mean they were *true* friends. True friends who were there for each other through thick and thin. Gunnar knew a guy who had supported Liverpool for years, and then he had suddenly switched to Manchester United, just because his new neighbor was a fan of Manchester United. *And what the fuck do you do with a guy like that? Is that a true friend?* And Gunnar had launched into a long and complicated speech about blood and pain and true friendship and other things he had obviously been thinking a lot about over the summer, concluding with this very dramatic idea that they become blood brothers. He had come prepared, had it all planned out—that too was just like Gunnar. The bits of broken glass were neatly wrapped in tinfoil—he had broken the bottle in the back garden at home and then washed the shards with dishwashing liquid because, said Gunnar, if you cut your hand with a dirty bit of broken

glass you might die, you might get blood poisoning and die—
and he had placed the lumpy little package between them in
the sunlight and carefully folded back the foil, as if it were diamonds he had in there, or scorpions.

And that was the moment when Christian came up with
the idea of burying treasure instead—as a symbol of true and
everlasting friendship. It was simple: All three of them would
have to offer up one thing, and that thing had to be precious, it
had to be a sacrifice. No mingling of blood, no cuts or grazes,
but stuff, *valuable* stuff, buried deep in the ground, as a symbol of their commitment to each other, to friendship, and to
Liverpool F.C.

They counted steps. When not on their bikes, they counted
steps. From Simen's house to Gunnar's house, from Gunnar's
house to Christian's house, from Christian's house to Simen's
house, from the top of the road, where Jenny Brodal's house,
old and ghostly white, hovered just above the ground, to the
bottom of the road where Simen's parents' summer cottage lay
partly hidden by a worn blue picket fence.

In Christian's parents' garden, located just sixty steps from
Jenny Brodal's house and four hundred and fifty-two steps
from Simen's parents' cottage, there was a shed. In the shed
there was an old light blue tin pail with a lid that Christian's
mother had picked up in a secondhand shop some years earlier. The pail was dented; it had sun-bleached, hand-painted
pictures of cows and pretty milkmaids on it, and on one side
the words: *Milk—nature's most nearly perfect food*. Christian
told Simen and Gunnar how his father had been mad all day

because of that pail, his father couldn't see the sense in spending two hundred kroner on something so stupid, and then Christian's mother had gotten twice as mad and said well, if his father had just built that terrace out from their bedroom door (as he'd been promising to do for years) she could have dressed it up with troughs and pots and climbing roses and cushions and throws—and she would put flowers in the pail. They could have had their own little Italian veranda. "What the fuck is an Italian veranda," Christian's father had said then.

"I don't know what an Italian veranda is," Christian said, and Simen and Gunnar had nodded, meaning they didn't know either, but they got the idea. They all had parents with stuff going on. The tin pail had been part of Christian's mother's great plan. But the terrace, Italian or otherwise, did not get built, not that year and not the year after either, so now the pail was tucked away at the back of the shed, partly hidden behind a broken lawnmower.

"The pail can be our treasure chest," Christian said.

The point in burying treasure was never to unearth it. Never. You know it's there. You know where it is. You know how many steps you have to walk to get there or how many minutes it takes on your bike. You know how precious it is and how much you sacrificed when you chose to bury it and never see it again. And you can never speak of it to anyone, ever.

"But," said Simen, Christian had to come up with something to put *in* the pail too. Christian had to make a *sacrifice*.

Simen felt uncomfortable uttering that word—*sacrifice*—it was a stupid word. Something a girl might say, or a woman, not an eleven-year-old boy. Uttering it made him think of Alma, Jenny Brodal's weird black-haired granddaughter, and how she, a few years earlier, had asked him into her room, told him to bend over, and then proceeded to brush his hair one long stroke after the other, one, two, three, four, five, six, seven, eight, nine strokes, she went on brushing forever, her weird little voice counting every stroke, "so that your hair will shine," she'd said, "and for this you must make sacrifices."

So that his hair would *fucking shine.*

"Brush your own hair," he had said when she wanted to do it again the next day, and she had said no, his hair was way longer than hers and shone more beautifully. And he, stupid little boy, had bent over and let her do it again. Anyway, the pail itself wasn't a *sacrifice*, Simen said. Hadn't Christian's grandmother just given him two hundred and fifty kroner? He ought to offer up at least two hundred of that. Gunnar nodded and made a mumbling sound indicating that he agreed with Simen. But no. Christian didn't want to give up his money, even though—even though!—the treasure had been his idea and he was the one who had said that their offerings all had to be *valuable, precious, priceless,* yes, he had used all those words, and even though he was the one who said they had to make a *sacrifice*. Simen and Gunnar both felt it wasn't enough to say that the tin pail itself was his contribution to the treasure. That wasn't a *sacrifice*. The pail wasn't a part of the treasure, the pail was the treasure chest. Only it wasn't a chest, it was a pail. If the truth be told (and, as Gunnar pointed out, this *was* the moment of truth), Christian didn't have anything of value *except* the money from his grandmother.

"This is not a game," Simen said.

"Well, it's kind of a game," Christian retorted, knowing already that he had to give up the money. "So okay, take it," he said.

And when it came to Gunnar there was no doubt what his offering ought to be. On this point Simen and Christian were in complete agreement. Gunnar had to sacrifice his Liverpool F.C. autograph book.

A few months earlier Gunnar had been to Liverpool with his big brother, who was twenty-two. They had spent a whole weekend there, stayed in a hotel, and gone to see a Champions League match between Liverpool and Tottenham.

Gunnar's big brother wasn't a real big brother, even though Gunnar was always going on about *my big brother* this and *my big brother* that. Gunnar's big brother was only a *half brother*, he was Gunnar's father's son from an earlier marriage and Gunnar didn't really see him all that often. Gunnar's father was a dentist, so was his mother, they had bought a summer house just down the street from Jenny Brodal's house. Gunnar's big brother was not really around that much, he was a grown-up and had his own life. Simen and Christian had seen him only once—the previous summer—when Gunnar had pointed him out. But that's how it was with Gunnar's family members. Simen and Christian hadn't actually met any of them, rather they had been pointed out. See, there's my big brother drinking beer with his friends and there's my father going out for a run again, and there's my mother in her garden, *my father has no idea she's doing it with weird Alma's father right under his nose*, and there are our dogs, they are my father's dogs, really, not like regular family dogs that you hang out with, they either lie very still in the backyard or go running with my father.

Steven Gerrard, Fernando Torres, and Jamie Carragher were just some of the players who had signed their names in Gunnar's autograph book. But that was not the autograph book's most precious feature. Simen knew that. Carefully glued to the last page was a photograph of Gunnar and his big brother outside Anfield Stadium; they were both wearing Liverpool scarves and his big brother was almost six foot six, with broad shoulders and long brown hair falling over his face; Gunnar looked a real daddy longlegs next to him. Under the picture in blue biro were the words: *To the world's greatest little brother: some people believe soccer is a matter of life and death, you and I know that it is much more important than that.*

Simen knew that Gunnar didn't want to put the autograph book in the pail. The two hundred kroner from Christian's grandmother was one thing, Gunnar's Liverpool autograph book was quite another. Forcing him to part with it was maybe asking too much, thought Simen. Christian's grandmother gave her grandson money all the time, but Gunnar's big brother hardly ever (or rather, never, apart from this once) took Gunnar to Liverpool to see a Champions League match. And how often did you get a chance to collect Steven Gerrard's, Fernando Torres's, and Jamie Carragher's autographs?

Gunnar, who was the skinniest of the three and whose family members were only pointed out and whose mother was doing it with weird Alma's father, had been close to tears when he promised the other two that he would offer up the autograph book and Simen almost said *Let's just forget about the whole thing.* But he didn't.

Instead he said, "I know what I'm putting in the pail."

He was the only one left and he wanted to show Gunnar and Christian that he too was prepared to make a sacrifice. *Bend over and I'll make your hair shine.*

Simen's mother had a small gold chain with a little diamond crucifix on it. His father had given it to her for Christmas two and a half years ago. Simen had gone with him to the jeweler's to buy it and had almost passed out when he heard how many thousands it cost. It was supposed to be partly from him too and it was supposed to make his mother really happy. He didn't know if it had worked, paying all those thousands to make his mother happy. His mother was the same after Christmas as she had been before Christmas. Simen had wondered whether to ask his father if it had been worth it. But he didn't. And now he had this whole other idea.

Every night before his mother went to bed she took off the necklace and put it in a blue bowl in the bathroom. He just had to wait until everyone was asleep—it would be the easiest thing in the world. No one would suspect him. Simen was not the kind of kid who stole stuff. His mother would be upset, she would turn the whole summer house upside down, searching for her diamond necklace, but she would never suspect him.

Gunnar and Christian stared at each other and then at Simen.

"How much did it cost, exactly?" Christian asked.

"Thousands. Seventeen, maybe."

"Shut up," said Christian. "You're lying."

"Well, if they're real diamonds," Gunnar said, "then it's possible. Diamonds are very expensive."

Christian considered this.

"Okay then," he said, fixing his eyes on Simen. "You get that necklace!"

The following evening they combed the woods, raced their bikes along the narrow, winding woodland tracks under the bright treetops, looking for the perfect spot in which to bury the pail. They rode past the green forest lake where, years and years ago, two little children had drowned. It was Alma from up the road at Mailund, exactly five hundred and sixty-seven steps from Simen's house, who had told Simen about the drowning in the woods. Alma was a few years older than Simen and had occasionally been paid by his mother to look after him for an hour or two. That was years ago, though. He looked after himself now. But a long time ago, before he even knew Gunnar and Christian. When he was little. Five, six, seven, eight years old. He was eleven now. When Simen grew up and had children he would never pay girls like Alma to look after them. Under no circumstances would he leave his future children with someone like her, not even for free. She was weird and dark-eyed and treated him like a doll and told stories, some true, some not, and he could never be sure which were which. The story about the children drowning in the green lake was probably true, he thought. Most of it anyway. The boy had drowned while the girl watched, and the mother of the two children had been so stricken with grief that she snatched the girl from her bed and drowned her as well.

"She must have loved the son more than the daughter," whispered Alma.

Alma and Simen on the edge of the lake, gazing across the sun-warmed water, each clutching a slice of apple cake and a plastic cup of red lemonade. It was Alma's mother who had packed them a lunch, but Alma didn't like red lemonade so she tipped it all into the lake. Alma's mother's name was Siri. She had a habit of stroking Simen's hair, saying, "Hi, Simen, how are you today?"

Alma continued, in that whispering voice of hers, to tell her story. "The little boy fell in the water and drowned while his sister just stood there and watched, and when the girl came home without her little brother, her mother didn't know what to do with herself. She cried and cried and cried, and no one could stay in the house because of all the crying. The girl put her hands over her ears and cried too. But her mother didn't care. Or maybe she did care, but she didn't listen. Then one night the mother went very quiet. And then the girl went very quiet too."

"What happened?" Simen asked. "Did the mother become happy again and stop crying?"

Alma thought for a moment. "No, not exactly," she said. "The mother took the girl into her big four-poster bed and read and sang to her and tickled the back of her neck and ruffled her hair and said *I love you so much, my little...little...*" Alma searched for a word.

"Little song thrush," suggested Simen, because that was what his mother called him.

"Little song thrush, yes, *I love you so much, my little song thrush*, the mother told the girl. Then she got out of bed and went to the kitchen and made a big cup of hot cocoa, which was the girl's favorite."

Alma turned to Simen. He had been eight years old then— that day when they sat at the edge of the green lake, eating apple cake.

"It's your mother, isn't it? It's your mother who calls you little song thrush," Alma said.

Simen didn't answer.

"Why does she call you little song thrush?" Alma asked.

"I don't know," said Simen, who was wishing he had kept his mouth shut. He didn't want to tell her anything at all about himself, and certainly not this. He didn't want to say, *Because every night before Mama kisses me good night and leaves my room she whispers: "What would you like me to sing to you before I go?" And then I whisper back: "I want you to sing 'Little Song Thrush.' All the verses!" That's why Mama calls me little song thrush.*

Alma turned to face the water again and continued with her story: "And once the mother had made the cocoa she poured a sleeping potion into the cup. It was colorless. Tasteless. There are such things, you know—sleeping potions that you can drink without even realizing that you're drinking them! You never know. It can happen any time. It could happen to you too. Your mother could put a sleeping potion into your cocoa without you knowing."

"Cut it out," said Simen.

"You cut it out," said Alma. "I'm only telling you that it *could* happen. These are the harsh realities of life."

"Well, cut it out anyway," Simen said again.

"And once the girl had drunk the cocoa," Alma went on, "she fell asleep in her mother's big four-poster bed. Fell into a deep, deep sleep. And the mother put her ear to the girl's mouth, and when she was sure that she wouldn't wake up, she picked her up in her arms and carried her through the woods to this lake and threw her in."

"I don't believe that," Simen said.

"That's because you're a little boy," Alma said, "and because you don't know what mothers do when they can't stop crying—and that girl's mother just couldn't stop crying."

It was years now since Alma had looked after Simen and told him the story about the boy and the girl who had drowned in the green lake, and even though he didn't believe the story one hundred percent, he didn't like to swim there. He swam in the sea instead. He never wanted to swim in those green waters, thinking about how that boy and girl, turned to water lilies, might clutch at him, a foot or an arm, and pull him under.

So Simen and his friends rode past the lake where he had sat with Alma when he was little and he thought to himself: *I know every inch of this forest.*

The treasure—two hundred kroner in notes, a diamond crucifix on a gold chain, and an autograph book from Liverpool—was in the light blue tin pail, lashed to Christian's handlebars. One shovel jutted out of Gunnar's rucksack. Simen had borrowed a saddlebag and found room for the other shovel in that. Three boys, all fine as pencil strokes, riding full tilt through the dim green light, on the hunt for the perfect hiding place.

The wood opened up and closed in and wrapped itself around them and suddenly Simen pulled up sharply and cried, "Look! Over there, under that tree!" They had come to a clearing in the woods and on the edge of this clearing was a clump of rocks shaped rather like the letter *S*—as in *sacrifice* or *Simen* or the greatest soccer manager of all time Bill *Shankly*—and in the middle of the clearing was a tree and the tree raised its branches to the sky as if it were cheering every single goal scored by Liverpool since 1892.

But everything looked different in the autumn. Nothing was the way it should be. It was raining and it was cold and dark and you had to wear hats and scarves and thick sweaters and you had to bring a flashlight, and the woods were brooding, dense, and still and there were no bright clearings with rocks in the shape of the letter *S* or cheering trees.

But they did find a clearing, and they did find a tree that looked a little bit like the one from the summer.

"So what was the point of burying treasure if we are just unburying it two months later?" Simen tried one more time. "I thought the point was to leave it there forever."

"Oh just shut up," Christian said.

"I wasn't the one babbling on about sacrifice and stuff," Simen retorted.

"I want my stuff back," Gunnar said. "Okay?"

Christian was quite sure that this was the right spot, he recognized it, he said. Simen regarded the tree with its bare branches raised to the night sky. No way! This tree wasn't anything like the other one. This tree looked like an old man shaking his fists in the air, very angry and close to death. And it wasn't just because it had lost its leaves. This tree was fucked. But he said nothing to the others. They had been riding in the wrong direction for what seemed like hours. He was almost absolutely sure that they had been riding in the wrong direction and that this was not the right spot. But if he was wrong and Christian was right, and it turned out that the treasure was buried under this tree, he wondered whether he should put the diamond crucifix back in the blue bowl in the bathroom or keep it, or maybe try to sell it. You could do a lot with seventeen thousand kroner. He pictured his mother looking all over for it, in the house, in the garden, never suspecting him. She had worn her red dress, she had smiled at him and asked him to help her look.

They dug the shovels into the ground.

"Just as well the frost hasn't set in yet," Christian said. "This would never have worked if it had."

"This is definitely the place," Gunnar said, "you can see that somebody's been digging here before—"

"Yeah, but the whole point was that we wouldn't ever dig it up again," Simen mumbled, knowing he was right about this.

"But whose point was that, anyway?" Christian asked.

"Well, the treasure was your idea," Simen said.

"Oh just shut up and dig," said Gunnar.

The boys worked in silence. It was pitch-dark now; they took turns digging and holding the flashlight.

An hour later when, breathless and exhausted, they shone the flashlight down on her, none of them got that it was Milla lying there, at least not right away. The grave looked like a bird's nest—a big underground nest of twigs and bones and skin and straw and grass and pieces of red fabric—and at first Simen, whose eyes did not take in the entire contents of the grave all at once, thought that was exactly what it was, that what he was looking at were the remains of some giant bird, the only one of its kind, black and surging, hidden from the world, lone and mighty on its heavy dark wings, swooping back and forth along subterranean tunnels, passages, and halls. A great, proud, solitary night bird that had at last come plummeting down, leaving only a few signs that it had ever existed—and he was not shaken out of this state until Gunnar, who was holding the flashlight, started screaming.

"Oh, Christ, it's a body."

Gunnar's face was green and not just from the ghostly beams of the flashlight.

Christian said, "Look at the hair, it's not grass, it's hair." Then he threw up.

Two years had passed since Milla disappeared and even back then Simen and his bike were as one, that was how he thought of himself, as a boy on wheels, a bike with a body, a heart, and a tongue, and if his parents had let him, he would have taken his bike to bed with him when, much against his will, he was told to go to sleep. From early morning he was out, zooming and skidding and swerving up and down the narrow dirt tracks around the white-painted church or screeched to a halt at the very end of the wooden jetties alongside the ferry wharf, inside the long breakwater; his handlebars flashed in the sunlight and he breathed in the sharp reek of shrimp shells and fish ends from the two fishermen who hadn't yet called it quits and chosen some other line of work.

On the evening she disappeared—July 15, 2008—there had been a shower of rain, the mist had thickened around him, and the roads were black and damp and looked as though they might yawn open at any minute and swallow him. Simen's parents allowed him to go out on his bike alone in the evening— as long as he stayed near the house. He was cold, but he didn't want to go home. His mother and father were fighting constantly and they couldn't stop, not even when he yelled, "Stop it! Please don't fight anymore!"

At the top of the winding road known as the Bend (but which everyone thought ought to be called *the Bends* because of the many twists and turns and which Simen knew took about a thousand and one steps to climb), that coiled like a rippling band up the slope from the town center, sat the big old turn-of-the-century house belonging to Jenny Brodal.

Every evening Jenny Brodal and Irma, the very tall woman who lived with her in her house, went for long walks together. Jenny was small and dainty and marched down the long road to the town center. Irma was big and broad and seemed to glide along a few steps behind her. Simen often came across the two women when he was out on his bike. Irma never said anything, but Jenny usually greeted him.

"Hello, Simen," she'd say, or something like that.

"Hi," he'd answer, never knowing whether he ought to stop and say hello properly or just ride on—in any case the two women were always long gone before he could make up his mind.

Irma was the woman whom Jenny had *taken pity on*. Simen wasn't sure exactly what that meant, to *take pity on* somebody, but that was what his mother had said when he asked who she was, the lady living at Mailund with Jenny Brodal.

Simen did his best to avoid Irma, especially when she was out walking alone. Once, he had come riding down the road toward her and she had grabbed hold of his handlebars and hissed at him. She didn't exactly breathe fire, but she might as well have. Irma seemed to be all lit up—he noticed this because the evening had been so dark. Glowing, as if she had just swallowed a fireball.

He had no idea why she did it. Why she hissed. He hadn't done anything, just cycling along, minding his own business. It wasn't as if he had gotten in her way. *She* had grabbed *him*.

His mother said that maybe Irma had been trying to have a bit of fun with him but just had a clumsy way of doing it. There was nothing wrong with Irma, his mother insisted, and Simen shouldn't let his imagination run away with him, shouldn't make up stories about people he didn't know. What Simen had to understand was that Irma was probably a very nice person. She was someone whom Jenny Brodal had rescued from all kinds of dreadful situations, someone whom Jenny had *taken pity on*, but because Irma was so large (Simen's mother hesitated before choosing a word that in her mind would accurately describe Irma's overwhelming physique) and did not, therefore, look like an ordinary woman, there was a risk of people judging her purely based on appearances. Simen's mother said, you must *never* judge people purely based on appearances. She said this because she always thought the best of people. But in this case his mother was wrong. Irma the giantess had glowed in the dark, grabbed hold of his handlebars, and hissed at him.

But on this particular drizzly July evening Simen luckily met neither Jenny nor Irma. It was Jenny's birthday and her big garden was full of people, he heard the voices and the laughter from a long way off. It was a big party, which Simen thought was strange, when you considered how old Jenny Brodal really was. Over seventy, at least, maybe even over eighty. He wasn't sure. But she was old. And was probably going to die soon. And Jenny Brodal obviously knew this, she wasn't the kind of person who skirted the truth. Nor was Simen. His mother was going to die, his father was going to die. And someday Simen too would die. He was well aware of this. He had discussed it with his mother—she always gave straight answers. His father was more evasive. So why have a big party when all you had to look forward to was death? What was the point?

Simen pedaled up the long, winding road to spy from the bushes. The mist lay over him and under him and ahead of him and behind him, and the voices from Jenny's garden seemed to leap out of it. The voices came from the mist. The chatter and the laughter came from the mist. The winding road came from the mist, and all the people at the party came from the mist. And only Simen and his bike were real. They were flesh and blood and bones and wheels and steel and chain. They were one—Simen and his bike. Or at least they were until his wheel rammed a rock and Simen flew headfirst over the handlebars. His scream was cut short as he hit the ground. He lay perfectly still for a few moments, until the pain kicked in. Grazes on the palms of his hands and his knees. Grit in the cuts. Blood. He hobbled over to the side of the road, slumped against a tree trunk, and cried. But no matter how loudly he cried his mother and father wouldn't hear him. Their house was way down the road, the party drowned out everything else up here, and he was alone and hurt all over, his knees hurt worst of all, his bike was probably wrecked, and his palms were grazed because he had put out his hands in an attempt to break his fall, protect his head. That was what you were supposed to do if you fell off your bike. And not only that, you were supposed to wear a helmet, his mother would be furious with him for not wearing a helmet and he wouldn't be allowed to go out alone on his bike in the evenings ever again.

His bike was still lying in the middle of the road. All funny and bent looking. Simen howled even louder. That was when she appeared. The girl in the red dress, with the long dark hair with a flower in it. She had a shawl around her shoulders. She was the prettiest girl Simen had ever seen—and the mist, now thickening into fog, didn't touch her, but appeared to shy away from something so beautiful. He went on crying even though a voice inside him was telling him that when something as pretty as this girl is coming toward you, you shouldn't be sitting in the ditch, crying like a baby. On the other hand, if he hadn't been sitting in the ditch, crying like a baby, the girl would never have stopped, she would never have crouched down in front of him and put her arms around him and whispered, "Did you fall off your bike? Did you hurt yourself? Can I see?" She would never have helped him to his feet, asked his name, and used her red shawl to wipe the dirt and the tears off his face. She would never have bent over his bike to inspect the damage. "It's not wrecked," she said, pulling it up onto its wheels. "Look, Simen, it's not wrecked." And she would never have walked with him through the fog, all the way down the long, winding road from

Jenny's house to his house, five hundred and sixty-seven steps—
with one hand in his hand, the other on the handlebars. "I'm
Milla," she said when they finally got there.

She propped his bike against the fence, looked at him, and
smiled. Then she bent over and kissed the top of his head.

"I'm Milla and you're Simen and you're not to cry anymore."

Then she turned and walked away.

II

YOUR
LIGHT
SHINES
MORE

JON DREYER HAD fooled everyone.

He was in the attic room at Mailund, that dilapidated white turn-of-the-century house, where the Dreyer-Brodal family spent their summers. He was looking at Milla.

The room was small and bright and dusty with a view of the meadow and the woods and of Milla picking flowers with his children. His wife, she of the asymmetric back (a little kink in her waist, that's all), owned a restaurant in the center of town, in the old bakery. Siri was her name.

Siri was at work.

He was at work too.

His work was right here. He had his desk, his computer, this is where they left him in peace. He had a book to finish.

But he was looking at Milla.

Siri's restaurant was called Gloucester, after the fishing port in Massachusetts where she and Jon and Alma had spent a summer when Jon was writing the first part of his trilogy. That was nine years ago, when Alma was three and Liv wasn't even born yet.

Oh, how he could write back then. Pages and pages, effortlessly every day. And now here he was, working on part three;

the first and second parts had been great successes, published in quick succession in 2000 and 2002. And then nothing. Part three—nothing!

He was supposed to have finished part three a long time ago but the days were frittered away and he had nothing to show for them. Maybe he was depressed. Siri said she thought he might be depressed.

Back then, when they were in Gloucester and he was still writing an average of ten pages a day, he'd lie beside his sleepless wife at night, hold her hand, tell her stories. He would remember things he thought he had forgotten long ago: the interior of his grandmother's apartment; his mother's colorful dresses, detailed one by one; the names and faces of his childhood friends. He told her about the silent ski excursions through the woods with his father, the sadness he sometimes felt when he was little, the snow falling everywhere on his trail, white, blue, silver, gray. And he lay beside her and talked and talked and occasionally she fell asleep, but more often than not she didn't, and he was nevertheless thankful for the warmth and nearness of her and he stroked her hand until he talked himself into his own sleep. And when Jon went quiet, sometimes dozing off mid-word, she took over. She told of dreams she'd had as a child and of dreams she had now. She told of films she had seen and books she had read, "And Jon," she whispered, "do you read and also write in order to become someone else?" He liked lying next to her, listening to her voice, but was too tired to reply. "Do you think it's even possible to put yourself in someone else's place, to suffer, breathe, feel as they do?" And when he still didn't answer she told him of when she was a little girl and of her father and how, instead of reading to her, he recounted snatches from books he loved. Siri was only six and her little brother, Syver, was four, but that didn't stop their father, who told the children about Karenin, Anna Karenina's husband, who was so strict that everyone was afraid of him, when in fact he was just very sad. And Siri remembered how she had understood what it must be like to be Karenin, even though she was just a little girl. And she told Jon, as she had so many times, about the time when Syver died in the forest, about her mother, who started drinking, who never staggered but simply moved fitfully around the house, suddenly popping up in a corner of the living room, suddenly on the edge of the bed, suddenly standing over pots and pans in the vast kitchen, suddenly in front of the mirror and "I tried to grab hold of her, but she slipped through my fingers and into the pots, into the mirror." And she told of how her father ran off to Slite on the island of Gotland and married Sofia, starting up his own stonemasonry, and of the time when he paid a visit to Mailund and had forgotten to bring a birthday present, so to make up for it he cut up his gabardine coat and gave it to her, telling her that it was an invisibility cloak. It was her father—on one of the few occasions in Siri's childhood when she had visited him in Slite—who had taken her to the lighthouse on the nearby island of Fårö. She liked Slite, liked the cement factory that seemed to loom over the whole town and the tired little streets in the center and the white dust that settled over everything and everyone, but Fårö was something else, Fårö was too beautiful, almost forbidding, with its red poppies and pebbled beaches and shifting lights of gray, and she remembered not wanting to go back there and she really hadn't thought much about that trip with her father until she and Jon and Alma were standing on Good Harbor Beach in Gloucester more than twenty years later and thousands of miles away, looking at the silhouettes of the two lighthouses, the twin lights, on Thacher Island.

And Jon would turn around and say to her, "Your light shines more." And she would make fun of him for coming up with a line like that, "You really do know your lines, Jon," she would say, but she'd let him get away with it. That was then. These days she never let him get away with anything.

Yet it was something he'd say to her from time to time: "Your light shines more." More than the lighthouses on Thacher Island, more than the bright rooms they had inhabited during those first years of marriage.

When Siri said, "I think you're depressed," it wasn't out of concern, it was more of an accusation, her voice demonstratively weary, telling him *Oh, I am so tired of you and all your crap.*

On a threadbare blanket on the threadbare couch lay Jon's dog, with his relish for the inner organs of beasts and fowls, hence his name, Leopold, after Leopold Bloom; regular dog food was out of the question, he'd rather starve than eat regular dog food. He was a big, black Lab mix with a white patch on his chest and a doleful look in his eyes. Leopold knew that Jon was never going to finish his book and this worried him.

The reason that this worried him—he was, after all, a dog and not a particularly pensive dog—was that Jon had stopped taking him for long walks. Jon was incapable of doing *anything* until the book was finished—apart, of course, from *not* writing, *not* beginning, and *not* finishing,

What Jon Dreyer said to himself and also to Leopold was that once the summer was over and the book was finished, everything would return to normal and then they would go for long walks. It was still possible to finish it this summer. It was only the end of June. If he wrote ten pages a day, he would have sixty new pages every week—he'd take Sundays off and spend quality time with his children—which meant that he would have about three hundred pages by the end of August. Three hundred pages was a book. It had worked before, it could work again. Ten pages a day starting tomorrow. So day after day Jon sat at his laptop intending to write, either that or he lay on the floor next to his dog and tried to sleep, or he gazed out the window, or he read newspapers online and wrote text messages to women who might or might not reply, and after a lot of all that he ate peanuts and drank beer.

Jon had a way of resorting to attic rooms. There was the attic study at Jenny's house, where he was now, with the window facing the meadow, and then there was the attic at his and Siri's home in Oslo, the extortionately expensive and drafty house on which they had a mortgage of more than eighty percent. Why the bank still trusted Siri and him and kept raising their credit limit was a mystery to him.

Jon leaned over the keys and typed:

10 x 6 is 60
60 x 5 is 300
300 is a book

Sometimes he spent the night in the attic room. In Oslo the attic was even more drafty than the rest of the house, but at least he could get some peace. Lie underneath the sloping walls and pointed roof and drink. Play his guitar. Google stuff. Send and receive text messages, which he promptly deleted. It's hard to say when Jon and Siri had started sleeping apart. It wasn't something he wanted and it wasn't something she wanted, it wasn't a permanent solution and it wasn't as if they slept apart every night either. And this summer they had even made love once or twice. He liked to run his hand over the sharp indent of her waist (which was so sharp because of her asymmetric back), he liked to run his finger down the nape of her slender neck.

Jon stood up and stretched a little. Leopold followed him with his eyes.

Walk time now?

Leopold let out a sigh.

No, apparently not, he's sitting down again.

Everyone except the dog was confident that Jon was going to finish the book, which was why he had been granted an additional advance of 200,000 kroner from his publisher. Yes, parts one and two of the trilogy had sold like hotcakes. That was what they had said, that was what they had written in the papers. But it was a while now since anyone had said or written anything about Jon's books, and the money had all been spent. Besides: Jon would never have used the expression "sell like hotcakes"—not only was it a cliché, it was also inaccurate. Hotcakes no longer sold like hotcakes. He had no statistics to back this up, but he was pretty sure that hotcakes fared poorly compared to smartphones or drafty houses in overpriced areas (like his own, for example) or antiaging creams. What a strange word, *antiage*. Jon typed it on his computer.

Antithis. Antithat. Antiage.

The point of an antiaging cream was that women and men who buy it and apply it to their faces will look younger. Feel younger. Be younger. Turn the clock back. Stop aging and start antiaging. *Antitime. Antihunger. Antianxiety* (that was already a word!). *Antideath.*

He remembered that much against his will, he had gone to a mall outside of Oslo with Siri to buy Christmas presents, and, that done, she had said that she had to stop by the cosmetics department to buy moisturizer.

"Feel how dry my skin is," she'd said, and she had taken his hand and run it over her cheek.

Antidry. Antidrought.

The woman behind the cosmetics counter, clad in a white coatdress, like a kind of trailblazing scientist, spoke softly and confidentially about the state of things in general. A demigoddess for our times, Jon thought. In his fifty years on this earth, he had witnessed and even participated in one or two political revivals and ideas about how to run the world and he could not help but admire her. The white skin, the white dress, the white voice, never uttering a word about fear, she talked only

about beauty. And Siri, his clever, cool, critical, hot-tempered
Siri, with her gracefully asymmetric back and dry cheeks, listened raptly and wound up paying 1,750 kroner of the million
that the bank had just paid into their joint account with their
drafty house as security, *antidebt*, for a cream containing pep-
tides, retinol, EGF (discovered, according to the white-clad
demigoddess, by a Nobel Prize winner), collagen, and AHA.

Leopold looked at his master: *Walk time now?*

The final part of his trilogy was to be about time. Jon planned
to write a hymn to everything that endures and everything
that falls apart. But truth be told he wasn't sure what he actually meant by "everything that endures and everything that
falls apart" or how he was supposed to write about it, but no
one argued with him, except the dog who was stretched out
on the floor with his leash between his teeth, waiting, and
reminding him that one human year is equal to seven dog
years and how is that for a thought on the nature of time? *Just
think how many years it's been since I had a proper walk, I'm a
humble dog, born with big muscles and long limbs and I need to
get out and run, I have no other wish.*

For a while Jon toyed with the idea of picking up where
Walter Benjamin's *Arcades Project* had left off. This would
be something quite different, of course, Jon was writing a
novel and not a massive, impenetrable work on the arcades
of nineteenth-century Paris (Walter Benjamin had been
somewhat disdainful of fiction). But something that took its
outset in shopping malls, the arcades of our own day, a depiction not merely of the people, of white-frocked women

with their gospel on how to turn back time, but of the things themselves.

Jon sighed and looked over his notes.

Siri was a chef. Siri cooked real food for real people. Not pretentious pap. People ate her food and were happy. And here he sat, year in, year out, writing a novel that might or might not have to do with a mall. Or with time. Leopold raised his big head and looked at him.

Jon had fooled everyone. The cover art was ready, the catalog blurb was written, he had agreed to do a reading from the book at his publisher's press conference at the end of August. And he had nothing.

Not "nothing" as a modest man might say about something, but quite literally nothing. Not a word.

Jon took a swig of beer and looked out the window. His girls were playing in the meadow. Alma and Liv. Alma black-haired and dark-eyed. Liv fair-haired and finespun. They were picking flowers and dancing about in the sunshine with the girl who Siri had hired to look after them. The girl called Milla. He had barely said hello to her the previous evening, after Siri had picked her up at the bus stop.

He regarded his daughters. They were jumping back and forth and Liv laughed and lay down in the meadow and made angel wings in the snow, even though it was summer and there wasn't any snow and she would leave no imprint. Something to hold on to. Something that was real. Alma turned and looked up at the window, but it was so dim in the attic and so bright outside that she could not possibly have seen him standing there looking down at her. Don't let go. Try to live a decent life. Hold on to my girls. Protect them. Don't let go.

And maybe Alma realized that he was standing there looking down at her, because she broke into a wild sort of dance in the tall grass, with her eyes fixed on the window. She spun around and around then suddenly fell down. Jon laughed. Alma got back onto her feet and looked up at him as if she had heard him laughing. Alma's short dark hair. Alma's chubby face. Alma's unformed body. She started spinning again. Around and around and around.

Jon shifted his gaze, looking for Liv, who was closer to the woods, having found a spot where there were obviously more flowers. Milla was right behind her, together they were picking an enormous bouquet.

Jon went on standing at the window. But now he wasn't looking at Alma spinning and falling, or at Liv picking flowers. He was looking at Milla. She had long dark hair and big eyes. A nice body. He had noticed that the evening before. About nineteen or twenty years old. Shy and a little bit awkward. Sweaty palms. Her eyes bright when she shook his hand and said hello. She had held on to his hand a little longer than necessary and something in her eyes told him that, young as she was, she had acknowledged him. And now she was running after Liv with a flower for her bouquet.

Her body full and young, she had held his hand a little longer than necessary. Something inside him quieted down. It was all going to hell anyway.

It was fine to just stand here and look at Milla and not think.

BUT SOMETHING WAS wrong. Siri held her breath. It had to do with Milla. Or something else. But Milla definitely had something to do with it. Her presence here at Mailund. The slightly lumpish body, the long dark hair (long dark hairs on the kitchen counter, in the bathroom sink, between the sofa and the sofa cushions, on the baseboards and doorframes), her face, sometimes pretty, sometimes not, beseeching eyes.

More and more Siri found herself having to concentrate in order to keep herself in check—was that the expression? Keep oneself in check? Be one. One body, one voice, one mouth, one thread, and not fall apart, dissolve, collapse in a heap.

"Your main responsibility," Siri said, "will be to look after Liv for five hours or so every day. But we'd be grateful if you'd keep an eye on Alma as well. Alma's twelve. She's"—Siri searched for the right word—"a bit of a loner."

Milla laughed hesitantly, brushed the hair back from her pretty moon face, and said that she thought it all sounded really great.

It was a mild, bright day in May and Siri had invited Milla to the house in Oslo. The idea was for them to get to know each other a little better before the summer. Alma was at school, Liv was at nursery school, and Jon had gone for a long walk with Leopold. Something about a chapter he was having trouble writing.

Milla had replied to the ad on the Internet for a summer job and Siri had been taken with her application. In her e-mail she came across as a happy, friendly, reliable girl. *It would be fantastic to get to know all of you and be able to be part of your family this summer. ☺ If I get the job I'll do my best to be a good "big sister" to your daughters so that you and your husband won't have to worry when you're at work.*

Maybe Milla could spread a little happiness? Maybe, Siri had thought, maybe, just maybe there were such things as happiness-spreaders? Siri may also have been influenced, or impressed, or intrigued, by the fact that Milla's mother, Amanda Browne, was a famous, or relatively famous, American photographer living in Norway. Siri remembered browsing in a bookstore and stumbling upon a book of photography by Amanda Browne—this was nine years ago, maybe even ten—and being struck by the stark beauty of the black-and-white images. Amanda Browne had, according to the book's introduction, photographed everything that was precious to her. Most of the photographs were of her young daughter, lovingly observed, intimately portrayed—playing, sleeping, eating breakfast and getting chocolate milk all over her face, running through tall, sun-scorched grass. The girl's name was Mildred. There were photographs of other people too. Amanda Browne's husband, her aging parents, an old aunt with illness written all over her face. And there were several photographs of the flat, blistering summer landscape surrounding Amanda Browne's house on the outskirts of Oslo.

But it was the photographs of the child that moved Siri. She remembered standing in the bookstore, looking at the pictures, and thinking of her own child, of Alma, just a toddler then. She remembered placing the book back on its shelf, jumping on a tram, and going directly to the day-care center where Alma spent a few hours every day. Looking at those photographs, Siri urgently felt the need to find her daughter, to hold her in her arms, touch her face, inhale the warmth of her skin.

And so here she was. Mildred. Or Milla, as she was called now. Nothing like the strong-willed, suntanned child in the book. Siri had offered her the job. And now she was regretting everything.

She smiled.

"My husband is a writer," she said. "He has a book to finish. I have a small seafood restaurant five minutes from Mailund, as well as a restaurant in Oslo. The seafood restaurant, Gloucester it's called, after a little fishing port outside of Boston, is only open during the summer months and I'll be spending most of my time there. It's a lot of work. I—"

Siri broke off. There was no point in trying to explain to Milla the amount of work involved in running two restaurants.

"Also, we like the house to be kept neat and tidy," she continued. "So it would be good if you could lend a hand with that too. It's best if everybody in the family helps out, that way it's easily done and takes little time. And while you're staying with us you'll be sort of like one of the family."

"Oh, yes," Milla said, looking bewildered. "It'll be great. I'm really looking forward to it."

She put a hand to her face, stroked her cheek. Her bracelets jingled. She had a whole lot of them on her wrist. (Fine.
Silver.) And every time Milla moved her hand, as when she
stroked her own cheek—why did she do that?—they jingled.

"And I'm throwing a party for my mother this summer,"
Siri said. "For her seventy-fifth birthday. I'm probably going
to need some help with that too."

Milla nodded uncertainly.

Siri never wore jewelry. No bracelets, no earrings, nothing
around her neck, only her wedding ring, which she removed
every night.

The sound of Milla's bracelets reminded her of when she
was a little girl, sitting opposite her mother at the kitchen
table. There was always complete silence when they sat together like that, except when Jenny turned a page of the book
she was reading and her bracelets jingled.

"We spend all our summers at Mailund," Siri said, again
regretting everything. Surely she and Jon could have split the
days between them? They'd done it before. She could have
taken Liv in the mornings and he could have taken her in
the afternoons when Siri was at the restaurant. Yes, that's how
they had done it in the past. But that hadn't really worked out,
had it? They always ended up fighting about who did what
and who didn't.

"A big old house," she said, interrupting her own train of
thought. "Oh, and we have this small house, an annex, in the
garden, that's where you'll be staying. With your own bathroom and lots of bookshelves."

"Okay," said Milla, and giggled.

Siri forced herself to smile. *Why on earth are you giggling?* Oh, she tried to curb her own impatience. Twenty years of running restaurants—it did something to you. To things like having patience. To things here at home. Jon, the children. She couldn't quite put her finger on it. *But what have I done with my life?*

"My mother and I lived in that big old house—Mailund, it's called—until I was fourteen and then we moved to Oslo," Siri said. She was babbling on. "My mother was a bookseller. She had a bookshop near the old bakery, where I've got the restaurant now. But you'll see all of that when you get there. We'll take you around and show you everything, the children and I will."

Siri could tell that Milla's mind was elsewhere, that she wasn't particularly interested in accepting Siri's little flower: *We'll take you around and show you everything, the children and I will.*

The veranda door was open and Siri could hear the neighbour's children next door, Emma's daughters, seven and nine years old (older than Liv but younger than Alma), who had been picked up from school early that day. They were clapping their hands and chanting a rhyme that she remembered from when Alma was younger.

Under an apple tree
Sat a boy and he said, said he,
Hug me,
Kiss me,
Show that you love me.

"And after that she worked for years in a big bookshop here in Oslo," Siri went on. "It's closed now. She was in charge of the foreign literature section. Now that she's retired she's moved back to Mailund for good. She lives with Irma, who helps her around the house. You'll meet both of them."

"Don't you have any brothers or sisters?" Milla asked. And then, as if she had already received a reply: "I don't either."

"No," Siri said. "I don't have any brothers or sisters."

She did not say: *But don't think that means we have anything in common, because believe me, we don't.*

What she said was: "I had a little brother, but he died when he was four."

"Oh," Milla said, lowering her eyes. "That's so sad."

Jenny's skin had been soft back then, so soft that you could snuggle right up close to her, poke your nose between her breasts inside the open neck of her well-worn nightdress. And she smelled nice.

Under an apple tree
Sat a boy and he said, said he,
Hug me . . .

Siri thought it would be a good idea to give Milla's parents a call and assure them that she was in good hands. Regular working hours. Good pay. The news was full of stories about au pairs and nannies who were treated badly: Filipino girls who were forced to work ten-hour days for next to nothing, young women who looked after other people's children so that they could support their own kids back home, Norwegians who liked the idea of having a servant in the house.

"We'll take good care of her, she'll be just like one of the family," Siri said.

"That's nice," Amanda Browne said, "but our sweet pea is a grown-up, you know, and does what she likes."

"Sweet what?"

Amanda laughed softly. "Oh, it's just a leftover from when she was little...sweet pea. That's what we used to call her."

Siri said, "If you and your husband wanted to come to Mailund during the summer to see Milla, we've plenty of room. You'd be most welcome. And I'd love to treat you to dinner at Gloucester—that's my summer restaurant—we're known for good seafood."

Siri had no idea what made her say these things. The last thing she wanted was for Milla's parents to come to Mailund, to have to socialize with them and give them dinner at the restaurant.

"Oh, no," Amanda replied. "Mikkel and I wouldn't dream of imposing."

Siri could tell that Amanda was embarrassed.

"Anyway, we made other plans months ago," Amanda continued. "Milla's nineteen, she can't wait to have a job and earn her own money and it will give her time, we hope, to think about what she wants to do next."

"Of course," Siri said, and added impulsively: "Your photographs mean a lot to me. I think they're beautiful, and true somehow. I just wanted to tell you that."

Amanda Browne was quiet for a few moments. And then: "Well, thank you very much. That's very nice of you."

And now here she was, Siri, with this rather lumpish, breathless teenage girl with one hand nervously fluttering on the tabletop. Siri had to concentrate hard to stop herself from placing her own hand firmly over Milla's. *Stop that! Pull yourself together. None of that fluttering, please, if you don't mind.* It wasn't too late. Siri could still say, *The nanny job's off. I'm so sorry, but it's all off.* They weren't at Mailund yet, they were still in Oslo. But she didn't have the guts. The girl was counting on this. It was already decided.

Later, Siri told Jon, "Her mother calls her sweet pea."

"Does she now?" said Jon, who had not yet met Milla and had been very much against bringing a nanny to Mailund. "Will we have to call her sweet pea as well?"

"No, no. It's just that…there really isn't anything very sweet pea-ish about her."

Milla was suffering from a spring cold that she couldn't shake off. She was pale and red-eyed and kept having to blow her nose. When they met that first time, Siri had tried to talk to her about all sorts of things and hadn't gotten much out of her, and she soon realized that where Milla was concerned there were two types of answers: a faint, hesitant "we-ell," which could mean yes, no, or I don't know; or a giggle, which could also mean yes, no, or I don't know.

Milla looked at Siri.

Under an apple tree

There was something about Milla's expression that reminded Siri of herself at that age. She had no wish to go back there. Siri smiled (instead of screaming) and wondered how to get out of this. Jon was right. It was a bad idea. A very, very bad idea.

Sat a boy and he said, said he,

Next door, Emma called to her girls *Come on in, you two!* and the girls laughed and ran inside.

"Well, that's agreed then," Siri said. "You'll come down on the twenty-fifth of June and I'll pick you up at the bus stop. So we have a plan then. This is great. This is just great."

MILLA HAD PROMISED herself that by the end of this summer she would have transformed herself into an entirely new person. Inside and out. From head to toe. When she got back to Oslo in August everybody would say, *Why, Milla, what's happened to you? You seem so different.* And she would smile demurely and say, *Nothing's happened, I've had a great summer, that's all.*

Here in the annex at Mailund all was quiet. So quiet you could think. And pray.

Mailund belonged to Jenny Brodal. "The mother-in-law from hell," Jon had said with a quick grin at Milla, and when he grinned at her like that she knew there must be something special going on between them. "Don't ever tell anyone I just said that," he had gone on, "I mean, she's my children's grandmother." She should pretend she'd never heard it, he had said, grinning again.

Just a few days after she had arrived at Mailund Milla found herself alone with Jon one morning in the kitchen. He had been in a world of his own and she wondered whether he was thinking about the book he was writing, whether he was so taken up with the book that he didn't even notice her there. He was making himself a cup of coffee. She was getting out bread and butter and ham and cheese to pack a lunch for Liv and herself. She positioned herself next to him and proceeded to butter the bread. *Are you going to say anything to me? Are you even aware that I'm standing here, right next to you?* Nothing. Not a word. Then out of the blue he reached out a hand and ran his fingers through her hair.

She raised her eyes and looked at him, but then he pulled away.

"Good," he said as if to himself. "That's good."

And without another glance at her, he picked up his coffee cup and walked out.

When she was younger, Milla had liked to brush her long dark hair, put on a pretty dress or a pair of tight jeans, make up her face, and walk into a room or stroll down the street to see how much attention she'd get. Boys and men turned to look at her, spoke to her, wanted her. She had breasts by the time she was ten. Her mother was tall and thin and firm and flat-chested. There was nothing there to curl up against. Her mother's body was a taut trampoline mat, if you ran into it you would bounce straight off again.

Her mother had tried to make Milla conceal her breasts under baggy, childish cotton sweaters. She would buy ugly clothes and have them wrapped in pretty paper. *Surprise, I bought you a little present, sweetie.* And always another sweater, size medium or large. White sweaters, pink sweaters, blue crewneck sweaters. But Milla had her own style, she saved up and went to rummage sales and flea markets where she bought long T-shirts that she wore as dresses over thick, laddered tights, or figure-hugging sweaters, brightly colored short skirts, scarves, and boots. Milla's mother and Milla were always fighting over how she ought to dress, arguments that started when she developed the breasts that men couldn't help staring at.

They called her Milla, which was short for Mildred, but she also answered to sweetie or sweet pea. She liked the fact that men stared. She wanted them to do more than stare. She wanted to curl up against someone, not be bounced back.

She didn't talk much, and for this reason many people would have described her as shy or timid. She told no one about when she was a little girl and how her mother had taken pictures of her when she was sleeping or swimming or playing. She avoided telling her friends that the pictures of little Milla had been exhibited in galleries all over and published in a book entitled *Amanda's*.

Look at me, Milla. That's it! Don't move now! Look at me! Stay like that a moment longer!

Amanda took thousands of pictures of her daughter as a child until the very thought of having her photograph taken had made Milla's stomach churn. She could count on one hand the number of pictures of her there were from after she grew up and put her foot down. No more pictures! Her mother was a blitzkrieg, invading Milla's little body, her bones, her pores, her vision, from every possible angle and Milla had laid down her arms, not old enough or smart enough or strong enough to defend herself, she was a kid, she didn't have the words, but one day she knew she'd get back at her. She'd get back at everyone who just assumed they could intrude on her and make up their minds about who she was. *Okay, Milla, now look serious, look happy, just pretend I'm not here, sweetie,* her mother's power, taking all those pictures, capturing stuff that was secret, untold, raw, *Right there, Milla, hold it right there,* deciding who Milla was, exposing her daughter only to show off herself, show off her sharp eye and brilliant artistry, selling Milla out. *The little suntanned girl in dotted underpants.* She hated that book, hated the pictures of herself, sometimes clothed, sometimes almost naked, it had robbed her of something, a part of her, how like her mother to call it *Amanda's,* as if Milla were merely an extension of her mother, an offshoot, an appendix.

"COULD YOU TAKE Liv out and pick some flowers," Siri said, twining her long hair around her fingers. "You could go out to the meadow behind the house."

No, she was not impressed by Milla's performance as a nanny. Milla could tell. Siri couldn't even decide exactly what to call her. Nanny? Babysitter? Au pair? Friend of the family? None of them sounded right. Mainly because Siri did not like to see herself as a woman who needed help with anything. Certainly not with taking care of her own children. Siri may have thought that Milla could not see her, but Milla saw her, saw all of Siri, saw Siri even though Siri didn't know she was being seen.

Jon was a different story. He had kissed her on the cheek once. At least she thought it was a kiss, it felt like a kiss.

She'd been at Mailund just a little over a week. She remembered how she had knocked on his study door and asked, "Is it okay if I run down to the shop and get some DVDs for Liv, since it's raining?"

He had turned and looked at her. "Where is Liv?"

"She's out in the garden. She doesn't want to come in, she just wants to run around in the rain, but I thought we ought to find something else to do until the weather clears up. She's soaked to the skin already and pretty cold."

"Couldn't the two of you read a book instead?" Jon asked.

"Well, yes," Milla said uncertainly, "I had a look through the big bookcase in the annex, but I couldn't find any children's books."

Jon got up.

"Let's go down to the living room and find something there," he said. "That's where the children's books are."

He edged past her and out of the narrow door, and it was then, in the doorway, almost by accident, that his lips brushed her cheek. Not a word. Not a glance. It was like that time in the kitchen when he had run his hand through her hair.

"They're books from when Siri and Syver were children" he said.

When they reached the foot of the long stairway, he pointed to the living-room door. She had thought he'd come in with her to help her find a book, but obviously not.

"Bottom shelf on the left," he said. "Now I have to work."

Halfway up the stairs again he called back: "And be sure to get Liv into some dry clothes."

When Milla looked at Siri she thought to herself: Siri's getting old. Over forty. There's something wrong with her back, she's lopsided, often in pain, and you almost have to lean a little to one side when you talk to her. I'm young. My lips are young. My hands are young. No one can see all the snapped bones inside me. It's a shame for Siri. She's lopsided, she's always in pain, and when she was a child her little brother drowned in a lake in the woods while she just stood there and watched.

Milla moved soundlessly around the house, gleaning snippets here and there. Jon had told her how, when Siri's little brother died, more than thirty years ago, no one had talked to Siri. She had been six years old at the time. Not even Jenny had talked to her, and Jenny was her mother.

Jon lowered his voice. "And you know what I think of Jenny."

Siri was always at the restaurant, was not to be disturbed. Milla hated the way Siri snapped at her no matter what she said.

Jon never snapped at her, on the contrary he seemed almost happy when she knocked on his attic study door to ask about things. He always invited her in, asked if she'd like to sit down—and then they would talk.

Milla had known Jon for only a few weeks, but she was quite sure that there was something between them. The sort of thing that could not be put into words.

THE TRUTH WAS that she had been unable to guard herself against him.

The first time she saw him he was standing on the corner of Akersgata and Karl Johans Gate, staring. The year was 1993 and Siri was twenty-five.

She wondered what he was staring at.

He was tall and dark and Giacometti thin with big curly hair, wearing battered jeans, a white linen shirt, and a billowing gabardine coat. He was a handsome man, but there was something unsettling about those glittering, staring eyes.

He was standing stock-still, steadfast you might say, calling to mind the statue of King Haakon VII a few blocks farther on, the one she greeted every night as she passed it on her way home from work.

So there he was, this man whom she did not yet know and who would very shortly turn his eyes on her: the billowing coat, a newspaper pressed to his chest, a slim, upright, wind-blown, valiant pillar of a man.

Siri was on her way to work, yet another function attended by customers who paid well and thought that ordering thousand-kroner bottles of wine was synonymous with fine dining. Until two years ago she had been the head chef at a restaurant on Frognerveien that had gone bankrupt. Now she ran her own catering company, Iris Catering, and had time to think, not that *thinking* was necessarily an advantage. Siri would rather not.

To the extent that Siri reflected upon her choice of career at all, she thought of herself as a craftsman, like her father who had worked with stone. No sensual culinary experiences from her childhood (apart from her mother's casseroles simmering on the stove and tubs of pistachio ice cream in the freezer).

But she was good, she was one of those who had done well for herself. First as a sous-chef, then as the head chef at the restaurant on Frognerveien (with no time to think), and just as she was really making something of it the place went bust. So now she had this stupid catering company, which had, it's true, been an instant financial success and had allowed her the time to *have a life*, that was the expression, wasn't it, but which in the long run seemed nonetheless *untenable,* which was the only word she could come up with.

Bachelor parties, weddings, office parties, business functions, holiday dinners. Fat middle-aged men who ordered Château Pétrus from Pomerol and expected her to go all weak at the knees. *Untenable.*

Her long dark hair was pulled back into a tight ponytail, she was wearing her corn-yellow high-heeled boots and the short, belted corn-yellow autumn coat that had been Jenny's, and her slightly asymmetric back that sometimes caused her pain. Other people did not necessarily notice this, she was a woman who was noticed for her beauty.

But if Jon, who would, year after year, stroke the aching spot and try to straighten it, were to say anything about her back he might say, "A lopsidedness, a graceful little kink in her waist—as if she had turned a cartwheel and stiffened just as she was about to straighten up, caught and held in the movement before it was completed."

He was standing on the opposite side of the street, staring: Neither the king's palace nor the Parliament building was on fire, so what was he staring at? Siri followed his gaze and, yes, there it was. On the square outside the Samson bakery was a young blond woman in a short, tight skirt, black, patterned with tiny white elephants, who appeared to be bending in his direction.

So that's what it was.

He was staring at a woman. It was very simple. A young and pretty one.

Siri looked from the one to the other. It seemed as though he was trying to stare her to him. And it was working. The young blond woman stretched and bent and swayed toward him, and it occurred to Siri that if this unknown man (who reminded her of a stone pillar) went on staring and the young woman went on bending, the tiny white elephants would eventually pull themselves free of her miniskirt and thunder deliriously toward him.

If asked, Siri could not recall thinking much else at that moment, other than about elephants charging through the streets of Oslo, but if she had been able to put into words what she felt when she saw Jon for the very first time (before he saw her and before she knew his name was Jon), she might have said, "Unbelievable. That a woman would fall for that. Unbelievable that she would fall for the oldest pickup trick in the world. *A man looking at her.* What does she think? That he *sees* her, somehow? That he sees right *through* her? That he somehow *fathoms* her? That he has decided she's the one for him, and that this fixity of purpose, or rather fixity of gaze, is just a taste of what he will show her once he has her to himself? That he, the great seducer, has already begun to make love to her as she stands there bending outside the Samson bakery?"

"Silly women and vain men," Jenny was prone to say when Siri was little. "And all of them lonely and wanting attention, like little children huddled in a corner of the living room, howling."

Siri felt like teaching this man a lesson, this man who evidently thought he could stare any woman to him. She removed her hair band and let down her long dark hair. Putting one foot in front of the other she walked across the road—from her street corner to his. One step, two steps, three steps. Now he had spotted her. Four steps, five steps, six steps. The blonde in the elephant skirt was history. Seven steps, eight steps. Now he was staring at her and wondering why the stare wasn't being returned. Why wouldn't she bend, stretch, sway? Nine steps. Siri tossed her hair back. Ten steps, eleven steps. Now she was passing him. Twelve steps. Now she was past him. Thirteen steps. *And now I will forget that I ever saw you.*

And it could have ended there, and everything would have been different, if Siri had not run into him again on a rainy night three weeks later, on the 7. Juni Square, where that selfsame statue of King Haakon VII stood in state, in all its valor. Siri was on her way home from work, it was pouring with rain, water gurgled under her feet, she was frozen to the bone, the chill late-summer rain a relentless herald of autumn. And all of a sudden there he was, standing in front of the statue of King Haakon VII, not looking at all like King Haakon VII. The king himself was quite unaffected by the weather. But Jon, whom she still did not know as Jon, was as wet and cold as a big black dog.

Siri peered at him. She immediately remembered him as the vain, good-looking man whom she had ignored three weeks earlier. The one she had recognized as the sort who thought he could stare all women to him and had put her in mind of the statue he was now standing in front of. Was he waiting for her? Siri did not believe in fateful coincidences, but this really *was* a fateful coincidence. That she should come upon him here, in the middle of the night, with King Haakon VII as witness. He could not possibly have known that she had thought of this particular statue, thought about him at all (she had ignored him!) when she saw him standing there on the corner of Akersgata and Karl Johans Gate. He could not possibly have known that she walked home this way every night after work. She, unlike the blonde in the elephant miniskirt, was not a woman who fell for tricks—not for staring eyes, not for pathetic pickup lines, not for the notion of fateful coincidences. (The very word—*fateful*—no, it was too stupid.)

"Hello," he said.

The 7. Juni Square was deserted. It was almost three o'clock in the morning and the nights were no longer bright. But Siri was not afraid. She never felt afraid in Oslo, this was her city. He had to shout just to make himself heard above the rain. They stood there, on either side of the statue.

"Hello," he repeated. "Did I scare you?" he asked.

"No," she said.

He pointed to himself, the soaking wet gabardine coat plastered to his body and said, "His clothes are dirty, but his hands are clean, if you know what I mean."

She did not know what he meant. And not until long after they were married did she realize that he'd given her a line from a Dylan song.

"Not dirty, but wet," she said. Siri was a stickler for accuracy, you had to get things right, not fudge facts, she spent a lot of time trying to get things right and was therefore much given to correcting other people too.

"Your clothes aren't dirty, they're wet," she said again and smiled hesitantly. "There is a difference."

He looked at her first, then he smiled back and walked up to her.

"Absolutely wringing wet," he said and gently touched her cheek, wiping away a raindrop, "and so are you."

ALMA DIDN'T GET IT. Her grandmother didn't want a party. Nobody wanted to have a party. But Siri was turning Mailund upside down. *Of course we will have a party.*

Jenny was speeding down the road to the jetties in the old Opel with Alma next to her in the passenger seat.

"Slow down Grandma, why don't you just tell my mother that you don't want it?"

"Tell your mother...?" Jenny shouted, almost driving into a ditch. "But you see, your mother is very insistent."

Jenny had brought Alma with her to buy a French novel she had read about in one of those literary journals to which she subscribed, but the girl who worked in the bookshop—the same one that Jenny herself had presided over for so many years—had not heard of it. Nor had she heard of the writer, nor of the literary journal, she obviously did not know who Jenny was and had no idea how to go about ordering a book from abroad. Alma had watched her grandmother get more and more agitated until she finally shouted at the heavily made-up girl.

"Spit out that chewing gum!"

"Wipe off all that black makeup around your eyes!"

"Read a newspaper!"

"Get a life!"

Alma touched her grandmother's arm and whispered that she would help her order the book on the Internet. It wasn't difficult. They could do it as soon as they got home. And Jenny had looked at Alma and said it was a good thing there were still some people in this world with a bit of *gumption*.

Alma walked behind Milla and Liv, and Milla had long dark hair, much longer than Mama's or Grandma's. Liv skipped about. The day was finally here—Jenny's birthday party and everyone, thought Alma, was going crazy. The day before, Siri had picked a long thick strand of hair off the kitchen counter, dangled it before Jon's eyes as if it were a worm or a slug or a snail, and screamed that she'd had enough. Hairs everywhere, Siri said. In the bathroom. In the kitchen. In the food. Jon asked her to keep her voice down or Milla would hear her, but that made Siri even angrier.

"Her hair in my hair!" she screamed, tugging at her hair.

Alma sat at the kitchen table, drinking tea with hot milk. They did not notice her sitting there.

Every evening Siri made tea with hot milk for Alma, to help her sleep. Soothing tea. She used to have cocoa, but now that she was older she had tea.

Alma had a habit of waking up in the middle of the night and coming in to Siri and Jon, even though she was twelve and too big for that. She didn't like being in her own bed alone at night, it was horrible to wake up the next morning in the musty adult bed, but more horrible to wake up in the middle of the night alone and scared.

Her mother was round and tender at night, so different from who she was during the day. At night she'd say *It's all right, Alma. Just you sleep here with me.*

It was the nightmares that woke her—hence the soothing tea with hot milk in which Siri had great faith.

More often than not Siri was alone in bed when Alma woke in the night and came in. Jon would be asleep in the attic room. Her mother and father pretended that they slept together in the same bed, it mattered to them that everyone in this family at least give the *illusion* of sleeping in the beds they were supposed to sleep in.

Alma loved to race toward Jon and throw herself into his arms, but she was too big for that too. She saw how he would brace himself to take her in his arms.

"Mind your father's back," Siri would shout every time Alma threw herself into his arms.

Twelve years old and things you can do:

You can sit quietly drinking tea while your mother dangles a strand of hair in front of your father's face and screams.

You can listen to your parents talk about you as if you weren't there.

You can run really fast into your father's arms and see him brace himself before he takes you in his arms.

Siri was always being complimented on her hair—and oh how she liked that. She acted as though she didn't like it or as if she didn't care, but she did. Siri's cheeks and nose reddened and her eyes narrowed into slender arcs whenever someone said something nice about her.

Now Siri said, "Go on out and pick some flowers to decorate the tables."

As if Alma and Liv were her little flower girls.

The meadow and the woods were behind the house. To the front of the house was the big garden and in the garden Irma had set up rows of trestle tables; Jon had helped her suspend two old cotton sails between the trees, in case of rain. Early on the morning of the big day Siri had covered the tables with linen tablecloths that fluttered in the breeze, but some hours later, when it started to drizzle, she ran out, removed the cloths one by one, and hung them around the house, over chairs, doors, the banister, and a little later, when the sun appeared she went back out to the garden in her well-worn, filmy white dress and spread the cloths over the tables once more, then the mist crept in and she removed them again.

Alma and Liv kneeled on the couch in the living room, still in their nightdresses, with their faces pressed against the window. They watched their mother, who could never decide whether to leave the cloths on or not.

"Tablecloth, cover thyself with all manner of exquisite dishes," Alma whispered to Liv, and Liv laughed and wrinkled her nose and said she thought Mama looked pretty out there in the sea of mist, drifting between the tables with all those white cloths swirling around her.

Liv wrinkled her nose when she laughed. She was the only one in the family who did that. And she laughed even more when Alma said, "What shines and shines and never becomes a princess?"

"Don't know," she said eagerly. "What?"

"Nope," said Alma. "Figure it out for yourself."

Siri and Jon worked constantly during the summer, Siri most of all. Siri knew exactly how much time she would have to spend at work and *I can't really rely on Jon, can I* (she would mutter under her breath, just loud enough for everyone to hear), which was why she had insisted on hiring someone to help with the children. Not that they really needed help with looking after Alma, but they did need help with Liv, who had only just turned four. Alma could look after herself. Alma could look after others too. Sometimes she looked after Liv (but only for short spells) and sometimes she looked after a little boy called Simen who lived at the foot of the road, but only occasionally and only for short spells, and this summer Simen was so big that he no longer needed looking after.

The day after her family arrived for the summer, Alma had rung the doorbell of the house where Simen lived. Simen's mother had opened the door. She wore a little diamond crucifix around her neck and looked very serious, she always did. Simen had once told Alma that his mother called him "little song thrush," like in the song. She wasn't sure exactly why. Simen didn't look like a song thrush, a crow maybe but not a song thrush, and his mother didn't look like a song thrush either.

"Hi," Alma said, and came straight to the point. "Maybe I could look after Simen for you this summer."

But Simen's mother was shaking her head even before the words were out of Alma's mouth. Alma wondered why. Did Simen's mother think she was odd? Sometimes that dark cowlick of hers stuck straight up and then she looked really odd. Or was there something wrong with her voice? Had her voice been too shrill? Had she said something stupid? Should she have gotten the conversation going with a few chatty remarks before coming to the point, said something like: Long time no see, Mrs. Dahl, hard to believe it's been a whole year, how have you been? Or something like that?

Simen's mother stood behind the door, which she was clearly keen to close again as soon as possible.

"No, Alma, Simen's too old to have a babysitter," she said. "He's nine now, you know. You're almost the same age, you two."

Alma looked at her feet, ran a hand over her bangs.

"No, we're not," she said, "I'll be thirteen soon, actually."

"Yes, well anyway," his mother said. "Simen has his friends to hang out with and doesn't need a babysitter. But thanks for offering. Talk to you soon."

Alma looked at Simen's mother.

"Yeah, but will you, though?" she asked.

Simen's mother was already closing the door on her, now she opened it again.

"Will I what, Alma?"

"Talk to me soon!" Alma said. "Will you? Or was that just something you said?"

Simen's mother gave a little laugh. It was the first time Alma had ever seen her laugh. She had a nice smile. They looked at each other.

"A bit of both maybe," Simen's mother said. "I'm pretty certain I'll talk to you soon, I mean we are neighbors during the summer and bound to be bumping into each other. But yes, it was also something I just said. Okay?"

The summer before, though, Alma had been paid two hundred kroner to mind Simen for four hours. For the first hour Simen had been at home with Alma, at Mailund. He had thought it great fun to run up and down the big stairway that went from the basement to the attic (and counting the stairs—twenty-seven) where Jon worked. Then they had played dress up in Alma's room and Alma had brushed his long blond hair and then he had started screaming and protesting like a little girl. After a while Jenny emerged from her room upstairs and told Alma and Simen it was time they went out or found something else to do, she'd had enough of them running up and down the stairs and screaming inside the house, they were getting on her nerves.

Siri was about to leave for work, which meant that Jon would soon have to stop writing in order to take his turn with the children. That was the arrangement the summer before Milla. They split the day between them. Before Siri left she made up a picnic basket for Alma and Simen. Sandwiches, apple cake, and red lemonade. Liv wasn't allowed to go with them. She was too young.

"Don't go near the lake," Siri told Alma.

"No, no," Alma said. "We know."

"And take good care of Simen," Siri said. "Don't let him wander off, out of your sight." Then she stroked Simen's head and said, "Hi, Simen, how are you today?"

"Fine," Simen mumbled.

Alma rolled her eyes. Her mother always had to interfere.

"*I'm* the babysitter, you know," she whispered. "Why are you always interfering?"

So Alma and Simen went off to the woods and ate their picnic by the lake. It was possible to swim there, as long as you watched out for the water lilies, and Alma told Simen about the time when Syver had drowned somewhere around here years ago, and then she tipped her red lemonade into the water. She didn't like red lemonade. How many times had she told her mother that she didn't like red lemonade? She only liked the regular kind. Not the red stuff. Red lemonade tasted like puke. But, and Alma said none of this to Simen, her mother didn't listen. Siri never listened to anything Alma said. Siri probably wished she'd never had Alma. Alma looked out across the lake. Simen sat close beside her and she told him about Syver, and as she went on the story changed into a kind of fairy tale. She liked it that Simen listened to her, that he pressed close against her and listened.

IT WAS IMPERCEPTIBLE and almost painless. The way she divided herself in two, sometimes in four. She was about three or four years old the first time it happened, and she remembered feeling dizzy—as though she had inhaled an invisible gas. After Syver disappeared, she ran through the woods to the lake looking for him, and it was as if one Siri remained standing by that still, water-lilied surface (and never left), while the other went home to get help.

The year before he drowned she said that he wasn't the only one, just one of many.

"I have lots of sisters and brothers," she said. They were playing in the yard. "Sometimes we're invisible and sometimes we're not."

"You're Siri," Syver cried, "and you don't have any other sisters and brothers, you have me."

"But I do," said Siri. "And we all have different names."

"You're Siri," Syver cried again. He pulled off his gray woolly hat and planted himself in front of her. "You're Siri and I'm Syver."

He tried to take her hand, but she shoved him away.

"It's just us," he insisted, reaching for her one more time, his voice very quiet, "and we're the only ones."

It had to do with her mother's anger. It was absolutely necessary to divide herself. After a while it became a habit. She didn't even feel dizzy. It came as a relief, all she had to do was breathe and let the invisible gas do its work.

Jenny's wrath was so vast and black and impossible to check once it began to build up that it was sometimes best to divide herself and become a whole army. One who kept a lookout. One who fought. One who cried and begged for mercy. One who tried to reason. One who danced and fooled about. One who said sorry. One who brought fruit and comfort and hot tea. One who tried to make everything all right again. And one who ran away but did not get very far.

Her mother's body was a beautiful and complicated structure, like an empress's palace. But every week it was attacked— by demons and trolls and a good deal of liquor—and each time it crumbled, everything, all of Jenny, had to be rebuilt. Brick by brick, plank by plank, nail by nail. It could happen on Monday, or maybe Saturday, or maybe not at all that week, and that was scary, because then there was the waiting and the dreading—Siri knew that sooner or later it *would* happen. The palace *would* fall apart. Sometimes, though, Siri would allow herself to relax. She would get sloppy, speak a little too loud, hug her mother's body a little too tight, barge through the door, muddy the floor.

Forget to tread carefully.

When Jenny was in one of her good moods, she would prepare sumptuous dinners in the huge kitchen. The dining table, which could seat twelve, would be set for two with the best china and crystal, and both Jenny and Siri would put on their prettiest dresses and patent-leather shoes and lipstick and perfume; the freezer was full of ice cream (green pistachio)— as many helpings as you liked for dessert—and Jenny made her special casserole, which consisted of one tin of pork hash, one tin of cocktail sausages, one tin of spaghetti and meatballs in tomato sauce, and one tin of reindeer meatballs, a generous dollop of tomato puree, corn niblets, chives, a chunk of brown goat cheese to give it a nice gamey taste, and a sprig of parsley on the top.

The main thing was not to be sloppy. But Siri kept forgetting. Was not sufficiently alert. That was the problem.

She'd lose sight of the bigger picture.

She'd mess up.

And Syver lay in the water and Siri stood at the water's edge and Jenny opened the door wide and gazed down wonderingly at the skinny girl standing outside, gasping for breath.

"Oh, Siri, darling," Jenny said, "what is it? What's the matter with you?"

And then, more softly, but without the slightest trace of disquiet: "And what have you done with Syver?"

WHEN ALMA WAS ten she changed schools. She wasn't happy in the old one and she wasn't happy in the new one either; she made no friends and didn't play with the other children at recess, just sat on her own in a corner of the school yard or locked herself in a bathroom. It wasn't a problem, she told Jon, she would rather be alone.

"And anyway, you're my best friend," she said solemnly, "you're the one I want to spend time with."

"But I'm your father," Jon replied. "It's good to have friends your own age too."

"I just want you," Alma said.

"How about we invite one of the girls in your class to come home with you one day after school?" He struggled on. "That girl Ingrid, maybe? Or Marie, or—"

"Papa," Alma broke in, "do you believe in God?"

"No," Jon said. "I don't. But a lot of people do," he added. "What about Gina or Hannah? Maybe one of them would like to come home with you after school?"

"Mama doesn't believe in God either," Alma said. "Why don't either of you believe in God?"

"I think we believe in people," Jon replied. "In all that we human beings are capable of doing—for good and ill. We

build up and we destroy and we build up again, and I think
that every day involves a choice—"

"I believe in God," Alma broke in again, wrapping her arms
around her father. "I pray to God every day. I pray that you will
live a long, long time, because you're the one I love, and I pray
that you won't get sick and die, even though you're getting old."

"Excuse me!" Jon retorted with a strained little laugh. "I'm
not old!"

These conversations with his daughter left him ill at ease.
Why couldn't she—just once!—talk about the things other
ten-year-olds talked about?

Jon remembered the time he had brought Alma a bag of
surprises—that's what he had called it—different kinds of
candy, a pink lip gloss, a DVD about a girl who in fact was a
princess. "I have a surprise for you!" he'd cried as he walked
in the door. "A bag of surprises."

Alma had raced up to him, torn the bag out of his hand,
and peeked inside. Her eyes had narrowed when she saw what
it contained. Jon looked at her: *Oh, my God, she's going to cry.*
She pulled out the lip gloss and held it up to him between her
thumb and index finger as if it were a dead mouse. By now her
plump little face was streaming with tears. She put the lip gloss
in the bag again, handed it back to him, and said, "You don't
know me at all, do you!" Then she turned on her heel and ran
up the stairs.

Another day Alma said, "Sometimes God talks to me."

"Oh, and what does he say?"

"He says I have to do things for him, and if I don't do them you'll die."

"Oh, Alma, no!" Jon straightened up, put down his book, drew his daughter to him, and whispered, "What kinds of things does God tell you to do?"

"He tells me I have to stay awake all night and not sleep. He says I have to go out in the rain and run around the house a hundred times even though I don't want to. He says I have to cross the street when the light is red, not green, even if there are cars coming. He says I have to give away my stuffed animals, he says I have to eat mackerel in tomato sauce even though it makes me sick."

"Hey, wait a minute, Alma. Your mother and I thought you gave away all your stuffed animals because you didn't play with them any longer. You said yourself that you were too big for stuffed animals."

"I *am* too big for stuffed animals," Alma said. "That's not the point. But I would never have given Flop away if God hadn't said I had to."

"You gave away Flop?"

"I gave Flop to Knut in my class."

"Knut, the boy who was so horrible to you a while back?"

"Yes, Knut! And he said he was going to pee on Flop and throw him in the garbage, he said he didn't want anything that my scabby fingers had touched, but I went down on my knees and said he had to take Flop, he could do what he liked, but please, please would he take him."

"But Alma, why do you do things like that? Why do you give away... Have you talked to Mama about this?"

"I don't talk to Mama. I talk to you."

Jon cupped his hands around Alma's face and forced her to look at him.

"Why do you give away things you love to people who're not nice? Did you just say that you *went down on your knees?*"

Alma nodded. "If I don't do what God says," she whispered, "you'll die."

Neither Siri nor Jon could understand where Alma, at the age of ten, had picked up her hectic faith in God. The school psychologist was called in. Her teachers were alerted. It could be that Alma would bring stuff to school again and try to give it away, or in some other way "put herself in situations that invited fellow students to behave in an offensive manner," as the school's principal put it. Various diagnoses and medications were considered for Alma's sudden faith in God.

But then Alma stopped bringing her belongings to school to give away, she no longer kneeled down for fellow students who bullied her, and after that Alma was left in peace, and for a while it looked as though things were going to be all right.

ALMA WHISPERED SO that nobody would hear her: "So Milla, what do you do when you go out at night? Do you meet people you know? Other kids your age? Do boys come and see you here at Mailund after everyone's asleep? Do you fuck them, one after the other?"

Milla, who stayed in the red-painted annex, had lots of nice clothes and a lot of nice makeup. One evening—this was several days before the party—she washed Alma's short black hair in the washbasin and blew it dry so that the black cowlick sat nice and flat over her forehead along with the rest of her bangs.

Milla sprayed the freshly blow-dried hair with lots of hair spray. "To keep the cowlick down," she said.

Alma and Milla were in the little bathroom, both of them giggling and huddling together in front of the tiny mirror on the wall, and Milla looked at Alma and said, "You're fine, you know, Alma, you're just fine." Then Milla got out all her cool makeup and asked Alma if she would like to have a makeover.

Milla went into the bedroom and motioned to Alma to sit down on the bed.

"This will be your transformation," she said. "That's your dream, isn't it? To go back to school when summer's over as a totally new person."

"Don't know," Alma said. "Maybe."

When, after about half an hour, Milla was finished, she handed Alma a mirror. Alma squeezed her eyes tight shut and counted to ten. *One two three four five six seven eight nine ten.* She opened her eyes and looked at herself.

"I don't know," she said. "I don't know."

If she cried, the mascara would run like black rivers down her face.

Alma liked what Milla had done with her hair, but she didn't like the makeup. She didn't want to be a new person, or at least, not if that meant having red lips and orange cheeks. Just being Alma was more than enough for Alma. She didn't want to be new. She wiped off the lipstick and rubbed her cheeks to get rid of the bronzing powder.

"Well, at least keep your eyes the way I've done them," Milla said, looking at Alma in the mirror.

There was a thick layer of gray eye shadow on the lids. Alma thought she looked a litle bit like a raccoon.

"Don't rub it all off," Milla said. "Smoky eyes, that's what it's called, that look. It's nice. It makes you look kind of mysterious."

"I don't know," Alma said, looking doubtful. "I think there's too much eye shadow."

"No, it looks good," Milla said. "Makes you look a lot older."

Milla lit candles and put on a CD; she used her computer as a CD player. Alma recognized the song.

"My father has that CD too," Alma said. "It's Bob Dylan, right? Papa listens to Bob Dylan all the time. I didn't think kids your age listened to that sort of music."

"Oh, yes," Milla said vaguely, and smiled. "Or, I don't know. But I listen to Dylan a lot anyway."

And then Milla asked Alma if she would like to dance and Alma did and so they danced. It was a slow song, so they danced slowly and quite close together. Alma laid her head on Milla's shoulder and Milla held her close.

"You're fine, Alma," Milla said again.

"You too," Alma whispered. "I like you so much, Milla."

THERE WERE STILL a few hours to go until the party would begin. Alma knocked on Milla's door. It was afternoon and the mist was threatening to envelop the whole of Mailund, the house itself and the annex and all the tables and tablecloths and flowers in the garden. Milla opened the door and Alma squinted at her.

"What are you doing?" Alma asked.

"I'm praying," Milla said.

"What?" Alma said, and she blushed. "Like to God?"

Milla looked serious. She didn't giggle as she normally did. She was wearing a red dress. One black bra strap was just visible. Sun-kissed shoulders. Long hair hanging down. And something dark and shimmering and freshly tuned that said: Look at this, play on it, savor it.

A few days earlier Milla, Alma, and Liv had been lying on the grass in the garden, sunbathing. It was one of the few warm, sunny days of that summer. Liv had not exactly lain still, but had quieted down when she was allowed to play with Milla's phone.

"Remember to put sunscreen on Liv so she doesn't get burned," Siri said as she was leaving for work.

As she was on her way out, she said, "There's a salad in the fridge for you."

Then: "Please don't give the children candy. Sugar is poison, okay!"

Then: "And keep an eye on Liv at all times, Milla. Don't let her out of your sight."

Then: "Don't go near the lake, under no circumstances are you to go near the lake."

"Okay," Milla said, stretching lazily on the grass.

The day was hot and Milla had opted for the black polka-dot bikini that Liv liked so much. Milla had three bikinis, a red one, a blue one, and the one with black polka dots, and Liv liked the black polka-dot one best. "I want a bikini like that too. Can I have a bikini like Milla's?"

"Answer me properly, Milla," Siri snapped. "Did you hear what I said?"

Milla was just about to answer when Alma got to her feet.

"Mama!" she cried. Her voice cut through the heat. It was the kind of day, she might have said, were she to describe it, when everything was white and gummy and warm and still, when everything moved a little more slowly than usual.

Siri looked at her daughter inquiringly. "What, Alma?"

Her mother seemed to be a long way off. But she wasn't. She was standing by the garden gate. They couldn't have been more than ten paces away from each other. But something had happened to the distance between them. Like in a dream. Siri's admonitions. Milla stretching lazily on the grass. The black polka-dot bikini. Liv, long-limbed and fair-haired, sitting on the towel on the grass, playing a game on Milla's phone.

Alma cried, "Why can't you just be nice!"

"You don't have to yell at me, Alma," Siri said.

"But you go on and on at Milla," Alma persisted. "You really should learn to trust people."

Siri opened her mouth to say something, her cheeks were scarlet. She shook her head and closed the gate behind her.

"We'll talk about this tomorrow, Alma. Text me if you need anything and remember to put sunscreen on."

Her voice and her shadow hung in the heat for a few moments before they evaporated. Alma munched a cookie slowly, Liv stared, mesmerized, at something deep inside Milla's phone, five minutes could have passed, or five hours, then suddenly Jon was standing there in front of them in the garden, waking them from their dream. He had Leopold with him.

Liv threw down the phone, ran as fast as she could, and leaped into her father's arms. Alma and Milla lay where they were on the grass. Jon took a few steps toward them, then stopped and looked down at them.

"So here are all my girls, soaking up the sun," he said, smiling.

Alma looked up at her father. Something about his voice. The slightly false note. The jolliness that wasn't genuine jolliness, just forced jolliness.

"A little touch of Saint-Tropez, eh?" he went on.

Alma tried to catch his eye, so he would see that she was rolling hers. *A little touch of Saint-Tropez*—please! What was the matter with him? But her father didn't notice her. He was looking at Milla. Alma followed his gaze and saw how it flicked swiftly over Milla's body—her feet, her legs, her knees, the polka-dot bikini, her arms, her hair, her eyes—as if Milla's body were the goddamned solar system. And Alma realized that Milla was letting him do it. That she was lying there perfectly still, letting him do it. This was not a dream. Alma saw it all very clearly. Jon looked at Milla, and Milla let herself be looked at by Jon. It didn't last very long. Alma noticed how Milla stretched out a little, there, beside her on the grass. Writhed over the heavens like the aurora borealis. And then it was over.

"Don't you all look nice," Jon said. And now he looked at Alma.

"What are you doing here?" Alma asked. "Don't you have a book to finish?"

Jon gave a quick laugh.

"Thank you, Alma. Yes, I do. But right now Leopold and I are going for a little walk. As long as nobody else can be bothered to walk him, I have to do it, right?"

He set Liv gently down on the grass between Milla and Alma.

"Take good care of this little one," he added, and then looked at Milla in a very different way from before. "Take care, all of you." He bent down to attach Leopold's leash and walked off through the gate.

"Have fun in Saint-Tropez," Alma shouted after him. She rolled over onto her stomach, so she wouldn't have to look at him.

"Your father's really nice," Milla said after a few moments.

"My father's an idiot," Alma mumbled.

And now here was Alma, a few days later, knocking on Milla's door; there were only a few hours to go until Jenny's big celebration and Milla had told her she was praying to God.

"Okay, you can come in," Milla said. "I have to go over and help your mother later on. But you can stay till I go."

Alma pushed the door open.

Milla sat down on the bed and beckoned to Alma to come and sit beside her. Alma sat down beside her.

"What do you pray for?" Alma asked.

"This and that," said Milla. "But I'm finished now. Do you want me to put on music?"

Alma shook her head and said, "Do you believe in God?"

"Yes, I always have." Milla turned and looked at Alma. "Do you?"

"I did when I was younger," Alma said. "But I don't anymore."

"Why not?"

"Don't know," Alma replied. "I just don't."

"I do," said Milla. "I think he sees me and watches over me."

Alma shrugged.

"God sees everything," Milla added. "When I was little my father used to sing to me every night."

She opened her mouth and sang in a clear, high voice:

Jesus bids us shine
With a pure, clear light.
Like a little candle
Burning in the night.
In this world of darkness
So let us shine,
You in your small corner
And I in mine.

"What's your father's name?" Alma asked.

"Mikkel," said Milla.

"And your mother?"

"Amanda."

"Can I have a glass of water?" Alma asked.

Milla frowned. "Get it yourself," she said. "There's a glass in the bathroom."

"Can't you get it for me?" Alma said. "Please." She swung her legs up onto the bed and settled herself more comfortably. "I'm so nice and comfortable here on your bed. I'll get water for you some other time, when you're thirsty." Alma laughed. "Swear to God, I will," she said.

Milla didn't laugh, didn't so much as smile, she merely got up and went into the bathroom. Alma heard the tap being turned on.

Hidden in her hand Alma had a long, fat Iberian slug. It stuck to her palm.

Alma detached it from her skin and laid it under Milla's duvet. A thread of slug slime clung to her fingers and she wiped her hand on the sheet. There! The slug drew in on itself and lay very still. Alma straightened the duvet and perched herself on the edge of the bed. When Milla got back tonight she would lay her bare thighs on top of the slug.

Alma smiled.

Milla emerged from the bathroom carrying a glass of water. "Here," she said. Her voice was cold. "Drink this and then you have to go."

Alma took the glass and eyed Milla. She had put on makeup and brushed her hair to a long, shining fall.

Milla said, "Okay, now I have to go help your mother, and then I've got other things to do. I don't have time for you."

She gave an impatient flick of her hand and her bracelets jingled.

"That's okay," Alma said. She drank the water. "I'm going now."

SIRI WANTED TO throw a big party for her mother. Jenny had said no, but Siri insisted. Of course she would throw her mother a party. Fifty guests, suckling pigs imported from Spain, long trestle tables in the garden, lanterns in the trees, she would not take no for an answer, she could roast the pigs in the big bread oven in her restaurant kitchen.

"We'll need five pigs," Siri said, and picked up her cell phone and called the supplier in Oslo. "And I'll roast some apples and root vegetables and potatoes. And that'll be it. We'll keep it nice and simple. The porch will have to be painted. Everybody will have to pitch in and help. The curtains will need to be taken down and washed. We'll have to scrub the floors. Where's the soap? I want the carbolic! This house," she said, spreading her arms as if to embrace all of Mailund. "We'll have to fix up the house. And the garden too. A garden party!"

She turned to Jon.

"It'll be a party to remember," she said. "And Jenny will be very happy. She can't see that herself right now, but she'll be so happy. She loves being the center of attention."

"Yes, but what Jenny wants most of all is to be left alone," Jon said.

And now the big day had arrived. That miserable seventy-fifth birthday. Jenny was drunk after having been sober for nearly twenty years. *A lifetime.* It had certainly *felt* like a lifetime. Jenny's speech was slurred when Jon ran into her on the stairs.

"Good afternoon, Jon," she said.

Jon stopped and looked at her. "Jenny, are you drunk?" Jon peered at her.

"I've been sober for more than twenty years. Which is more than can be said for you, is it not?"

"Well, you do pick your days," Jon mumbled.

"Yes," Jenny said, "that's right. I *do* pick my days!"

He glanced around and lowered his voice. "Does Siri know you've been drinking?"

"I'm seventy-five years old and I do what I like."

Jenny ran a hand through her hair and signaled to Jon that she wanted to get past—they were still on the stairs—but Jon stayed her with his hand and stepped right up close to her.

"I'm going to say this just once, Jenny, so listen," he whispered.

She nodded while at the same time trying to push him away. Jon carried on whispering: "Siri has worked very hard to arrange this nice party for you. How about showing a little..."

He searched his mind for the right word. Consideration? No, that was too much to ask for. Gratitude? No, he refused to resort to emotional blackmail. And, to be fair, it wasn't as if the old witch had asked to be celebrated. Decency? Maturity? Maternal feeling? He began again, released her arm, and spoke in his normal voice.

"Jenny, how about *pretending* that you appreciate what Siri has done? I mean the party and all. It would mean a lot to her."

She shook her head and began to walk away.

"Did you hear what I said, Jenny?"

Jenny made no reply, but simply continued her descent of the stairs, slowly and with exaggerated dignity.

The suckling pigs were vacuum-packed and crated. Jon pictured them lying in the supplier's freezer room in Oslo: pink, bordering on white, their snouts creased in a gentle grin. The skin of their necks and front legs lying in folds like that of a well-fed infant. They were deep-frozen, imported from Spain. Five pigs, 170 kroner per kilo plus VAT, six kilos per pig. Siri got them wholesale.

"Okay, we'll have them some other time," Siri said, having either changed her mind at the last minute or succumbed to pressure.

Because nobody wanted those suckling pigs. Alma had googled "suckling pigs" and found pictures of whole pigs burning on barbecues; she had begun wailing, and did not stop until Jenny took her to the beach for a swim. Irma had muttered something about the slaughter of animals and cannibalism and disappeared into the basement. So now, instead of the pigs, Siri was in the kitchen putting the finishing touches to a menu that she *had no heart for*: scampi, chicken skewers, meatballs, salads, and *other stupid fiddly finger food. Happy now, everybody?*

Days, no, weeks before the birthday, Jon had done everything
he could to talk Siri out of the suckling pigs idea. He had done
all he could to talk her out of the party. Jenny didn't want it!
No one wanted it! He had sat his wife down on their bed,
kneeled in front of her, and taken her hands in his.

"Why are you arranging this party, really?"

"Well, who else is going to do it?" Siri said. "Her birthday
has to be celebrated."

"Yeah, but does it really?"

"Of course it does!" Siri looked at him. "Why are you
bringing this up now?"

"She won't thank you for it, you know."

Siri stood up, her voice shrill: "Come on, Jon. I'm organiz-
ing a party for my mother, both you and I know that deep
down she'll be happy about it, she loves the attention, she's already decided what dress she's going to wear, this is my present
to her, it's as simple as that. And now here you are, doubting
my motives, insinuating that I'm, I don't know, crazy or something, stupid little Siri, throwing this big party for her mother.
Well, to hell with you!"

"Would you listen to yourself?" he said. "You're getting so
wrapped up in this, it's like I'm losing you."

"*You're* losing *me* . . ." Siri gasped. "*You're* losing *me?* You're
the one who's lost, Jon, you're the one who's never around, out
with the dog, out buying bread and milk, out, out, out, and
concocting some crappy theory about me and my mother and
this whole fucking party . . . ?"

Jon took a deep breath. "It's getting totally out of hand, Siri." He waved his arm. "This...all this...this whole celebration, it's tearing you apart. She doesn't want it, I'm telling you, she doesn't want it!"

He put his arms around her. She tried to wriggle free, but he would not let her go.

"Let me go, Jon," she said.

He held on to her, tried to rock her back and forth, whispered, "Why don't you sit here with me? Just for five minutes. Don't say anything. Just let me hold you." He laid his head on her breast, whispered, "Stay with me."

Sometimes he could get through to her like this.

"Come back, Siri."

But not this time apparently. She wrenched herself free, grabbed a fistful of his hair, and pulled, screaming, "Let me go!"

He just had time to remember the pain of hair being yanked before he slapped her face. She hit him back.

And at that moment he could have killed her. "I hate you," she screamed, and he yelled "No" and hit her and held on to her and pushed her away and he would never, never, never be able to beat his way out of her, into her, and she shouted "I hate you" and all he could say was "No, no, no." So he shouted it out loud, howled "No, no, no," held on to her until suddenly, without any effort, she wrenched herself free of his grasp, his arms seemed to wither, she simply broke free, as if everything had grown withered and weak, he didn't know what to do with his arms, or his hands, and she got up off the bed and shook herself (the way Leopold did after he'd been swimming) and took a deep breath.

Her cheeks went scarlet when they fought like this. It wasn't the blows that turned them red. He hadn't hit her hard. She had hit harder. But he was afraid that one day he would hit too hard. He was not a man who hit women. But he was afraid that one day he would strike Siri and the blow would be irrevocable. But the red flush was not brought on by the blows. Her cheeks always turned scarlet when she got angry like this, looking as though she had clawed her face.

"You haven't lifted a finger, Jon, to help me with this party." She was shaking. "This party that I'm arranging while at the same time working at the restaurant. Would you like to know how it's going? Are you interested? Have you actually worked lately? Or do you just sit there staring at your phone? Taking walks with the dog. And guess who was up most of last night, after coming home late from work, paying the bills? Are you at all aware that we receive bills, and that they get paid?" And then, in a perfectly normal voice, she added: "A life without you, Jon. I dream about it, you know. A life without you and those cold hands of yours."

He had done everything he could to talk her out of it, but it did no good, and now the dreaded day had arrived. Jon looked out the window.

He peered down at Alma, Liv, and Milla out there picking flowers for the trestle tables. More than once Milla turned around and seemed to look straight at him; he closed his eyes, did not want to meet her gaze, even though he knew, of course, that there was no way that she, so far below and so far away, could see him standing there. And yet maybe she did know after all. He had mentioned to her that sometimes, when he could not bring himself to sit still in front of his computer, he would stand at the attic window and look out across the meadow and the woods.

But then he looked at his daughters and felt like crying.

He had messed everything up, hadn't he?

JON RETURNED TO his desk, but the image of the girls in the grass stayed with him. He thought of Alma, remembering *her* birthday. What was it, he wondered, about the Brodal women and their birthdays?

When Alma turned eleven, Siri and Jon invited all of the girls in her class to a party—and almost all of them said they would come. The day before the party Jon took Alma into town to buy her a birthday outfit. Alma was small and chubby and together they settled on a skirt and blouse in the same shimmery silver fabric. They also bought shoes. And had scones and cocoa at a coffee shop. Then they went to the hairdresser to have Alma's short black hair trimmed.

"Maybe you could feather the edges around her face," Jon whispered to the young female hairdresser. He studied his daughter in the salon mirror. "Soften it up around your face so you don't look so gruff. Don't you think?"

Jon smiled lamely, patted Alma's cheek, and went off to sit by the door, where he found a woman's magazine to hide behind.

Why wasn't Siri doing this? Taking her daughter clothes shopping, getting her a hair cut? Because she was working, yes. Earning money. Paying the bills. And he wasn't working.

His book, his volume number three, his grand finale, was no longer considered work.

He looked at his computer screen.

Today he had written the following: *Note to self: Must elaborate.*

When the girls from Alma's class began to arrive for the party, Alma ran up to her room, got into her bed, and hid under her blanket. Jon followed her, sat on the edge of her bed, and told her, as gently as he could, that her guests had arrived, that they had brought presents, that Alma really did have to come down now. Reluctantly she followed her father downstairs to the living room where eleven girls were waiting for her.

The sound of high-pitched voices, giggling, and squeals of excitement had filled the house, but silence fell when Alma walked into the living room with Jon right behind her.

The eleven girls looked at Alma, Alma looked at the eleven girls.

Jon thought they looked like two armies facing each other across a plain, with Alma the only soldier in her regiment.

But then the silence was broken.

"Hi, Alma," said one of the girls.

"Hi, Alma, happy birthday," said a second.

"You're hair's really nice," said a third.

"Aren't you going to open your presents?" said a fourth.

"I like your silver skirt," said a fifth.

The group of girls broke up and flocked together again—this time around Alma. They patted her, they hugged her;

suddenly, for a moment, she was their chosen one, their best beloved, they could not get enough of her. It reminded Jon of the day when he had gone to pick up Alma from school and had taken their puppy, Leopold, into the schoolyard and how he had been besieged on all sides by small, avid, affectionate, pleading little girls, all wanting to stroke the dog's fluffy coat with their soft, eager little hands, he remembered the girlish mouths, so much tender skin at one time, a choir of piping voices: *Oh he's so cute! Can I pet him, please? His ears are so soft!*

All the girls in Alma's class were at least a head taller than Alma, most of them had shoulder-length or long hair adorned with beads and clasps, and now here was Jon's daughter, in the living room, surrounded by them, Alma with her pitch-black hair and shining eyes, engulfed by them.

She had deigned to be petted, had offered no resistance, had made no faces, she had opened her presents (four books, a board game, a hairdressing set, lip gloss, sparkly tights, a blue short-sleeved top, a glass-bead necklace, a bracelet) and given each and every girl a polite thank-you hug. Siri whispered to Jon, "I think Alma's enjoying herself," and Jon had nodded, but he could not tear himself away from his daughter's eyes, burning.

After an hour the birthday girl and her guests took their seats at the long, festively decorated dining-room table to continue celebrating Alma's special day with pizza, lemonade, and cake. Siri and Jon worked their way slowly around the table, pouring lemonade into paper cups and helping to lift slices of pizza onto paper plates. The girls were all babbling and chattering, all except Alma, who sat quietly watching her guests.

They were now oblivious to her. She was no longer their best beloved. They no longer loved her shimmering silver skirt, or her short black hair with its new bangs, or her eyes, burning. The birthday party was almost over, after the pizza there might be some dancing and then everybody would be presented with a goody bag and home they would go. The guests had done what their parents had asked them to do: They had gone to Alma's birthday party and they had been nice! It had gone well.

Yes, we had a great time.

Yes, yes, we had pizza.

And yes, Alma liked her present.

But then Alma got up from her chair and put her arms in the air. Her cheeks were red, her eyes burning. All the girls stopped talking and stared at her.

"Look, Papa!" she cried. Her body was trembling, tears spilled from her eyes.

Siri dropped what she had in her hands (a slice of pizza, a yellow paper napkin) and started to run around the table, Jon got to her first and caught Alma in his arms as she collapsed onto the floor.

"Alma, darling. What's wrong?"

Alma looked up at her father, eyes brimming with tears, and laughed. "I know everything's going to be okay now. I'm so happy."

Alma flung her arms around her father's neck and he sat down on the floor with his daughter in his arms. Siri stood over them, but what was she supposed to do with her hands? There was silence. Eleven speechless, big-eyed girls waited to be told what to do. Jon looked at Siri and saw his own despair reflected in her eyes. Alma clung tightly to her father, laughing loudly against his chest. Her laughter was full of light. Jon felt her breath on his skin, through the thin fabric of his shirt.

He nodded to Siri, *Straighten up, see to the girls, you have to say something. Say something, for God's sake, Siri, do something, don't just stand there!*

Siri straightened up and looked at the girls—soft hair, soft skin, soft voices. She forced herself to smile, although Jon could see that all she really wanted to do was put her hands over her ears, as if she were just a little girl herself.

She looked at the girls.

"Alma..." she began helplessly, spreading her arms. "Alma isn't feeling... well."

The girls stared at Alma lying on the floor in her father's lap.

Then one of them said, "But if Alma's not feeling well, why is she laughing?"

AND AGAIN HE looked at the screen. *Note to self: Must elaborate!*

Fuck that!

Then he wrote: *I love my family. I am an asshole. I will never finish this book.*

He got up from his chair for the fiftieth time that morning. He was more restless than usual today, dreading the party. The large majority of the guests were old, many in their eighties, one or two past ninety. The thought of these very old people coming here to dance with cobwebs in their hair, and of Jenny there on the stairs, quite clearly drunk, of himself as a dead man in a swimming pool (not that there was a swimming pool in the garden at Mailund, but this is how he imagined his life at the moment), reminded him of *Sunset Boulevard*, which he had made up his mind to see again as soon as possible, and the thought of this cheered him up. He and Siri could watch it together.

Jon logged on to Amazon and ordered *Sunset Boulevard* to be sent express, it cost three hundred kroner extra, but that way he would have the film in just two days. He envisaged his wife, her asymmetric form, her slender bones, her white filmy dress, tablecloths billowing around her.

Did she know that Jenny was drinking in her room?

He didn't have the heart to tell her. Or maybe he just couldn't get up the courage. As far as this party was concerned, he had no fight left in him.

Leopold got up and put his paw in Jon's lap. It was Siri who had wanted a dog. He hadn't wanted a dog. But now they had a dog and he was the one who took care of it. And even as he felt his annoyance at this rising (he hadn't wanted a dog, had put his foot down, had said "I think we should wait," yet now the dog was his responsibility, no one else bothered with it, why was that?) a text message from Karoline chimed in on his cell phone: *What are you doing?*

Without hesitation he replied: *Thinking of you.*

Which was not exactly true. He wasn't thinking of Karoline at all. But that was probably what she wanted to hear.

He put down the phone and looked at the computer screen: *Must elaborate!*

Then another message came in. He picked up the phone. It was her again: *That's nice to know, and kind of wistful too.*

What the hell did that mean? What was nice and kind of wistful too? Jon clicked on MESSAGES SENT. There it was: *Thinking of you.*

Oh yes, right. He had written that he was thinking of her and she thought that was nice and kind of wistful. *Because they were both married? Because the world could never know about their romance?* Darling Karoline! *Wistful?* Really? He laughed. Leopold raised his head and looked at him. *What kind of a laugh was that?* Jon wasted no time in deleting his messages, both the messages in his INBOX and those under MESSAGES SENT, and he remembered to delete the ones in the DELETED MESSAGES box too. He knew that Siri read his e-mails and also the texts on his phone, so he never forgot to delete the DELETED MESSAGES, although it felt equally pointless every time.

The whole idea behind deleting a message was to actually delete it, no? Not to assign it to another box, or file, or whatever, called DELETED MESSAGES.

Because your message was not, in fact, deleted if you pressed DELETE. It was simply reassigned to DELETED MESSAGES. It was not deleted, effectively and decidedly deleted, as in *gone*, until you clicked on DELETED MESSAGES and answered the question: *Are you sure you want to delete this message?*

Jon liked the idea that she, Karoline, had a summer house just down the road. He liked that they could run into each other at any time and that he could run his hand down the inside of her thigh whenever he felt like it and under anyone's nose. He liked that he could take the dog for a walk or go to the store for some milk or bread and she'd be there. He could just send her a text. It was so easy. She was so close. Just down the street. Nobody had to know. It was right there in front of them—his wife, her husband—but nobody had to know. Difficult romances were overrated. To Jon, Karoline represented the thrill of convenience. She was always available and nobody had to find out.

Once—last winter—he had invited this woman to his house in Oslo; an arts journalist who had written an admiring piece on his books in *Dagbladet*. He had sent her an e-mail, thanking her for such an insightful and well-written critique. And so it began.

Some months later Siri flew down to Copenhagen for the day. She had a meeting with a talented new chef. Something like that. Or maybe it was something else. He didn't remember exactly what had taken her to Copenhagen. The main thing was that she was going away and would be away for a whole twenty-four hours, and in another country at that. He could hardly wait. He made plans. He sent a text message to the arts journalist, inviting her to his house. He was going to fuck her right there in the middle of his and Siri's drafty, heavily mortgaged house. Until then, he had underestimated the erotic power of the betrayal itself. That all-surpassing power of knowing what he could do, anywhere and anytime he pleased, there was so much pleasure in store for him if he just lighten up and let himself experience it.

He pictured her on the expensive gray couch in the living room, her legs splayed. Jon was not going to skulk around the edges any longer. What he wanted was to be able to destroy everything and still endure. Wrecked, sanguine, alert. He had been tired for a very long time. The taste of tired. The smell of tired. Irene was her name, the arts journalist, freelance and free for that entire day and he was going to have her—have her and have her and have her until she was all gone and he would rise up, finally awake.

She had rung the doorbell. Had parked a few blocks away. Taken care not to be seen by the neighbors. All of this they had agreed. The quick text messages full of anticipation. What they had not agreed, however, was that she would bring her dog. A stupid little mutt that stood in the hall and barked when it saw Leopold. Jon was all at once keenly aware of where he was, of the things surrounding him, of the scene being played out: the clothes cupboard from IKEA, the colorful baskets full of scarves and mittens and woolly hats—one basket for him, one for Siri, one for Liv, and one for Alma—the dark hardwood floor, the shoes and boots and sneakers spread all over, which were supposed to be kept on the shoe rack but were never put on the shoe rack, a child's begrimed drawing of a pink girl under a beaming yellow sun, signed LIV. And in the midst of all this, in Siri and Jon's house, Irene the arts journalist's stupid mutt, barking at Leopold and at Jon. As if *they* were the intruders.

"Why did you bring the dog?" Jon asked.

"Julius needed a walk," said Irene. She tugged at the leash, trying to control the little creature. "I couldn't leave him for the whole day," she added.

"You're not staying the whole day!" Jon snapped.

He tried to summon up the picture of this woman, Irene the arts journalist, with her legs splayed on the sofa. But she did not look as he remembered. They had met a few weeks earlier, briefly, at a café, and since then he had inundated her with text messages and e-mails. *All the things he was going to do to her.* During the week following that first brief meet at the café he had been all aflame. Yes, exactly that. All aflame. But the woman standing here now, in his and Siri's house, was podgy and had a hint of a mustache.

Leopold sat quietly next to Jon, staring at the stupid mutt. It wouldn't stop barking and Jon thought of their neighbor. He knew that Emma, who lived in the adjoining house, was at home during the day, working on her dissertation. She was bound to be hearing all of this. The house wasn't just drafty, the walls were paper thin as well. You could hear everything your neighbors did.

"Julius, is that your dog's name?" Jon asked quietly.

"Yes…"

"Wouldn't Brutus be better?"

"What… I don't… what do you mean?"

That was as far as she got. Because at that moment Leopold growled, bristled, and got to his feet. He lunged at the smaller dog, picked it up between his teeth and shook it from side to side. Irene screamed and hauled on its leash, the mutt whined, Jon made a dive at Leopold and managed to drag him away and up the stairs to his study in the attic.

"Stupid mutt!" he muttered. "Fur ball! Ratty little runt."

Jon patted Leopold and scratched him behind his ear.

"Not you," he whispered and closed the door.

The big mongrel gave him a doleful look.

"You're a good dog, Leopold, but stay here, okay?"

He opened the door again and went back downstairs, expecting to find the ground floor transformed into a battlefield with blood and bits of stupid little dog splattered everywhere, but all was well.

"Maybe this wasn't such a great idea," Irene said when she caught sight of him on the stairs. She was cradling her dog in her arms, like a baby. He saw her looking around. *What the hell are you gawking at? Our stuff? Siri's and my stuff? My children's stuff?* Jon picked up Liv's drawing from the floor, it was lying halfway under a boot, and smoothed it out. The pink girl smiled. So did the yellow sun.

"I think I'll go now," said Irene. "This was probably not a good idea."

Jon cleared his throat, folded the drawing, and put it in his trouser pocket.

"Couldn't you stay a little while?" he said. "I'll make us some coffee."

He hoped she would say no. That she would leave now. She had said she was going, and so she should honor that. But she nodded and said, "Coffee would be nice—and maybe some water for Julius. It scared him, being attacked like that."

She moved in close to him. She smiled. She still had the tubby little rat cradled in her arms, like some sick parody of a Renaissance painting of the Madonna and child.

"Maybe you should keep that dog of yours under better control," she said softly, and stroked his cheek. "He could be put down for less, you know."

But now there was Karoline. The one he had been exchanging text messages with this particular summer, and also the summer before and the summer before that. Karoline who had a summer house just down the road with her husband, Kurt. Karoline whom he had known since he was fifteen.

Not an arts journalist, but a dentist. Fortunately not a book person at all. Karoline didn't have opinions about books, not his books, not other people's books. This was one of the things he liked most about her.

Karoline and Jon had been neighbors many years ago, when he was a kid. And best pals. And teenage sweethearts. She had short fair hair, long pretty fingers, was very athletic, very good-looking. The problem with Karoline was that she was boring—*humorless*. But she thought *he* was funny and that mattered more.

He had introduced her and her husband, also a dentist, to Siri and Siri had treated them to a fine dinner at Gloucester. The two couples had hit it off right from the start and began doing the sort of things together that grown-up couples do with other grown-up couples and even talked about how easy it was, how uncomplicated, how great it was to make new friends after forty. It was rare for Jon and Siri to get along so well with others as a couple.

Once they had tried socializing with another set of Mailund neighbors. There was this couple, a little younger than they, who had bought the summer house practically next door to Jenny's house. That couple had a son. Christian was his name. But oh, his parents were always arguing. And they were always renovating their house, starting projects they couldn't or wouldn't finish, among other things a hideous veranda outside their bedroom, and their entire outside area looked a mess.

Siri and Jon began making excuses for why they couldn't meet up or have dinner. It was too exhausting. The arguing. The mess. The junk. Their overall hopelessness. Jon remembered feeling sorry for the boy, though. He was their only one. They didn't have any other children. But then he remembered how he would see Christian rummaging around his parents' garden and in their shed finding old planks and nails and broken pottery—all kinds of forgotten treasures—which he obviously knew how to make something of. This was a comfort, Jon thought. The boy would be all right.

It was an art: to be able to be adults with other adults, effortlessly. But Jon and Siri and Karoline and Kurt managed just fine. At least for a while. They invited each other to little gatherings, went for long Sunday walks in the forest and on the beach, and even tried arranging joint outings with their respective children. The Mandls were very outdoorsy.

They too had a son, Gunnar, who was a few years younger than Alma, but the same age as Christian, and there was a grown-up son too, Morten, from a previous marriage, but he wasn't around all that much.

Gunnar made it very clear that he wanted nothing to do with the Dreyer-Brodals.

Once Jon overheard Gunnar whisper to his father, "I don't want us to be with these people, Dad."

Jon ran the words over in his mind.

I don't want us.

I don't want us to be with these people.

These people.

From a ten-year-old boy.

But despite this—children behaving in such a way that embarrasses the parents and the parents pretending not to notice—the Dreyer-Brodals and the Mandls tried planning things to do together with the children, things that were always canceled at the last minute.

Once there was a plan to do a picnic at the beach, and again Jon overheard Gunnar: "No fucking way!"

"You do not..." Kurt hissed back, looking desperately around to see if Jon or Siri had heard or seen anything. "You do not use that kind of language... okay?"

Jon turned around and stared out the window and pretended not to have heard anything.

Siri and Karoline were discussing what kind of food to buy. They had all met at the grocery store by coincidence one late afternoon and, in a matter of minutes and a little too enthusiastically, come up with this idea of a picnic—and yes, right away.

"Listen, Dad," Gunnar continued. "Alma is weird... She's a freak, you know... that's what Simen says. He knows her. She made him dress up like a doll and brushed his hair and treated him like... she's a freak, Dad. They all are. We don't want to hang out with them."

Excuses were made and plans to go on a picnic "very soon" were immediately agreed upon. Jon was always relieved when the couples-and-kids things were canceled. He didn't much like the couples things either. What he was interested in (he pondered the word *interest* and how he felt that he really wasn't interested in anything at the moment and wondered if that was a result of the sadness he felt) was this: that he could text *Thinking of you* anytime it suited him, the convenience of being able to fuck her pretty much under anyone's nose, and that she thought he was funny.

Jon eyed Leopold. And then he texted: *I'm taking the dog for a walk. Meet me?*

Back came the prompt reply: *Yes.*

And then he wrote: *Do you have a little time? Do you have to get back right away?*

And right back: *No. I have time.*

Jon looked at his computer screen again.

Must elaborate!

He clicked his way out of the document and stroked Leopold's soft ears. Then he looked out the attic window. There was mist and rain in the air. Milla and the kids were still out picking flowers. Milla had on a woolen jacket. She hopped and danced about, clumsy and heavy, he noticed that she had a big ass. She was an oversized child who had started leeching onto him. *Have to put a stop to that!*

He turned to the dog. "Come on, Leopold, time for a walk."

Leopold jumped up and loped after him down the stairs. Siri was in the kitchen on the ground floor; she called out when she heard him on the way down.

"Are you all done writing?"

She met him at the bottom of the stairs, gazed at him with that mystified look of hers.

"No, but the dog needs to get out too, you know," he replied.

Her dark hair was pulled up into a loose knot. She was wearing a thin summer dress, the white one that he liked so much. The front door was open onto the garden, it had grown dark outside. The air was both cool and damp. Siri looked as if she'd been crying—her eyes always shone after crying.

"Where are you going?" she asked.

"Out with the dog," he said again. "Somebody has to take the dog out."

111

Siri lowered her eyes.

"I'm just worried about the party," she said. "I'm afraid it might rain."

"Well, then it'll just have to rain, won't it?"

He wondered if she knew that Jenny had been drinking.

"It's my mother's seventy-fifth birthday," she said, "it *can't* rain."

"No... well, we'll just have to wait and see," Jon said.

He pulled Leopold out the door and made to shut it behind him. She ran after him.

"Where are you going?" she asked.

"Out with the dog, Siri," Jon said. "Leopold's dying for a walk. I'll be back in half an hour. Or an hour. Is there anything you want me to help you with when I get back? You need me to slice things? Carry anything?"

Siri shook her head, stood in the doorway, shivering slightly in the mist-damp breeze. She looked up at the sky.

"It might clear up" she said.

"I think it will," he said and stroked her hair. "I'm quite sure it will, Siri. I think it's going to be a great party."

ALMA SAW HER father walking down the hill with Leopold in tow. Where was he off to now? Out buying bread. Out buying milk.

She didn't care. No one cared. And here everyone was getting ready for the party. Grandma didn't want to celebrate her birthday. But you could scream I DON'T WANT TO at Alma's mother and she would carry on as though nothing had happened. Alma's mother wanted to have this party and that was all that mattered.

Jenny said, "Alma, tonight we'll get out of here. Once the party's in full swing we'll take the car and run away from it all, we'll take a couple of deck chairs, some food, and something to drink and we'll sit on the beach and look out to sea, and the thicker the fog gets, the harder it rains, the better."

"We'll get wet," Alma said.

"We'll take umbrellas and fix them to the deck chairs and pretend they're parasols," Jenny said, "and then we'll let it all come down."

JENNY OPENED BOTTLE number two and cursed the fact that she had not succeeded in putting a stop to all of this. Goddamn it! Who were all these people who were coming to her house? Jenny wanted none of it, Irma wanted none of it. But Siri hadn't listened to anyone.

"Of course you have to have a celebration," Siri had said. "Of course your birthday has to be commemorated, Mama!"

Siri had actually used the word *commemorate*. As if Jenny were some precious inanimate thing in a glass cabinet.

Jenny drank her wine and shot a glance out the window. She rested her eyes on her youngest grandchild, little Liv of the tousled blond locks. From there her eye moved to the lumpish, moon-pretty teenager whose name she could never remember. *The nanny!* Couldn't Jon and Siri look after their children themselves? Jenny had not had any help in the house. Jenny had not even had a husband. Her husband had run off to Sweden. Jenny had done it all on her own. She bent down to scratch the lump on her toe. It was hard, like a walnut, not squashy like a cyst or growth, like the one they removed from her breast ten years ago, which had turned out to be benign. She wondered if she'd even feel anything if she jammed something into it—the thing on her toe—a piece of broken glass or a pair of scissors.

This was just a thought. She had no intention of jamming anything into anything. She got up. She could bend down and get up like she was a twenty-year-old girl, still quick and limber. But write a speech—that she could not do.

It grew darker as she stood there, she smacked her lips, tried to draw the fog to her with her eyes, to dissolve herself in it and become one with it.

"Her name's Milla," Siri had said. "But she's also called sweet pea."

"Sweet what?"

"Sweet pea."

The grass was cut and the house scrubbed. Irma had spent seven whole days on her hands and knees, scrubbing the broad floorboards with carbolic soap. The week before she had washed down the ceilings and walls. The week before that, drawers and cupboards. She had left the windows to Siri.

Jenny shook her head.

Irma was good to have around the house. No fuss with her. Took care of all the odd jobs now that Ola, Jenny's neighbor and friend, was too old for that. Maintained the house. Mowed the lawn. And, above all, Irma left her in peace.

Jenny went on standing there, looking out the window.

And Irma had set out long trestle tables in the garden and on the tables were the freshly ironed white cloths that Siri had carried in and out, then in again and then out again, so they wouldn't get wet when it rained, and on the freshly ironed white cloths were glass vases filled with the flowers that Liv and Alma and Milla had picked in the meadow behind the house. The trees were hung with lanterns, which was good, because even though it was summer and the nights normally were bright, the fog was rolling in over Mailund, getting thicker and thicker as the afternoon wore on.

The fog mingled with the aroma of dishes that Siri had been preparing in the kitchen, slipped around the serried ranks of wine bottles, the plates, cutlery, and glasses standing at the ready on the big white-clothed table under the apple trees, stole under the doorsteps and windowsills and through every cranny of the old house, drifted through the bedrooms and living rooms and kitchen and out into the garden again and over the meadow behind the house where Liv and Alma and Milla had picked flowers, but Liv had not acknowledged the fog, even though it had acknowledged her, and not until she and Alma and Milla had picked a whole bucketful of wildflowers did it begin to drizzle again and the fog blended with the scent of the rain and summer evening and Jenny's perfume, because now the birthday girl was almost ready to come down the stairs and greet her guests, and the fog melded with the light from the lanterns hanging in the trees and from a distance the garden might almost have seemed to be hovering several feet above the ground.

The old house at the top of the road could have done with a coat of white paint, but in the misty light no one noticed that. And the grandfather clock in the living room, the one that had belonged to Jenny's paternal grandmother, would strike seven and by that time everything would be ready. The garden would come to life. The house would come to life. The doors would be flung open. The rain would ease up a little and even if the fog did hang around the treetops, light would shine from lamps and lanterns both inside and out. And they would all be out on the front steps to welcome the guests. Jenny and Irma, Siri and Jon and Alma and little Liv and the moon-pretty girl whose name was Milla.

Jenny gripped one of the curtains. Let the festivities commence! Almost fifty guests from far and near. They came with presents and flowers and champagne and rain in their hair and laughter and summer dresses and white pocket handkerchiefs to wish Jenny Brodal happy birthday.

SIRI TURNED TO Milla. They were all out on the front steps now, waiting for the guests to arrive. They were also waiting for Jenny. She should have been downstairs by now, lined up there on the steps with them. It was her party after all. She was the guest of honor, she was the birthday girl, the star of the show. An hour earlier Siri had stomped up the stairs to her mother's room and knocked on the door.

"Mama, how are you getting on? Are you about ready? Do you need help with anything?"

She received no reply. Siri put her ear to the door and listened. All she could hear was a faint humming sound. Was her mother singing in there? She opened the door a crack and peeped inside. Jenny was sitting on the bed. Her makeup was half done (powder and lipstick, but nothing on her eyes), she had on her black dress and those thick, gray woolly socks of hers. In her hand she had an almost empty glass of red wine.

Siri flung the door open and caught the flicker of pure fear in her mother's eyes before Jenny raised her glass to her. They stayed like that, eyeing each other. Siri had to try to find a voice that did not cry, did not actually scream, a voice that said, "How much have you had to drink?"

Jenny scratched her head, looked at the ceiling, drank the last drops.

"To be honest, Siri," she said, "I don't know the answer to that question. Quite a lot, I think. But definitely not enough."

"Why?" Siri asked.

"Well, why not?"

Siri took a step closer, but Jenny raised her hand to say stop. *Don't touch me.*

"You shouldn't be drinking," Siri whispered. "It'll kill you."

"One day at a time, Siri. One day at a time. I never said never."

"So why now?"

"Because you're a grown woman," Jenny replied, setting her glass back down on the bedside table. "You are, in fact, a middle-aged woman of forty...and you'll be fine no matter what I do. You don't really have to worry...You and I..."

Jenny looked away.

"You and I what?" Siri said. "You and I what?"

Jenny shook her head. "Forget it," she said. "Would you please go. Would you please close the door and leave me be."

Siri turned and started to leave. Before closing the door she said, "The party will be starting in an hour."

Jenny laughed loudly. "Oh, yes, we mustn't forget that. The party. The celebration. It *will* start in an hour! Of this we can be sure!" She waved Siri away, still laughing. "Of this we can be very, very sure."

And now here they were, out on the front steps of the house, waiting for the first guests to arrive. All of them, except Jenny.

Milla had long hair hanging down her back, a red umbrella, red lips, and high-heeled shoes that squelched in the drizzling rain. She had pinned a white peony from Siri's white flower bed behind her right ear.

Her dress was of thin red cotton and draped around her shoulders was the red silk shawl she had borrowed from Siri.

Siri wanted to say something about the flower in Milla's hair. She felt Jon's eyes on her and she knew she ought to let it go.

"Don't you look lovely, Milla," Siri said.

Milla's face lit up. Jon knew there was more to come, he could tell from Siri's face that she couldn't let it go. Alma looked on with interest. Jon squeezed Siri's hand hard. *Don't say it.* Siri forced herself to smile and pointed to the flower in Milla's hair.

She couldn't let it go.

"But, you know, I'd rather you didn't pick the flowers in the garden. That white peony in your hair—that's from one of my beds. It's like you … wreck things, you see."

"Oh!" Milla said and lowered her eyes. Her hand began to tremble. "I didn't know."

"Leave her alone," Jon said.

A lapwing—noted for its wavering flight—was heard chirping in the distance.

Milla looked away and smiled. *Leave her alone,* he had said.

BUT NO ONE saw Milla's face hours later when the young man they called K.B. pressed her head down into the grit. His hand was clammy and hard, his breath hot.

"You want it, don't you," he whispered. He drove into her from behind, ripping her apart.

She didn't want it, but she couldn't turn around, couldn't shake her head no, couldn't answer clearly choking on grit.

"Can't hear you, darling," he said.

And Jenny's guests circulated in the garden, trying to master the art of balancing a small white plate in one hand and a wineglass in the other, they swayed to the music, they laughed loudly at something someone said, they strolled off on their own, up to the meadow where flowers had been picked that afternoon: bluebells, cow parsley, daisies, buttercups, globeflowers, purple clover, rosebay willow herb, and stork's-bill, and some guests stood quite still and looked up at the sky and debated among themselves whether the rain would soon come pouring down after all.

III

SWEETHEART
LIKE YOU

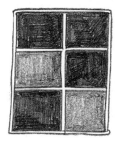

SHE CONSIDERED NOT leaving the party, she considered staying, even though most of the guests were a hundred years old. Milla glanced around, looking for Jon, but instead her eyes found Siri, standing alone under a tree. Siri could often be seen like that, alone, lost in her own thoughts. She was wearing a long, pale blue dress, an old silk dress that had once been Jenny's. *A lot of people probably think Siri is good-looking,* Milla might have said to her friends, if she had lived long enough to show them her pictures from that summer. Although Milla seldom showed anyone her pictures. She liked to keep them to herself, put together secret scrapbooks. She was always on the lookout for nice, big sketchbooks with hard covers and thick, white, unlined pages that she could fill with photographs, drawings, quotations and song lyrics, diary entries, dried leaves and flowers and grass. Milla had not traveled to all that many places in the world (not yet!), but her plan for the years ahead was to go far, far away, and no matter where she was in the world, no matter how far from home she was, she would always pull a little tuft of grass out of the ground, paste it into her scrapbook, and write the date and the name of the place underneath it.

And this summer Milla had taken lots of pictures of Siri. Dark and slim and delicate and tough all at once. Tall and a little lopsided with lips that were large and full. The lopsided-ness caused her a great deal of pain, sometimes for days at a time, Milla knew that, and she knew that Siri struggled not to show it, she had seen her when she thought she was alone, crouching down, closing her eyes, not moving.

Milla took a lot of pictures of people who were not aware that they were being photographed, and these pictures too she stuck in the album. She felt safe behind the camera. There was nothing heavy and moonish about her when she moved around with her little black cell phone clicking away. All those years watching her mother watching her, the camera between them. *Oh, yes, Milla, that's a nice shot, sweetie, don't move.* Baking cookies and getting sticky flour all over her face and in her hair and on her hands and clothes. Sleeping (or pretending to) so her mother could get her shot of the sleeping child, lounging around on the grass wearing nothing but those stupid dotted underpants.

One day, Siri had been fast asleep in the wicker chair in the big garden. Milla had just gotten back from the beach, in her arms she carried a big watermelon she had bought at the market. She was planning to cut it up and share it with Liv, who was hopping and skipping and dancing around her, singing, "We're going to have watermelon, we're going to have water-melon, we're going to have watermelon in the mo-o-o-orning."

"Ssh," Milla whispered, pointing to Siri in the wicker chair. "Look, Mama's sleeping!"

"Mama's sleeping," whispered Liv.

"Can you look after the watermelon?" Milla went on, gently placing the melon on the ground. "Can you sit here on the grass and look after the watermelon? I just have to do something."

"What are you going to do?" whispered Liv.

"Ssh, don't wake Mama," Milla replied softly, putting her finger to her lips. "It's a surprise. Shut your eyes and count to twenty in your head and afterward we'll go into the kitchen and cut up the watermelon."

"What's the surprise?" Liv cried.

"Ssh, ssh. I can't tell you that, because then it won't be a surprise, will it? So you've got to sit very quietly here on the grass and look after the watermelon and count to twenty in your head—and maybe the surprise will have something to do with ice cream."

Liv sat down on the grass, squeezed her eyes tight, and whispered, "One, two, three, four..."

Milla took her phone from her shorts pocket, crept over to the wicker chair in which Siri lay sleeping, bent over her, and took a picture. She looked at the picture, she looked at Siri. Siri did not wake up. Milla took another picture. And another. Siri had covered herself with a light blanket and this had slid to the ground, a little thread of drool ran from her open mouth. Milla slipped her phone back into her pocket, picked up the blanket, and laid it over her.

"...fourteen, fifteen, sixteen, seventeen..."

Liv opened her eyes and in a whispered shout said, "Can I stop counting soon, Milla?"

Milla turned to the girl on the grass and told her she could stop counting now, because it was time for watermelon.

"And ice cream!" Liv cried.

"And ice cream," whispered Milla, putting her finger to her lips again. "Remember now, don't wake Mama. Let Mama sleep."

Siri was constantly on the verge of getting really angry with Milla—and then she would regret it and try to be particularly nice instead. And when she was feeling regretful she let Milla borrow things of hers, like the red silk shawl that went so well with her red dress.

Milla wanted Siri to like her, but she was never good enough. It wasn't Milla's fault that Jon sometimes preferred to talk to her rather than Siri, or that Liv and Alma would rather be with her than with their mother. Siri was always in a bad mood. Alma had told her that all chefs were bad-tempered. Especially those who were trained in France.

But the chicken skewers were delicious. To begin with the plan had been to have suckling pigs, that was what Siri had decided, she'd had a vision of the sort of celebration this would be, as if it were a play or a painting, but no one wanted her vision. And that made her even more bad-tempered.

Milla had eaten a lot of chicken skewers on the sly before the party, taken a couple here and a couple there from the freezer and heated them up in the oven after everyone else had gone to bed.

"And what I'm making now, Mama, is chicken skewers with satay sauce," Siri had said in a loud, shrill voice. She was standing in the big old kitchen, sweating in the heat, her shoulder-length hair loosely pinned up with a lovely old clasp.

Milla wished she had a clasp like that.

This was a few days before the party and Milla was in the pantry, hiding behind the half-open door, observing the scene unfolding in the kitchen. She had been on her way in to get a jug of lemonade for the children, but when she heard that Siri and Irma and Jenny were there, she stopped and hid behind the door.

Jenny leaned against the wall with her arms folded. She stood like that, perfectly still, watching Siri and not saying a word. Irma sat on a kitchen chair, chuckling. Her cheek bulged with tobacco.

Then all at once Jenny said, "Satay what?"

"Chicken skewers in satay sauce," Siri said. "It's a Thai dish made with peanut butter and coconut milk and—"

Irma snorted loudly.

"I don't want any goddamned Thai dish," Jenny interrupted.

Irma looked at Siri.

"You should have listened to me," she said.

"What?" Siri asked, confused.

She looked at her mother, then at Irma.

"What are you saying?"

"I don't want any goddamned dish!" Jenny shouted.

Irma laughed even louder.

"Are you listening, Siri?" Jenny was still leaning against the wall.

Siri turned to Jenny with tears in her eyes.

It occurred to Milla that, had she dared, had she been sure not to be discovered, hiding there behind the door, she might have taken a picture of Siri at that moment. Siri with tears in her eyes. Siri being yelled at by her mother.

"I don't want a party!" Jenny screamed. "I don't want a party! I don't want suckling pigs and I don't want your dish! I don't want anything from you! I don't want this!"

Then she stormed out of the kitchen in her high heels and did not acknowledge Milla or even notice that she almost knocked her over in the pantry.

A few days later, when the party was finally under way and Liv was dancing on the feet of some distant uncle, Milla decided to stay, at least a little while, even though it was her night off, she'd get to maybe exchange a few words with Jon. She could mention to him that she had played the song he had said she ought to listen to. He had given her a CD (not a new CD, but one that had been lying around in his study, and he hadn't exactly *given* it to her, it was more of a loan), and then he had sent her a text in the middle of the night and asked her to listen to "Sweetheart Like You." Just that, nothing else.

Dear Milla, it said. *Listen to Sweetheart Like You—you'll like it. J.*

Milla had played the song several times. She wondered why Jon was up in his attic study, sending texts to her, instead of being asleep in bed with Siri. Could it be that he wasn't happy with Siri? Was he thinking of her—of Milla? Late at night? Was that why he couldn't sleep? Milla played the song over and over, she found the lyrics on the Internet, read them again and again, wrote them down on a separate sheet of paper, and glued this into her scrapbook. Maybe there was a secret message from Jon to her in there somewhere.

By the way, that's a cute hat

129

And that smile's so hard to resist
But what's a sweetheart like you doing in a dump like this?

Milla knocked back a glass of white wine. And then another.
She walked with studied care across the garden in her high
heels (the stilettos piercing the lawn and sinking into the
earth with every step she took) and into the bathroom off
the hallway, the one reserved for guests; she stood in front of the
mirror and took her mascara from the little fringed gold evening bag over her shoulder. She smiled at herself in the mirror,
adjusted the red strap of her dress. Surely there was something
she could do this evening. She had seen people her own age in
the Palermo Pizzeria, and she knew there were usually lots of
people at the Bellini. Let Jon party with the geriatric set and
maybe at some point in the course of the evening he would
stop and look around the garden, searching for her, and wonder where she had gone.

Sweetheart like you
Sweetheart
Sweet like you

She took a last look at herself in the mirror and stepped
back out into the garden. The old trees sighed in the breeze.
The fog coiled around clusters of festive people. Here and
there, someone gazed up at the heavens, to see whether they
were about to open and wash them all away, fragments of
the same conversation heard everywhere. *Is it going to rain
soon? Does Siri intend to move the whole party indoors if there's
a downpour? Is there a plan? What about all the food?* And
then a woman's singsong voice rising loudly above all the

others: *A spot of water in our hair is just good luck.* Milla felt a drop of rain land on her shoulder and could not help smiling. She stepped under the outstretched sails that Jon and Irma had slung between the trees and stopped by the buffet table. She sneaked one chicken skewer and then one more, she couldn't seem to get enough of them, that salty taste, she felt a flutter of excitement in her stomach, maybe it was the wine, maybe the salt, maybe the text message from Jon, she had this feeling that something wonderful was about to happen.

She looked around her and again her eyes met Siri's. Milla felt sorry for Siri. Lopsided Siri who lay alone at night while her husband was thinking of other women. Milla smiled at her. Lopsided Siri who was never happy. *Come on, smile back! I know how sad you are!* More drops of rain landed on Milla. She felt them on her shoulder. In her hair. On her cheek. Running down her spine. She felt like laughing. It tickled. But when, after locking eyes, Siri turned away, as if repelled by her, she suddenly felt more like crying.

Bitch! Fucking bitch!

She didn't say it out loud and no one could hear what she was thinking. She was just a girl in a red dress standing by the white-clothed trestle table with her mouth full of chicken. Milla swallowed, tossed her hair, and made her way toward the gate at the end of the garden. She turned around one last time and looked straight at Siri, now surrounded by her guests. Milla wondered what Siri would say if she knew about her and Jon. Milla took out her phone. Could she send him a text right now? Or should she wait? She knew how he liked talking to her, even if he was thirty years older than her, liked the fact that she popped into his study when he was working. He liked showing her things. Liked telling her things. About himself, about music and books.

Milla thought about the time he had given her the Dylan CD. This was several days ago. How he had looked at her and spoken to her.

"Sorry to disturb you, Jon. I was just wondering if you knew where the sunscreen for Liv is? I can't find it and I was thinking that we might go to the beach since the weather's so nice."

Jon swiveled around on his office chair and looked at Milla. He had his own special way of looking at her. His eyes sparkled. She felt like telling him that he was cool. That he had this kind of cool energy. Or would that sound stupid? He was a writer, and she wasn't sure how you were supposed to talk to writers. She didn't want him to think she was stupid, that she was just this immature young girl.

"No, you're not disturbing me, Milla. In fact I'm bored to death here!"

He had a pile of CDs lying on his desk. He picked up one of them, the Dylan CD, and tossed it to her.

"This is good. You should listen to it."

"Thanks," Milla said. "Thanks a lot."

Jon made no reply. Milla went on standing there.

"What are you writing?"

Jon looked away. "I'm writing a novel that will never be finished. I simply do not have it in me to finish this book."

"That's nice," Milla replied, then corrected herself: "I mean, it's nice that you're writing a novel. It's not nice that you can't get it finished. I'm sure you will, though."

Jon laughed again. Not at her, though, she thought. He was laughing to himself, as if she wasn't there, as if something funny had just struck him. But suddenly his eye met hers again and he said, "You look very pretty today, Milla, look how pretty you are, standing there like that in the light from the window."

Milla smiled.

"I think you're cool," she blurted out, "you've got this incredibly cool energy and I'm absolutely convinced that you're going to write a brilliant novel."

Jon gave a curt laugh, it was hard to interpret that laugh. Milla blushed. It had probably been stupid to say that bit about cool energy.

"Looking at you gives me energy, Milla," he said, but he wasn't looking at her. "You're beautiful," he added. "Luminous."

Jon had turned back to the computer screen. She didn't want it to end yet. She said, "I'm not very good at writing, never have been, but I have so much respect for the way you sit here writing, day in, day out, and you've written lots of books before, it was so hard for me at school, I just couldn't do it, but I've often thought that if I *had* been able to write a book then it would have been something really special."

Jon turned to face her. A different look in his eyes now. Not the friendliness of a moment before. Something more challenging.

"Oh—a book about you? About your life?" he asked.

"Yes, kind of. There's so much I'd like to describe, if you know what I mean."

"I think I know what you mean," he said.

He laughed out loud, but she had no idea whether he was laughing at her or at himself or if she was supposed to laugh along. And then he looked at her and said, "Are you an elf, Milla?"

"What?"

For a moment Milla thought she hadn't understood what he'd said. Had he in fact asked her if she was an elf? What was she supposed to say to that?

"What...an elf? ... Yes, maybe I am." She giggled, "There's a lot of magic in my life, kind of."

"Good," Jon said tersely, "that's great." And suddenly he looked very tired.

But Milla stood her ground.

"What I wanted to tell you is that I make books too. Not like you do, I don't mean like you. It's just something I do for myself. Secret scrapbooks. Secret because I don't show them to anyone, have never told anyone about them either. Only you, now. You're the only one who knows. I take pictures. I photograph everything I come across—people, animals, scenery. But mostly people. When they don't know they're being photographed. I glue all of the pictures into my book, and I put other things that have some meaning for me in there. Everything from tufts of grass to good quotations. And I write a little bit too, but not much. Diary entries."

Milla took a breath. Jon swiveled around on his chair again and this time he looked straight at her.

"Do you have pictures of yourself in there, too?" he asked. "In your book?"

He had that provocative look about him again, as if he were challenging her once more.

Milla wavered. "No, how do you mean?"

"I mean, this is a book *by* you and *about* you and you're telling me that you take lots of pictures of other people, and I was wondering whether you have a picture of yourself, I mean, whether you've glued a picture of yourself in there, in your book?"

Milla was still wavering. "I don't like to look at pictures of myself. I'm not very photogenic. My mother used to take pictures of me all the time when I was little. I hated that—"

"Give me your phone," Jon said, cutting her off.

"What?" Milla giggled.

"Give me your phone, come on, give it to me."

She drew her cell phone from her jacket pocket, crossed over to him, and placed it in his hand.

Jon waved her away.

"Stand over there in the doorway. That's it. Now look at me. Don't pose. Just look straight at me. Never mind the sun in your eyes, it's fine. That's it, yes!"

Jon snapped a shot and at that same moment Leopold got up off the floor and sat down by the door. Milla stood there in the doorway, looking at Jon and conscious of the sun in her eyes. He wasn't doing anything, but it felt as if he were stroking her.

"There now, look at this," he said, studying the picture. "You're luminous. You can glue this into your book. And look here," he added, pointing to a black smudge in the bottom corner, "there's Leopold's tail."

Jon handed the phone back to her. She studied the picture. She looked pretty—she could tell right away. He had taken her photograph and she looked pretty. The blue denim dress hugged her figure so neatly, the ponytail suited her, her lips were red, and there was no uncertainty or awkwardness in her eyes. *Luminous.*

"Thank you," she said. "Thank you. It's a nice picture. I'll make an exception and show it to my friends. I'll post it on my Facebook page."

"Yeah, well," said Jon. "Just don't mention who took the picture. Okay? Let that be our little secret."

"Okay," she said, looking at her cell phone. "Anyway, it looks like a picture I could have taken myself."

He didn't answer.

"I mean, I never let anyone photograph me."

He turned to face the computer screen and said, "Well, Milla, now I'd better get back to work. Okay?"

"Okay," she said.

She stared at his back, hoping he would turn to look at her one more time.

"And I guess Liv is waiting for you," he said, not turning around. "Weren't you going to the beach?"

"Yes," Milla said. "Okay. Bye, then. Thanks a lot for the CD. And the picture."

"Bye," Jon replied absently, still with his back turned. "Take care."

Milla opened the garden gate and left the party. She told herself that no one would notice she was gone. She had no business there anyway. In the mist, dancing, with the old people. She was young. *Sweetheart like you.* She was beautiful. She was *luminous.* And soon she would text Jon and maybe even meet up with him.

The road twisted, snakelike, from Jenny's house at the top of the hill to the jetties and the sea at the very bottom. It was lined on both sides with summer cottages and houses, all of them small and all but invisible in the mist. But Jenny's house was neither small nor invisible. Light shone from the windows, lights glowed in the garden, and the voices and laughter could be heard a long way off.

Milla started walking. *Don't look back in case anyone's watching.* The silky red fabric of her dress wafted around her, barely brushing her skin, the breeze brought soft rain with it. *Don't look back!* She seemed to hear her own voice in the mist, her own voice as it had sounded when she was a little girl out cycling with Mikkel, her father, the man who always had to turn everything into a competition.

"I want ice cream, Papa!"

She had to pedal hard to keep up with him, even going downhill she had to pedal hard.

"Can we buy ice cream?"

Mikkel accelerated, turned to look at his daughter. Long dark ponytail. Pink girl's bike. Pink helmet.

"You want ice cream?"

"YES!"

He was going faster now.

"If you beat me down this road we'll buy ice cream, if *I* beat *you* we don't buy ice cream. Okay?"

"Okay."

"Are you ready?" he said.

Milla had picked up so much speed that she was now neck and neck with him.

He glanced down at her. He had a nice, wide mouth, his forelock was blown by the wind. They sped down the hill.

Milla let go of the handlebars. She could cycle downhill without holding on. Her father had taught her to do that.

"One! Two! Three!" they shouted together, and they both stuck their arms in the air.

"Rock! Paper! Scissors!"

Milla chose rock. She always chose rock. Papa had told her she ought to vary it now and again. Be smart. Not always choose the same thing. It made her an easy target, he said, and smiled. But rock was rock. There was nothing more solid than rock. If you wrapped a rock in paper it would hit every bit as hard as when it was not wrapped in paper. Rock did not lose its force. Milla was eight years old and sure that she was right. Paper was for wimps.

"ROCK!" she cried, punching the air with her fist triumphantly.

Milla felt how the bike almost seemed to take off, to take wing, like a huge bird, she whooshed past her father.

"ROCK," she cried again and looked back to see if he was watching her.

When she lost her balance and the bike came crashing down, the ground seemed to come alive. It punched and clawed and bit and beat and battered her bones.

Out of the corner of her eye she saw her father's lips—as he swept past forming the word *paper*. He had the palm of one hand raised as if he was waving to her.

Don't look back. If you look back you'll fall off your bike. If you look back you'll be turned into a pillar of salt. If you look back the one you love will die. *You're beautiful. You're luminous.* Milla looked back, there was no one there, no one had seen her go. The big, white, brightly lit house she had just left had a lonesome air to it. She could hear voices, party guests shouting and laughing, but the sounds were swathed in thick velvet. Soon the fog would envelop them all. The house, the garden, the people. *Sweetheart like you.* Milla walked on.

In the middle of the road lay a buckled bike and in the ditch a little boy was sitting, crying. Milla drew closer, the boy looked up, caught sight of her, and cried even louder. She went over to him, crouched down beside him, and saw the grazes on his knees and the palms of his hands. He was bleeding. There was grit in the cuts on his knees. The grit would have to be picked out before his wounds could be cleaned and dressed. Her legs went watery, as if it were her own knees that were hurt and bleeding.

The cuts were seeping red, rimmed with black, and criss-crossed by stinging pink streaks, it looked as though someone had drawn on his knee with a sharp pink pencil, but she didn't think he would need stitches. She hadn't needed them either, that time when she fell off. She laid a hand on his shoulder.

"Did you fall off your bike? Have you hurt yourself?"

The boy cried even louder and nodded vigorously. Milla looked up and down the road, wondering whether he was on his own or with his parents or someone. But he was clearly alone. She took his hand and helped him to his feet, then she used the red shawl she had borrowed from Siri to wipe the dirt and tears off his face. The boy had gone very quiet.

"What's your name?" she whispered.

There were bloodstains on the shawl. It didn't matter, she told herself. She would tell Siri that it was not her blood, it wasn't as if she had been careless or anything, she had just helped this little boy who had fallen off his bike.

"Simen," he sniffed. "My bike's wrecked, I'm sure it is, and I can't afford a new one."

He burst into tears again and rested his head gently against her. Milla let him stay like that for a few moments before extricating herself and going over to his bike, which was lying in the middle of the road. She hunched over it and inspected the damage. The bike had survived the crash well, it was a bit muddy, but nothing was broken that couldn't be fixed.

"It's not wrecked," she said, pulling it up onto its wheels. "Look, Simen, it's not wrecked."

And then Milla asked if she could walk him home. Simen nodded, his face brightening a little as he let her take his hand.

"Where do you live?" Milla asked as they started down the long slope.

She had one hand in his hand, the other on the handlebars of the bike. Her umbrella was slung over her shoulder alongside the evening bag.

"Near the bottom of the hill," he said. "It's the second house on the left as you come up the road."

"But we're not coming up the road," Milla laughed. "We're going down it, so your house must be on the right. Which means we'll have to look to the right to find the house where you live."

They said no more after that. But Milla glanced at him every now and again, walking beside her, upright as a little tin soldier. The mist wrapped itself around them.

"It's like walking in a cloud," Milla whispered.

When they got to his house she said, "I'm Milla."

She propped his bike up against the fence. He looked at her and almost burst into tears again. Maybe because she was about to go.

She bent and kissed the top of his head.

"I'm Milla," she said, "and you're Simen and you're not to cry anymore."

Then she turned and walked away.

JENNY HID BEHIND the bedroom curtain and looked down on the garden and all the guests in their finery milling around in the fog. They didn't stand a chance. The fog was too big for them. Too heavy, too gray, too impenetrable and too beautiful. Jenny screwed up her eyes. Her head hurt. The bump on her right toe burned. Her hands shook. More Cabernet would alleviate the shaking. And possibly also the headache. What more could one possibly ask for? Her feet were leading their own fleshy existence down there in the nectarine sandals, she had put them on, but now she kicked them off again, and her dress strained so tightly across her belly that she could hardly breathe. Jenny peeped out the window. Oh, look, there were Daniel and Camilla and their hapless daughters, and there was Steve Knightley from Seattle and dear old Ola, her neighbor, who had turned gray and sad after his wife, Helga, died, and what on earth was her dear friend Julia wearing—some sort of caftan? And bright green? It was far too short, surely? And then her eyes fell on Siri wearing a blue silk dress that had once been hers. Jenny drained her glass and watched her daughter walking around the garden, playing the hostess. Siri would be all right. Siri had her restaurants and she had Jon and she had both her children. They were not dead. And look there was

her old friend Mary Olsson and that ridiculous little husband of hers. Jenny took another swig. Who on earth were
all these people? Was this the gang that would show up at
her funeral? Jenny could see several who—and she observed
this with some satisfaction—were sure to go before her. Definitely! And in the spirit of feeling momentarily immortal,
she decided she would make a speech. There were a couple
of things she wanted to say. Jenny stumbled over to her bed
and stretched out on it. Pen and paper. Somewhere in her
room she had pen and paper. Why was it always so difficult
to find pen and paper? She had a speech to write. Not a long
speech. No. She was going to write a short speech. And it
would begin as follows:

Nothing.

Jenny sat up and stared into space. It would begin as follows:
Nothing.

Jenny got down on the floor and looked under the bed.
Well, what do you know—a pen under the bed. And over
there on the dressing table—a couple of receipts. She would
write on the back of them. Jenny climbed back onto the bed.

It would go like this:

*Dear family and friends. Dear Siri, who has organized this
party for me. Dear Irma. Here we are, standing in the fog and
wondering whether it's going to rain...*

Yes, that was good.

Another little drink and maybe she could make the rest up
as she went along.

SIRI SHUT THE front door behind her and everything went quiet. Her knees buckled under her and she flopped to the floor, like a puppet, then she sat up again because, she thought, *I'm not a puppet and I control my own movements, I just need to sit here for a minute and collect myself and rest,* and then she put her face in her hands. Disastrous. Disastrous. Disastrous. This whole party was a disaster. *What have I done with my life?* Something had gone wrong. The long pale blue dress that Jenny had given her slithered down over her form and streamed and spread across the hardwood floor into a pool of silk. *You look so beautiful,* Jon had whispered as they had arranged themselves on the steps outside: Siri, Jon, Alma, Liv, and Milla, and even Irma (Irma the giantess with a face that Jon had once compared to the angel Uriel in a painting by Leonardo), they had stood there, as if on a stage, and greeted the guests and bade them welcome. *You look so beautiful.* And the next moment: *Leave her alone!* So curt. So harsh, his voice. And only because Siri, in the gentlest of fashion—softly, quietly, lightly—had expressed her objection to the flower in Milla's hair. The meadow behind the house was full of wildflowers that Milla could pick for her hair. Milla—this big clumsy child who had come to Mailund with all her sadness and all her loneliness.

Leave her alone!

So curt.

So harsh.

The white flower bed at Mailund was Siri's pride and joy,
and not there for Milla to be picking flowers for her hair. Goddamned child.

Siri blamed Milla. Something had gone wrong and Siri
blamed Milla. Milla was there to help but was turning into a
nuisance, a big, clumsy, needy nuisance, lurking around, snap-
ping pictures with her cell phone. And she blamed Jenny who
decided to fall off the wagon on this exact day, in front of all
these people, triumphantly announcing this family's defeat—
why? *Because she didn't want a party and had said so many
times and Siri hadn't listened?* And she blamed Jon who smiled
foolishly every time he saw Milla come into a room. Just because she was young and pretty. It was too stupid. But then
she pictured him sitting there in the attic room not writing.
Yes they joked about it. *All work and no play makes Jon a dull
boy.* She hated him for joking about it. The not working. The
giving up. The lies. The cheating.

Sometimes at night Siri would go upstairs to the attic to say
good night to Jon. They slept apart almost every night now—
and he looked so lonely lying there on his bed, staring at the
ceiling or reading a newspaper on his cell phone, or flicking
through novels he'd written himself.

There was a stack of Jon Dreyer books on the floor.

"So, now all you read are books you've written yourself?" she asked him once.

"Leave me alone, Siri, just leave me to read whatever I want."

"Maybe if you actually read a book written by someone other than yourself, you would be inspired to write again."

"Thanks. Why don't we make the following agreement right now: I don't tell you how to cook and you don't tell me how to write. Okay?"

It was wrong to call this room the hallway, Siri raised her head and looked around, they had always called it "the hallway"— *I will not have a lot of mess in the hallway, Siri, help Syver hang up his outdoor things*—when in fact the room was grand and lofty, with old wooden flooring and no furniture. There was the stairway, set like a throne at the room's center, the broad stairway that wound up from floor to floor. On the first floor Jenny was perched on the edge of her bed (or maybe she was standing behind the curtain, looking out the window), refusing to come down. And Siri had come to take matters in hand. *She was going to take matters in hand.* This was not an expression she had ever used before, but suddenly she had found herself plodding around the garden in her long, blue silk dress and high heels (that had sunk into the ground with every step she took, squelch, squelch, squelch), behaving in a manner that seemed foreign, using words and expressions that were not like her at all. Occasionally, for a fleeting, horrified moment, she caught a glimpse of herself. The shrill note in her voice. The stupid words. It was as if there were something

heavy weighing on her tongue that had to be removed immediately—that expression, *It's time I took matters in hand*, uttered in such a phony way—and out of her mouth she plucked
a big, shiny bug. And then another. And one more. Her mouth
full of big, shiny bugs.

"Well, I think it's time I took matters in hand," she said
with a smile to old Mrs. Julia Herman, who was swanning
around, talking to everybody and dressed in a rather odd-
looking green caftan that emphasized her old, skinny, blue-
tinged, varicose-veined legs. Had Julia Herman perhaps
forgotten to put on her trousers?

"Right, now I'm going to take matters in hand," Siri said.
"I'll go and get her. Mama has to come down now, of course
she must. We can't wait any longer."

Siri listened. Out in the garden the party was running its
course, but the heavy front door muffled the sounds of it. The
silence in this house was deafening, it had been that way ever
since Syver died. She had tried so hard to fill it with sound.

"MAAAAMMMMAAA!"

As a child she'd had a clear, high-pitched, penetrating voice,
but she had learned to control it.

"Not that voice, Siri, if you please!"

But sometimes she forgot, whooped and sang and danced
around the house, ruining everything.

Fifteen men on a dead man's chest,
Yo, ho, ho and a bottle of rum.
Drink and the devil had done for the rest.

Yo, ho, ho and a bottle of rum.
Hey!

And all at once Jenny would appear on the stairs, somewhere between the ground floor and first floor, her face chalk-white, with her red lips, her long flowing hair, her high heels, her neat little figure, and whisper, *"Your voice, Siri, could you take it somewhere else? Please. Please! I can't take it."*

The stairway reared up, it had always been scary to walk those stairs, up or down, as if the stairway were out to get you, as if you and it would never see eye to eye, as if at any moment it might withdraw a stair here or insert an extra one there. Over the years the stairway had been sanded down, oiled, and painted, it had been furnished with carpet, stair rods, and a new banister, the carpet had been replaced by another carpet, but no one in the house wanted carpet, *I don't like carpets*, Jenny said, so now the stairway had been sanded down and painted again, cobalt blue, the same color as it had been long ago, before she, Siri, was even born. She had counted the stairs time and again. One stair. Two stairs. Three stairs. Four stairs. Until she got to twenty-six. Sometimes she got to twenty-seven, on one occasion she counted thirty. When Jon counted the stairs he got twenty-seven. And only a couple of days ago, just before they had that big fight about the party, the two of them had taken each other's hands and walked slowly, like a bride and groom, up the stairway, and together they had counted the stairs in between kisses: *One, two, three, four, five, six, seven*—they got to twenty-six, but Jon insisted that they had miscounted, that he had kissed her too many times and that neither of them had taken the counting seriously, so he wanted to do it again, and this time there was to be no talking, no laughing, no kissing. So they turned around and started to walk back down the stairs: *One, two, three, four, five, six, seven, eight,* but when they reached *eighteen* Siri tripped and twisted her ankle. It hurt, but not very much.

"Ow!" she said with a little laugh. "Sorry," she added and gave him a kiss. "I know we're not supposed to laugh. Or say 'ow.' "

"We'll turn back," Jon said. "I'd better take a look at your ankle."

So they turned and walked back up the stairs. Jon helped her to their bedroom, which was on the second floor, set her down on the bed, undressed her, propped pillows under her leg, packed ice cubes in a towel, and packed the towel around her ankle. Siri laughed and said that it didn't hurt *that* much, and he kissed her ankle and then her knee, as if she was a little girl who had injured herself, and then he put his lips to the inside of her thigh, and then they fucked.

Jon was still in the garden, wandering from guest to guest, *I'm putting the finishing touches to a book at the moment, it's coming out soon, at least I hope so, if I get it finished,* she had seen him talking animatedly to Ola and to Steve Knightley from Seattle and to Karoline and Kurt Mandl and it struck her that she had never liked Karoline, Jon's vain little dentist friend from when he was young. Why couldn't Karoline and

Kurt, *the Mandls*, have found a summer house somewhere else? Did they have to come here? She pictured Karoline's face—so much insecurity and vanity squeezed into something so little and blond. Jon didn't like her either, he had called her "humorless" and Siri had agreed. Sometimes they would laugh at how humorless Karoline had been on this or that occasion and how they really didn't like her very much at all.

And Milla—she's not helping. She's in the way. It's not working. *People are in the way. People must leave us in peace.* She repeated these phrases inside her head. *People are ruining things.*

Siri sat on the floor in the hallway and tried to summon the courage to climb up the stairs and fetch her mother, but something was not right. She lay down on the hardwood floor in a rustle of silk and closed her eyes.

Three years earlier Siri and Jon had gone to Gotland to see Sofia, her father's Swedish widow. Sofia was going to sell the house in Slite and move into a two-room flat. According to Siri's father's will, some of the money from the sale was to go to her, so there were papers to be signed—and Siri and Jon and Leopold were going to have five days together on Gotland without the children.

Siri remembered laying a flower on her father's grave, saying "I'll be back!" even though nobody was there to hear her, she remembered picking *kajp*, a sort of wild chive that only grows on Gotland, and making soup for Sofia and Jon, and she remembered Jon and her taking the car out for a long drive on the island and Jon hitting the brakes, whispering, "How about buying a house here on Gotland, a little limestone house where you and I and Alma and Liv could live?"

They had explored the island from Burgsvik to Fårö, visiting the medieval stone churches. Bunge church, Lokrume church, the cathedral in Visby, Hörsne church, Gothem church with its tall tower, Follingbo church with its painted ceilings, Eskelhem church, and Hamra church.

"You could start up a restaurant," he said, "one that's only open in the summer months and I'll become a writer again, one who actually writes, we'll sell the house in Oslo and clear our debts, we'll know no one, bother with no one, it'll just be us, you and me and Alma and Liv and Leopold and our love and all this." He flung out his arms, embracing everything around him. The shifting lights of gray that were typical for Gotland, the grassy moors on Fårö that called to mind African savannas, the impressive rock formations—*raukarna*—that were four hundred million years old, the sand dunes, the cement works in Slite, the phantom ship out at Norsholmen.

"A little limestone house," he said again.

Siri laughed and shook her head. She didn't say anything, but if she had, it would have been: *You can't just move to a strange place and think, oh yes, here I'll be happy, here I'll find peace, here I'll be able to write my book.* They had climbed out of the car to take in the ghostly landscape that had unveiled itself to them on the way to the old limestone works at Furillen.

"Alma could go to a Swedish school and Liv could start at nursery school here," Jon went on. "I bet there's no problem getting your kids into a good nursery school here, and they can both run in the woods and on the moors and pick scarlet poppies and swim in the sea until late in September."

Siri stroked his hair and said that he should put it all in his book. It was nice. The limestone house, the love, and the poppies.

"I mean it," he said softly. "I'm talking about something we could actually do."

"But we don't belong here, Jon," Siri said. "We can't just pack up and move. That's not something we can do. I want to be with you, I want to be with Alma and Liv, I belong with the three of you, but I don't belong here. This island has nothing to do with us. It doesn't work that way."

"Why can't we just pack up and make a new start somewhere else?" Jon asked. "Why not? Where does it say that we can't do that?"

"I don't know," Siri said. Her patience had run out. She got back into the car. "You just can't. End of story."

But Mailund was another matter.

After all the dreary summer cottages and houses lining the long road up from the little town, Mailund appeared like an oasis from another age, the age of white lace dresses, the age of straw hats, of handlebar mustaches, Rhenish wine, and croquet. Never mind that on moonlit autumn nights the place seemed to shine with an almost uncanny glow and in misty weather could look somehow forbidding, as if it were hovering a few feet above the ground. This was her childhood home, it had been in the family since 1947, Alma

and Liv had spent every summer here—this is where she belonged, for better or for worse. Siri knew every room, every
bedroom, every inch of the vast kitchen (she could have
cooked a meal blindfolded in there), every window, every
threshold, every single wall, and every single floorboard on
every single floor, at any time she could call to mind the
various sounds that each room and each stair made, and the
blue moonlight that caressed the furniture and ornaments
in the front room or flickered over her big bed in the over-
large bedroom on the second floor on all the nights when
she could not sleep.

Siri looked up. She had been lying on the floor long enough.
Now she must go and get her mother, drunk or sober.

Up the stairs, first door on the left.

Drag her out of her bed, down and out into the garden,
kicking and screaming.

Here's the birthday girl, everyone! Here she is!

When Siri was a little girl her legs often buckled under her
and she would sit in the hallway like this and look around.
As if she were readying herself. She came home from school,
pulled off her satchel, shut the door, and flopped to the floor.
After a little while she'd begin to listen. That was the whole
point. To listen. The ticking of the grandfather clock in the
living room. Faint rustlings on the first floor or in the kitchen.
Where was Jenny? Was she back from work? Had she gone to
work at all? Was she in a bad mood? Had she been drinking?
It was the guessing game.

153

Where are we today?

Who are we today?

What do we do today?

What do we say today?

Every day was different, so Siri needed this time after she came home from school. To flop and ready herself. To dissolve and re-form. To lie or sit or stand perfectly still and listen. Become one big ear. Were those crying sounds she heard from Jenny's bedroom? Singing? Snoring? Angry mutterings?

"*Siri? Is that you?*"

And you had to be able to interpret the tone of voice.

"I love you more than anything in all the world, Siri," her mother might say and then burst into tears. "I don't blame you, I really don't, I just miss him so much."

Her drinking escalated as the years after Syver's death wore on, but then, when Siri was seventeen, Jenny stopped drinking quite decisively and hadn't touched a drop until today, her seventy-fifth birthday, the day of the party, her fete.

Siri listened to the noises from the garden.

The voices, the music, the clinking glasses, the plates, the cutlery, the fluttering white tablecloths (she had put them on the tables, then taken them in, then put them on the tables again), snatches of conversation, *Have any of you seen anything of the birthday girl, No, neither have I*, all the different ways in which people laugh when they are gathered at a party, high and low, all the sounds that the guests don't even hear: the wind, the sighing in the treetops, the first drops of rain, *I don't think it's going to rain. The forecast said rain, but you can't trust the forecast.*

Her plan was to run up the stairs and knock, no, *bang* on Jenny's door, and say that now she really did have to come downstairs, now it was time to honor her guests with her presence. Her plan was to take matters in hand. But Siri was still sitting on the floor, eyes fixed on the stairway.

She said: Get up and go to her.

Nothing.

And then she said: I'll sit here awhile longer.

Siri gazed up at the stairway. It coiled its way through the house like a rattlesnake. *And together they had counted the stairs in between kisses.* She could hear Jenny moving about in her room. Siri stood up and stretched until the kink in her waist was barely noticeable under her long, pale blue silk dress.

Then she shouted at the top of her voice wincing at its shrillness: "Jenny Brodal! Mama!" She walked to the foot of the stairs. "Listen to me now, you've got to come down! The party's started and your guests are all waiting for you!"

THE RAIN FILTERED down, thin and gray, and the wind picked up and pulled and tugged at Milla's red umbrella. No one could say exactly when she had left the party and gone down to the jetties. Maybe there were other parties that evening. The quayside was shrouded in mist. Milla bought a hot dog at the kiosk, she spilled ketchup on her red dress and gasped softly. A young man with fair hair turned, looked at Milla, and smiled.

"Love the red umbrella."

Milla smiled back.

"Thanks. But I've stained my dress. Look."

The boy, known to his friends as K.B., shrugged and spread his arms.

"Some summer evening, this, huh?"

"It was my birthday a few weeks back," Milla said, thinking that he was good-looking, and that she should say something. "I'm nineteen now and about to start a new life."

"Oh, *good*. How old are you?"

"Nineteen," Milla said again.

"Shame about the weather, though," he said. "Oh, and happy birthday."

"Thanks." Milla stared at the boy. "But that was weeks ago."

The boy went on talking: "Good, good. Well, see you later maybe. I'm off to the Bellini to meet some people. Ever been to the Bellini?"

Milla shook her head.

"Well, see you there, maybe. Bye."

"Bye," Milla said, smiling. "See you, maybe."

"I'M LEAVING NOW," said Jon. He felt raindrops on his fingertips. He thought: If it started to rain everyone could crowd together under the sails he'd strung up in the garden.

"Are you leaving...?" The bespectacled professor of literature who might or might not have been Jenny's lover some time in the last century looked surprised. "But you can't leave now?"

"Oh, but I can," Jon replied.

"But the birthday girl hasn't put in an appearance yet."

"Well, that may well be," Jon said, "but I have to go."

The man Jon was talking to, Hansén his name was, had the vexing habit of throwing his head back and roaring with laughter every time he said something he deemed amusing. He was a literary critic for *Bergens Tidende* and was known for once having plagiarized an obscure American essay on William Faulkner and to have gotten away with it. He had a big belly, a big nose, and a big beard. Jon had studied the beard closely while listening for what seemed like an eternity to the critic's pessimistic views on contemporary writing and literature (contemporary writing in general and Jon's writing in particular), and to his delight he had discovered a ladybug living in that soft, hairy indent between Hansén's lower lip and his chin.

"Yes, well, nice talking to you," Jon said, tearing his eyes off the ladybug.

"Maybe we can pick up where we left off some other time?"
Hansén said.

Jon smiled noncommittally.

"My dog, Leopold," he said, "relishes the inner organs of
beasts and fowls—a well-read man like yourself will get the
reference, right?—anyway, the dog must have his evening
walk."

Hansén nodded curtly and walked away. Jon glanced
around, looking for Karoline. She and Kurt were standing a
little way off, talking to Steve Knightley from Seattle. Karoline felt his eyes on her and made a little gesture with her hand
that he found hard to interpret. A wave, perhaps, or a caress?
He smiled at her and strolled off to find Siri. She was talking
to some distant aunt who'd just had a hip operation, and Siri
was listening and nodding and being sympathetic and looking
stunning and slightly aloof in the pale blue silk dress with her
dark hair in a silver clasp. Jon went over to her, put his arm
around her. He kissed her on the cheek, whispered in her ear,
"Where's Jenny?"

Siri smiled and nodded, outwardly giving the aunt her full
attention, and whispered back, "In her room, plastered."

Jon squeezed her hand, they had not had a chance to talk
about it, had not talked about Jenny, upstairs in her room,
drinking her brains out, but this was not the right moment.
Jon flashed his most winning smile and asked the old lady
with the newly operated hip a few hip-related questions before
excusing himself and leaving.

"Our dog needs his evening walk," he said. "He's shut up in
my study, feeling a bit lonely and neglected…"

The aunt nodded, but Siri shot him a puzzled look.

"You're taking the dog out again?"

"Well somebody has to," Jon replied. "Don't worry, I'll be back in twenty minutes or so. Maybe half an hour. I'll pick up some milk and bread for tomorrow's breakfast."

Siri nodded and turned away. He reached out to touch her shoulder, but she wouldn't let him, and walked a few steps and turned her attention to one of the guests, an elderly woman of about eighty wearing a very short, apple-green frock.

Jon opened the door and entered the house, the silence inside was deafening. He ran up the stairs and collected Leopold from the attic.

"Okay, Leopold, let's go. Come on," he muttered. "We'll slip out the back way." He scratched behind Leopold's ear and the dog wriggled and squirmed and dragged him down the stairs.

Out on the road it was very dark for that time of year. He decided to walk to the shore, maybe pick up a hot dog at the kiosk and a couple of beers at the grocery store, sit on the beach and look at the sea. He checked the time, the store was open until ten. He loathed parties. He hated to see Siri becoming someone else, the perfect hostess, swanning around the garden, laughing to all and sundry. What was there to laugh about? It was bullshit, all of it, a pack of lies. He had tried to talk to her about it once. Her duplicity when they had company. And she had laughed and said, "My duplicity, Jon? *My* duplicity?"

He had tried to tell her that he hated it when she put on an act.

"It throws me," he said, "when you act all sweet and obliging and charming and witty."

"You hate it when I'm sweet and obliging and charming and witty?"

He nodded.

"You prefer depressed and unfriendly?"

"I think you know what I mean."

"No, Jon, I don't know what you mean."

What he meant was that he wanted the real Siri. The naked Siri with the kinked waist whom he could stroke and fuck and lie close to. Not the Siri with the swift, shrewd gaze and fine creases of dissatisfaction around her mouth or the Siri with disappointment and contempt choreographed into every single, graceful little move. But no matter how he worded it, it would come out wrong. He knew that.

A hot dog with all the trimmings and a couple of beers. Half an hour on the beach. No more.

"Just you and me, Leopold, okay?"

The dog looked pleased.

"And a hot dog for you too," Jon said.

His cell phone trilled inside the pocket of his suit jacket. He took it out and read: *Why Sweetheart Like You exactly?*

He sighed and told himself that he would have to get out of this: little Milla, nineteen years old. The *nanny*. He couldn't...

Jon slipped his cell back into his pocket. Leopold strained at the leash, letting him know that he couldn't wait to run free on the beach. Jon pulled out his phone again. He looked at the text message he had just received and eventually wrote: *Dear Milla. I don't really know why that song reminded me of you.*

Something to do with the title. Sweet. Sweet like you. Sweetheart you. Something like that. J.

Back came the immediate reply: *I'll be around this evening if you feel like getting away from the party and having a glass of wine with me, at the Bellini, maybe?*

Jon tied Leopold to a post outside the shop and went inside. He grabbed a six-pack then wrote: *Some other time, maybe, Milla. My presence is required elsewhere. See you tomorrow. J.*

JENNY HAD NODDED off on the bed but was woken by Siri calling her. "Listen to me now, you've got to come down! The party's started and your guests are all waiting for you!"

She opened her eyes with a groan. Her head was pounding. Siri. My little girl.

It was as if she could see the two of them right here in this room many, many years earlier, herself in front of the mirror, her little daughter right behind her, and she smiled remembering how she had let Siri brush her hair every evening. She could hear her daughter's voice back then: *Bend forward, Mama,* and she would bend forward, sending her hair cascading to the floor. *One. Two. Three. Four.* Oh yes, there had to be a hundred strokes or it didn't count. *Five. Six. Seven.* And Jenny remembered that it had hurt her back, standing like that, bent forward, but that it had been absolutely essential that Siri be allowed to finish brushing. The warm scent of her daughter's skin, the eager little hands, the brisk strokes tugging through her hair. *Eight. Nine. Ten. Eleven.* And how she had tried to think of other things: books she had read, men who had made her laugh, the trip to America that she had dreamed of making but that had never come to anything, Siri's father who had run off and moved in with that Swedish whore in Slite, no, don't think about that, think about something good, to help forget that she was doubled up like this with her back aching. *Forty-four. Forty-five. Forty-six.* That she was still young and beautiful, well, not quite so young, maybe, on the wrong side of thirty as Jane Austen would have put it, but beautiful, of that there was no doubt. *Sixty-seven, sixty-eight, sixty-nine, seventy.* And how in the end all her thoughts twined together to form one thought, the one, constant thought. *Eighty-four.* Her boy. Syver. All thoughts ran into Syver. *Ninety-one.* Why had she let the children out on their own? Why had she insisted on their being outside? They'd been huddling there, knocking on the door, wanting to come in, but she'd needed a little time to herself, she'd needed peace, it was a lot to cope with, having two young children when you longed to do something else, she remembered how she had looked forward to both children being old enough to start school so that she could go back to work, and she had told them that *in this house we have inside time and outside time, and right now it's outside time, come back at two o'clock.* Her only boy. Those blue eyes. That gray woolly hat. Those slender, delicate hands and long fingers. That soft body. That piping voice. Those heavy bangs, with the cowlick that always stuck straight up. And that it wasn't possible to end it all, even though life without him was, and would always be, bereft of light. It wasn't true what they said, that it gradually became easier to cope with loss, that time would work in her favor. It had become something of a sport to tell her this and every time they said it she had wanted to lash out, she had wanted to scream, what the hell did they know about time, they hadn't lost a child, but she couldn't end it all, she had one more, she couldn't...*A HUNDRED!* Siri cried. And every time Siri cried *A HUNDRED* Jenny straightened up and tossed her hair back and let it fall down around them both, because that, to Siri, was the most beautiful thing in the world.

Jenny met her own eyes in the mirror. The hairbrush lay on the dressing table along with two clasps and a perfume bottle. She pinned up her hair, put on lipstick, and stood up. She staggered slightly. The black dress fit neatly over her breasts, yes, but was a little too tight across the stomach. She could hold that in though. In a woman's posture lies her beauty. If it hadn't been for her thundering headache this party might have been bearable. She looked around the room, the Cabernet was all gone. She had no choice but to squeeze her feet into her sandals, descend the stairs, go out into the garden, and greet all her guests. Because in the garden there was more wine and here in her room there was nothing. And she had never said never. She had said one day at a time.

Jenny got out the receipt on the back of which she had noted down her speech.

Dear family and friends. Dear Siri, who has organized this party for me. Dear Irma. Here we are, standing in the fog and wondering whether it's going to rain...

Was that all she had managed to write before she nodded off? She had the very clear impression that she had written a lot more and possibly also something a little more meaningful. A few words about Siri, for instance, would have been in order. Siri, who had arranged all this. This celebration, which no one wanted, it's true, least of all Jenny, but all the same. Jenny was

sure she had jotted down a few key words for what to say to Siri
in any speech she might make. Something that would make Siri
happy. Something that meant something. She glanced around
the room as if looking for another sheet of paper, although she
knew very well there was no other sheet of paper.

*Here we are, standing in the fog and wondering whether it's
going to rain . . .* No, that wasn't very good. Not good at all. She
would have to come up with something much better than that.
Or not bother at all. She had made it clear that she wanted no
speeches from anyone, so maybe it was all right that she didn't
make a speech either.

Although it would have been nice to say something to Siri.
Something proper.

Jenny looked at the speech.

*Dear family and friends. Dear Siri, who has organized this
party for me. Dear Irma. Here we are, standing in the fog and
wondering whether it's going to rain . . .*

No, this would not do and Jenny took one day at a time, as
in fact she had always done, ever since the day Syver died. Garden parties were not for speeches, anyway. She could always
tell Siri a thing or two when she had her to herself. *I know it
wasn't your fault. You were just children out playing. It wasn't
anybody's fault.* Siri should have watched her little brother,
shouldn't have taken her eyes off him, but she was only six
and it wasn't her fault and Jenny would tell her that. She ought
to hear it. Not now, but when all this was over. Jenny held her
breath. And now . . . She twirled in front of the mirror. The
black silk fit perfectly over her breasts. Yes, now it was time to
go down and greet her guests.

LEAVE HER ALONE, Jon had said, and everyone had quieted down and listened to the song of the lapwing, but Siri hadn't cared about the bird, she had wondered why he had defended Milla.

The girl had picked a flower from the white flower bed and put it in her hair. And then she was gone. Siri remembered seeing Milla, all alone, bent over the buffet, piling her plate high with those little marinated chicken skewers. Siri had lingered, watched. It was she who had made the chicken skewers, but not for Milla to eat them all. Siri saw one chicken skewer after another disappear into the girl's mouth and down into that bottomless maw. All over the fog-bound apple orchard, festively clad people were chatting and drinking toasts and it seemed none of them noticed Milla. At the time, Siri thought *I'm the only one who notices her*, but as it turned out, lots of people had noticed her. Lots of people would say that they had seen the girl in the red dress and red shawl (the one she had borrowed from Siri), with the flower in her hair. Milla was there, at Jenny Brodal's seventy-fifth birthday celebration, she was seen. And then she disappeared so definitively that, try as they might, no one could find her.

There were, in fact, many who went missing that night. Jon slipped away and didn't come back until around eleven. His suit was damp and creased and he said he had fallen asleep on the beach. He had needed a bit of time to himself, he'd said, had gone off with the dog to listen to the waves and had fallen asleep.

Jenny and Alma had also been gone for a while. Their plan had been to go to the beach and sit on deck chairs under parasols, but no, they hadn't gone to the beach (well, if they had, they would have met Jon), Jenny had taken Alma for a drunken joyride, up, down, and around the narrow country roads in the Opel. They hadn't gotten back until very late. Drinking and driving with Alma in the car, "Unforgiveable," Siri said. "Just fucking unbelievable." But then, when it transpired that Milla had disappeared, not just temporarily disappeared, as Jon and Alma and Jenny had, but well and truly disappeared, the showdown with Jenny had been postponed.

According to Alma, her grandmother had been "perfectly sober the whole evening," which was more, she pointed out, than could be said of her parents.

A first thought was that Milla had gone home with someone, some strange boy or man, and Siri remembered making up her mind to have a serious talk with her about the risks of going home with strangers, although in fact what she had really felt was rage. Milla running off. Milla flaunting herself. Siri couldn't understand why this should make her so angry. Milla wasn't a child. A child-woman, maybe. But not a child. She wasn't somebody who Siri was supposed to take care of. Moon-pretty, needy, flaunting herself. And what had happened, why hadn't she come back? And just before noon the day after the party, after many fruitless attempts to call Milla's cell phone, Siri had sent Jon out to look for her.

"But where will I look?" Jon said.

"I don't know," Siri snapped. "Everywhere, anywhere. Down at the jetties or outside the Bellini, she's bound to have been at the Bellini."

"But it'll be closed now, won't it?" Jon looked at his watch and Siri sighed.

"Look everywhere for God's sake! Just find her! She's our responsibility. And I've got to go to the restaurant. She's probably sleeping off whatever stupid thing she did last night. Just find her, okay!"

And that morning became the first day without Milla. Jon walked up and down the long road, around the jetties, knocked on the door of the Bellini Bar, which was obviously closed in the morning, and by two o'clock that day, Siri left the restaurant and looked with him, and it was almost evening before Jon rang Milla's parents, wondering if they might have heard from her, that surely there was nothing to worry about, but she had been gone since last night and was this something she'd normally do, hook up with friends, perhaps. Did they know whether she had friends visiting town or if she might have gone somewhere and not told anyone.

Amanda and Mikkel came to town that night and began searching for their daughter. They asked Siri and Jon again and again when they had last seen her.

"But surely, you must know something?" Amanda screamed the following morning, when Milla had been gone for two nights. "You can't just stand there and not know. It's not good enough! Please! She lived in your house! You were supposed to watch over her! Where is she? Where is she goddamn it? Tell me where she is!"

By now the police were brought in, search teams were formed, and with that, reporters from every corner of the country descended on the little town a few hours south of Oslo.

Simen hadn't told anyone that he had seen her on the night she disappeared, hadn't wanted to tell his parents that he had been out bicycling without his helmet on. That he had fallen and hurt himself and nearly wrecked his bike. They would never let him take it out in the evenings again. His mom and dad joined the search team and looked for her, but Simen thought those search teams would just scare her. It was better to look alone. Maybe he'd be the one to find her and fix whatever it was that needed fixing and that had made her hide.

The young man known as K.B. soon became the focus of police attention and was called in for questioning several times, but was eventually released. He'd had a couple of drinks with Milla at the Bellini, he said, and they had left the club together and parted as friends. K.B. gave interviews to the press in which he confirmed that they had strolled around for a while, hand in hand, kissing a little, but that he was tired and hadn't felt like walking all the way up the long road to Mailund, so they parted at the foot of the slope and K.B. went back to his parents' house and fell asleep on his bed. The part about coming home and falling asleep was confirmed by his mother, who claimed she had been awake and looked at her watch. K.B. was sorry now that he hadn't been more of a gentleman, he said, looking distraught in all the photographs that were taken of him, he hated himself for not having walked her all the way home. "I liked her so much," he said, "I hope she's all right."

More than a week went by, and now it seemed everyone knew or had known Milla in some way. There were many stories of people who had seen her after she disappeared, in a coffee shop in Kristiansand, on a crowded street in Oslo, outside the cathedral in Trondheim, and one young woman claimed to have spotted her in New York. A Norwegian student named Karin, majoring in fashion design, swore she had seen Milla in Central Park and she had a picture on her cell phone to prove it. Not a very good picture, but a picture nevertheless. A dark-haired girl on a bicycle, turning her head toward the photographer, a red scarf around her neck, blurry. "I saw her from afar," Karin said to the Norwegian journalist who was taken off an entirely different story involving the indictment of a United States senator in order to interview the girl witness. The story about the girl in Central Park was discredited the next day, but it made all the headlines and did its rounds on social media. "I know you can't tell from the picture," Karin said, "but I know what I saw. I'm sure it was her. I tried following her, but she was on a bicycle and I lost her. Look at the picture, I know it was her. I know it."

In August 2008, a month after she vanished, Milla was the most famous person in the country.

It was always the same photograph.

"Oh, she hated when people took pictures of her," a girl claiming to be a good friend said in a television news story. "Maybe because her mother took so many pictures of her when she was little."

"But then she posted a picture of herself on her Facebook page," another girl, also claiming to be a friend, said. "She looked so pretty, she posted it just a few days before she disappeared. And I remember noticing it, because she never posted pictures of herself."

The photograph graced the front pages of the newspapers and was flashed on television news reports. Siri, who had always called her moon-pretty, stared at it and saw that in this picture her face was no longer quite as moonish. No, right then, at the moment the photograph had been taken, Milla was young and beautiful. And that was how she would be remembered. Beautiful Milla, who disappeared and left this one picture behind. Blue denim dress, ponytail, full dry lips smeared with lipstick a little too red. It's a light, bright picture. No background to indicate where the picture was taken, just a black smudge in the bottom left-hand corner.

Siri asked: But who took the picture? Was it taken here in our house? While she was here with us?

And Jon shook his head and said he had no idea, probably she took it herself. She was always taking pictures and maybe she took a picture of herself.

Milla is smiling, and squinting in the strong summer light. She is eyeing the onlooker with a faint glimmer of flirtatious annoyance, as if she were saying *Come with me, let's go have fun.*

"So full of life," her friends said and lit candles. "A ray of light."

Many talked of her radiance. And a Facebook page entitled "Finding Milla" was created.

Siri tore the photograph from a newspaper and looked at it again and again. *Let's go have fun.* No one could say for certain that she was dead, there was no body, but hopes of finding her alive gradually faded. As the nights grew darker and the summer vacationers started packing up their belongings and cramming into their cars and driving away, another Facebook group was formed, titled "Light a Candle for Milla."

Siri looked at the photograph. Why is she laughing? I never saw her laugh like that when she was here. Who is she looking at? Did she really take it herself? *Light a candle for Milla. It was dark when she disappeared, light a candle to help her find her way back to us.*

Always there. Always that same photograph. *Come, let's have some fun!* Lovely and lost.

SHE HAD BEEN like a little doll, much smaller than other girls her age, and she was in her mother's arms and they were running through the long grass, and she remembered her mother's warm breath and big mouth as she sat her down in the grass and got her camera out. She remembered the sun burning. Her body all hot. Her dotted underpants soft and loose against her skin. She pulled and tugged at those underpants so they might cover a little more of her. *Now Milla, I'm right here, see, I'm not going anywhere, I'm right here—and stop pulling and tugging.* Her mother ran backward while shouting to Milla, her face flushed, her trampoline body taut, her voice out of breath, eager. *Okay, sweetie, now you get up and run, run toward me, like you're in a hurry, don't look back, just hurry up and run,* but Milla couldn't hurry. She wasn't in her mother's arms. She wasn't sitting in the grass in the hot sun. She couldn't run. And she wasn't as little as a doll. No one was as heavy as her. And her mother wasn't there. No one was there. And ahead of her stretched the long road to Mailund and she didn't know if she could make it all the way up to the house at the top. Her legs weren't working the way they should. Cuts and bruises on her knees. On her thighs. On her stomach. On her face. He had jabbed his knee into her ribs, this was while she was still standing upright, all the breath had been knocked out of her and she had dropped to her knees, skinning them. He wouldn't listen to her when she said she wanted to go home. His mouth was slobbery and wet, his tongue had swollen inside her mouth and she had pushed him away and said she wanted to go home now, this wasn't what she wanted, he had misunderstood her, and that was when he jabbed his knee into her ribs.

"You want it, don't you?" he whispered, and then he drove into her from behind, ripping her apart.

She didn't want it, but she couldn't turn around, couldn't shake her head no, couldn't answer, clearly choking on grit.

"Can't hear you, darling," he said.

They had left the Bellini and he had whispered in her ear that he knew a nice spot where they could be alone and they had ended up on a narrow footpath near the ruins behind the school, not far from Brage Road. Gravel and stones and sand everywhere and that was why her hands were ripped up.

But she hadn't died. Here she was, walking, and he was gone. The rape had been quick and afterward he had actually made to help her back to her feet, offered her his hand. She hadn't taken it, just shook her head.

"Can you find your own way home?" he asked politely.

"Yes," Milla whispered. She meant to speak clearly, but all she could find inside of her was that little whisper.

She was still lying on the ground, curled up like a tiny animal.

"Good, good," he said. "See you. Okay?"

"Okay," said Milla.

"I'm going to get the car now," he said almost as if to himself and then he left and Milla couldn't understand why he had said that about the car. It crossed her mind that this was important, that this was the sort of thing she had to try to understand, what it meant, but she didn't want to think about that now, hadn't the strength to think about anything.

She had used her torn panties to wipe off his semen. Then she had stood up very carefully; a stab of pain ran through her pelvis and stomach and she was scared that something inside her might come loose and fall through her, and then she had taken a couple of steps and picked up her gold evening bag that was sprawled on the ground a little way off the path. A gold evening bag with fringe. How stupid. Milla would never use it again. But she had to put her underwear somewhere, she couldn't be seen carrying it in her hand, and the little evening bag was all she had. He'd taken her phone too. She wondered why. What was the point in taking her phone? Surely he had his own phone? Now she couldn't call her mother and ask her to come and get her. She rummaged in the bag again. But no, it was gone. She'd known that, though. That her phone wasn't in there. She'd been lying on the ground and he'd asked her if she could find her own way home and then he'd turned and walked away, and then she had seen him pick up her evening bag, take her phone, and toss the bag back onto the ground. She wanted to try to sit down again, but it hurt to sit, so she lay down, the way she'd been lying before, curled up, just for a minute, because she'd have to go soon. He had done this to her, but she was alive, she wasn't dead, he was just going to get the car, why did he say that, and Milla told herself that it was not impossible to stand up and go home. But it was unfathomable to her, that he had taken her phone and that she couldn't call her mother and tell her to come, and then she began to sob.

She couldn't see a thing, but she put one foot in front of the other and walked. It wasn't just that it was very dark or that she was crying; her eyes hurt. She had gotten sand in them, a bit of grit in one eye. There wasn't too much blood. Not from her eyes, not from her hands, not from the grazes and cuts, not from between her legs, and it was odd, she thought, that she wasn't bleeding more.

The roads were deserted. It was darker than usual for the time of year, and cold, and raining again. Milla wrapped the red shawl around herself. Although she'd rather have left it lying there on the dirt path. He had nearly killed her when he stuffed it into her mouth. But she was shivering and had nothing else to wrap around her and it occurred to her that she'd better get rid of it when she got home. Think of what to say to Siri. It was Siri's shawl after all. She could say she had lost it. That someone had taken it. And that she would, of course, buy a new shawl to replace the old one. Milla looked up at the sky. It must be very late. It wasn't the sort of summer night to be out in and the narrow streets were deserted.

After he had jabbed his knee into her ribs and she dropped down in front of him he had struck her on the back of the head, not very hard, just hard enough to make her fall onto her stomach and lie there with her face in the dirt. He didn't say a word as he pulled down his jeans, tugged her dress up over her thighs, ripped her underwear and drove into her from behind. When she tried to scream, her face in the dirt, he tore off the red shawl, the one stained with Simen's blood, crumpled it up, and crammed it into her mouth.

"Okay?" he said. "Is that better?"

His cock ripped apart everything that kept her up, cartilage, bone, joints, flesh, all that held her insides together was crushed and began to seep out of her. There was no stopping it.

Milla stood at the foot of the road that wound upward, dark and narrow, from Simen's house, second from the bottom, to Jenny Brodal's at the very top. Simen was the boy on the bike. He was probably in bed by now. But she wondered whether she could ring his doorbell and talk to his parents, say something like: *My name's Milla, I know your boy a little bit, he fell off his bike earlier this evening and hurt himself and I was just wondering how he was doing.*

But no. They would probably look at her funny. She wasn't wearing any underwear and stuff was still running from between her legs. It smelled sour. She had no shoes on her feet and her dress and the shawl were covered in all sorts of stains. She'd lost her umbrella. What would they think? Somewhat difficult, as things were now, as she looked now, as the girl she was now, to explain that she and Simen were friends, that she had walked him home, that she didn't mean him any harm, that the girl she was now, the one they saw standing before them, the one they smelled, was not the real her, and that she simply needed some help. Could she, say, borrow a phone so she could call her mother? And why couldn't she use her own phone? Yes, why couldn't she? What would she have to say for herself? How to explain? Because he had taken it? No, it wouldn't do. She would break down and start babbling or crying before she was even halfway through all that had to be said.

She walked a little farther, then she stopped. She had to gather herself. Wasn't that the expression? Wasn't that what old people said when they were tired? That they had to gather themselves? Once Milla had helped an old lady cross the road and several times the lady had stopped, looked up at Milla, and said, "I just need a moment to gather myself," and Milla had waited and the cars had waited and everything had seemed to come to a halt waiting for the old lady to gather herself. She wished that she could gather herself back to hours earlier. But she couldn't, so there was nothing for it now but to shuffle like an old lady, up the road of a hundred bends, and then, yes, there it was, she heard the sound of a car.

She looked back. It was speeding along, lighting up everything around it on the road. For one crazy moment she thought it was her mother coming for her. But then she had to jump out of the way and throw herself onto the verge. The car was going flat-out. It sounded like Jenny's Opel, Milla pulled herself up and peered. It *was* Jenny's Opel. The car stopped, and it was hard to see who was in it, the outlines of two people in the front, she hadn't been able to see them face on, but Milla was pretty sure it was Jenny and Alma. Why were they out driving at night? Why weren't they at the party? Was the party over? What time *was* it, anyway? The car started up again and drove on slowly, it turned the bend and carried on up the last stretch of the road to the house. Even when she could no longer see it she could still hear the drone of the engine. She heard it cease when the car reached the house. And it was good, she thought, it was good that they hadn't seen her. What on earth would she have said if they had seen her like this?

Milla picked herself up and walked a little farther.

She looked up at the dark sky.

"Mama!" she whispered. "Papa!" And then she sat down on the verge again, clasped her hands, and tried to pray. She had heard another car approaching and knew that it wasn't her parents in that car. She had known it all along, that they wouldn't be coming and that she wouldn't make it home in time. He had said he was going to get the car and she had known this was important and had tried to understand what it meant, and now she understood that he was coming for her, and so she shut her eyes and covered her ears. Didn't want to hear the car. Didn't want to see it. Now all she wanted to do was sit here and breathe until she was no longer breathing.

The car drew closer and even though she had closed her eyes, she was aware of everything around her being flooded with light.

IV

APPLE OF
MY EYE

THE SUMMER DISAPPEARED along with Milla and already it was October and she had been gone for three months. Jon's book was postponed. The dog needed a walk.

Leopold raised his head and looked at his master: *He is not writing. And pretty soon he will rest his head on his computer keyboard and cry.*

Jon's writing room in Oslo was in the attic, just like at Mailund. The room was partially renovated, the walls painted white, and a double-glazed skylight had been installed in the sloping ceiling so that he could look out. He had a desk in the corner and a mattress on the floor.

Jon stared out the window facing up to the sky and down onto the driveway, but the sun was too bright to see anything so he grabbed the dog's gray blanket, pulled it out from under its long black forepaws, forcing Leopold up onto his feet. The animal staggered slightly, shook himself, and Jon draped the blanket over the old curtain rod so that it covered the window completely. There! Now it was dark!

He will never finish that book. Leopold lay down warily on the floor, this time without his blanket, his muzzle against Jon's feet. *Never!*

Jon and Siri were still living off the income from the Oslo restaurant, plus the money from a huge bank loan and a rapidly
disappearing fourth advance from the publisher. All Jon had
to do now was write the third part of what had once been described (on the basis of the two parts that were already written
and published) as the "great turn-of-the-millennium trilogy"
and "the most important novel of the decade about our na-
tion." Expectations were overwhelmingly high, or at least they
had been, it was in part three that he would prove to be at *the
very height of his powers.* Jon should have completed the manuscript five years ago, but no, the days went by, his marriage
went down the drain, his daughter Alma was troubled, and
then there was Milla who came and disappeared and after
that, it had been impossible to write anything at all.

Jon was himself over fifty, confronted every day in the mirror with a slightly shriveled, prune-like face and a not incon-
siderable paunch that stuck out from or, rather, drooped from
his otherwise skinny frame. The attractive young mothers he
met every morning when he took Liv to nursery school looked
straight through him.

Every Thursday evening Jon went running with his dentist
friend Kurt Mandl, the husband of his dentist mistress, Karoline. Once, twice, three times around the lake and guess
who was out of breath and struggling with steamed-up spec-
tacles after the first round, and calling to cancel more often
than not?

"We're not getting any younger, Jon!" Kurt Mandl shouted.

"No, of course not," Jon shouted back.

Kurt's dogs were, like Kurt himself, admirable in most every way. Kurt only had to make a clicking sound with his tongue for the dogs to be there by his side. Taking Leopold for a run like that was quite out of the question. If Leopold were allowed to go loose, he would simply take off. If he were on a leash, he would drag and tug and bark at other dogs and make a spectacle of himself and his master.

Jon ran his fingers over the keys and wrote:

Miseries, October 16, 2008
1. I have no money and lead a wretched life, am financially dependent on my wife.
2. I hate Kurt Mandl.
3. My daughter hacked off her teacher's hair and is a topic of discussion in the news media: "Thirteen-year-old girl attacks English teacher." Expelled from school. Why????
4. I am a philandering bastard.
5. I have a stupid dog that pulls and tugs at the leash when I take him for walks: daily proof of my lack of control and character.
6. I don't exercise and I drink too much.
7. I can't write.
8. Milla?

And it was only going to get worse, everything coming undone. He thought of Milla's mother, Amanda, wandering from room to room, screaming out her grief for her lost daughter.

He and Siri had often talked about how they must write a letter to Milla's parents, they had to try to make amends for those awful summer days in July and August right after she had disappeared and they were all out looking and they hadn't known what to say. He remembered that on the second day, Amanda—until then holding herself together—shouted at them: "You can't just stand there and not know! It's not good enough! Please! She lived in your house! You were supposed to watch over her!"

Write them a letter. But with what words? What could you possibly write in such a letter?

Jon slid the mouse up to point four and point eight in his misery list and pressed DELETE. Siri checked his mobile, she checked his e-mails, she opened the documents on his computer entitled "TRILOGY PART THREE," partly searching for traces of what she in arguments referred to as his "untold life," but also to check whether he was, in fact, *writing*. They didn't talk about it and he didn't stop her.

Sometimes he did write something. A page maybe, precisely because he knew that she would read it. He wrote for her. And he wouldn't let her find out about the other women. That was nothing. Or not nothing. It was beside the point.

He deleted the entire misery list and wrote a new one, fit for Siri to read.

Note to self, October 16, 2008
1. Alma expelled from school for cutting off her teacher's hair. Why did she do that? How do we deal with this? How can we help her? How can we get through to her?
2. I don't exercise and I drink too much. (Make a plan!)
3. I'm not writing. Solution: Call Gerda at the publisher's, agree on a schedule, write minimum five pages every day (no more self-loathing!), deliver the next hundred pages in about six weeks. Ask for another advance???
4. Write a letter to Milla's parents.

Milla left the party and had texted him and he had texted her, but her cell phone had never been found and he hoped to God it never would be.

Jenny and Alma got back to Mailund as the party was winding down. They had been on a frenetic ride around the country roads. Jenny had been drunk and Jon and Siri had been furious at her. How could she go off drunk with Alma like that? How could she? But the celebration was still going on in the garden and Jenny ignored both of them, went and sat down next to Steve Knightley from Seattle.

And when the last guests were gone, and Jenny had gone to bed, and Alma had gone to bed, and Siri had gone to bed, Jon sat down at the end of one of the trestle tables and finished a bottle of red wine.

Eventually he got up and wended his unsteady way over to the annex where Milla stayed while with them. To see if she had come home? To see if she was all right? Why wouldn't she be? It was her night off and she could stay out as long as she wanted. She wasn't a child.

Jon made sure that no one saw him, he knocked on the door and waited a few seconds before stepping inside. He stood for a moment in the dark room, the pent-up smell of perfume, the unmade bed, the untidy desk, the overflowing bookshelves, the dirty clothes on the floor. He walked over to the desk and ran a hand over the magazines and makeup and a pink book that he realized must be her diary, that secret scrapbook she had told him about. He tucked it into his waistband, under the thick sweater. He felt his heart pounding. He opened the two clothes cupboards. Did he think that she would be hiding in there? He pulled the blue-and-white striped duvet off the bed and noticed a dark lump lying on the sheet. He took out his mobile and studied the lump in the light from the screen. He jumped back and let out a quiet scream at the sight of the black slug on the white sheet.

JON NEVER STOPPED admiring his wife. Her graceful movements, her asymmetrical back, her slender wrists. Siri bemoaned the lines on her face and what the years had done to her (as if the years had asked her to dance and then rudely stepped on her toes), and he noticed how she was always checking her reflection in shopwindows and in the dark, gleaming paintwork of parked cars.

Jon told her often that she was prettier than ever before.

The first time he saw her had been from afar, and it was the very way she moved that had made him fall in love with her. She had walked straight past him, not noticing him at all, or at least pretending not to notice him, and he remembers thinking that he had never seen a woman move so gracefully.

Leopold got up and left the attic room. Jon heard him padding down the stairs, it was the same padding sound he heard every morning and every night. When Leopold was dead, when the dog was gone, he'd still hear it.

Over the past fifteen years the drafty house had somehow come to encapsulate the sounds of his family—Leopold's pad-pad on the stairs, Siri's cheerful hello every time she came home, Alma's tireless rendering of "Little Song Thrush." He could still hear it, his daughter singing, that bright, childish voice of hers, like a little flute in the house, distinct from the girl herself. Alma had just turned thirteen and it was years since she had sung anything at all.

Jon had the house to himself for a few hours and could do what he liked. He could lie down on the floor and sleep. That would be nice. Just sleep it all away: Siri, Alma, Milla, all those female glances, his intolerable friend Kurt, and his intolerable friend's humorless wife.

Note to self: Must break it off with Karoline!

He had downloaded all the music from the seventeenth-century Purcell opera *King Arthur* on his computer and played it over and over again. There was an aria in particular he couldn't stop listening to about a cold man waking up. The man pleads with the higher powers—What power art thou?—that they leave him alone and let him go back to that unconcious state of mind where he had dwelled. He is excoriated. Alone. Freezing. Trembling.

I can scarcely move or draw my breath,
I can scarcely move or draw my breath.

Purcell died a few years after composing his masterpiece, supposedly having caught a chill after his wife, Frances, angered by something, locked him out of their apartment.

A man wakes up and for a few moments he experiences everything exactly as it is.

Jon wrote: *A man wakes up and is lucid.*

It doesn't last long, though, he thought, that kind of lucidity. If it did you wouldn't be able to stand it, it would kill you.

Let me, let me, freeze again to death

Jon blinked and turned the music up, he didn't want to fall asleep, because then Siri would come into the attic room and just look at him until he woke up, and say things like *The writer at work, I see.*

And still: It took only a minute or two. He called Leopold's name and heard him pad-padding back up the stairs. "Come here, boy! Come lie down here." And then Jon lay down on the floor beside his dog, inhaled the calming scent of him—grass, Bourbon, tar, and something hot and sweet and alive—and fell asleep.

"FUCK YOU, MAMA!" Jon opened his eyes and sat up sharply as Alma's voice cut through the house. It was half past one and he had slept for hours and now they were back from town. Siri had taken Liv and Alma shopping. "Don't worry," she had told him. "Just write." Those precious hours alone—wasted. "It will all be fine," she'd said and touched his hand. Wasted. That gift. Those hours. And what had he done? Surfed the Internet. Thought about Karoline. Listened to the entire libretto of John Dryden who in contrast to Jon Dreyer had gotten down to the business of working. And slept on the floor. All this and now they came tumbling back into his life. The front door slamming. The chorus on his computer singing. "FUCK YOU, MAMA!" Siri shouting, "Jon! Jon! Have you remembered to walk Leopold? He probably needs to go."

What Jon needed was a long spell on his own. No children. No Siri. No dog. Borrow that house in Sandefjord that an acquaintance had offered him. Jon got up from the floor and sat at his laptop and pounded away on the keys. This so that Siri, if she put her ear to his door, would hear the sound of working. Click click click! He looked at the book on the desk. *Danish Literature: A Short Critical Survey* by Poul Borum (Copenhagen: Det Danske Selskab, 1979). He turned to page seven and proceeded to type what was written there. *Preliminary Remarks: This book is a short survey of contemporary Danish literature, preceded by an even shorter sketch of the first thousand years of Danish literature* click click click.

"Okay, whatever," Siri shouted. "Can you send him down? I'll take him out."

Jon got up from his chair and opened the door for Leopold and shouted, "Great! Here he comes. Thanks! Nearly there!"

He heard her sigh. He heard it through all the other noises. She was mad. He knew it. Later, he would ask her about her afternoon; he would pretend he hadn't heard their daughter's "FUCK YOU, MAMA," engrossed as he was in his writing, and he would listen to her. His fingers danced over the keys. *In a significant lecture on the aesthetics of literary influence at the second congress of the International Comparative Literature Association (reprinted in his book* Literature as System, *published in 1971), the Spanish critic Claudio Guillén put it very succinctly: It is important . . . that the study of a topic such as, say, Dutch poetry be encouraged not for charitable but for poetic reasons.*

Jon heard the door slam and a moment or two later he peeked out the window and saw Siri and Leopold on the street outside their house, Leopold tugging and straining at the leash—that dog was strong as an ox—and Siri doing her best to stay on her feet, tugging and straining in return. Leopold squatted in order to shit while Siri looked on peevishly, clutching a small black plastic bag. She drew the bag over her hand, bent down, and picked up the turd. But instead of getting up again she stayed where she was, crouched down with the plastic-wrapped turd in her hand, her head bowed. Leopold wriggled and squirmed around her, but she stayed crouched down, didn't move, and Jon wondered why she wasn't getting up, had she hurt her back or been struck by anxiety, lost her ground, and he was all set to run out to her and take her in his arms and comfort her, but then she stood up, tugged on the leash, dropped the turd bag into the nearest trash can, and disappeared around the corner—half walking, half running to keep up with the panting dog.

Leopold was every dog's revenge on mankind. It is humiliating not to be able to control your dog. It is a sign of weakness. Lack of willpower. Lack of perseverance. It proves that you're lazy. Slothful. Sloth. One of the seven deadly sins: acedia (or accidie or accedie, from the Latin *acedia* and the Greek ἀκηδία meaning neglect, indifference, nonchalance, carelessness). Rather like a writer who doesn't write. But unlike a dog owner who can't control his dog, a writer who doesn't write can hide behind the excuse that he is *thinking*, that *literature takes time*, he can even allow himself a yawn or snigger of contempt at fellow authors who spew out a new book every year. Jon had used these very words himself just a few weeks ago, when asked by a journalist why it was taking him so long to write part three. Writer's block? Might the whole notion of a trilogy have been a mistake in the first place? The journalist was a young female summer temp named Charlotte. She had a PhD in literature and had had two collections of poetry published. Jon had decided in advance not to sleep with her, she was twenty-seven, had milky thighs and a tattoo, but then he changed his mind. Her line of questioning was driving him crazy and maybe if he fucked her, she'd shut up.

"Well, here's what I think," said Charlotte, "I think there is something very contrived about the whole notion of a trilogy. I mean, this is something you decide on beforehand, along with your publisher, before you've even written a single word, possibly simply in order to sell more books, sell the idea of this very big literary event, and I guess what I'm asking is if your trilogy was motivated more by commercial concerns than literary ones?"

It is impossible to act as if everything is fine, when the dog is straining at the leash and setting the pace and won't sit when you say *Sit* or heel when you say *Heel*. It is there for everyone to see: You've got no control over your dog, you're a spineless little man. Ulysses's dog didn't question Ulysses's authority. Argos didn't tug and strain at the leash, but waited patiently for his owner for ten long years, while Ulysses himself fought and won a lengthy war and then slowly wended his way home to Ithaca. Homer, Shakespeare, Kafka, Pynchon, Jules Verne, Poe, Steinbeck. They all wrote about dogs. *Literary* dogs. Click click click. But Jon's dog just strained at his leash and had no idea how to be a literary dog. Jon's dog had no idea of how to be a dog, period.

But here they were. His family. Liv calling, "Papa, Papa, I gathered some shells for you." And Alma's "FUCK YOU, MAMA." He noticed that his daughter had yelled *fuck you* and *Mama*—such a tender word, mama—in the same breath.

The thing was: Alma had cut off a chunk of her teacher's hair. First Milla disappears and then Alma cuts her teacher's hair off

Jon tried to block out the image of the teacher with hacked hair, a big nose, and red-rimmed eyes.

Why, Alma?

They had asked her again and again and all she did was shrug or say, "I don't know why. Her hair was just really long."

It wasn't as if they hadn't talked to Alma about the difference between right and wrong, good and bad, white lies and black lies. Siri and Jon weren't bad parents. Jon wasn't a bad father. He loved his children.

On his computer he wrote: *I want to write about fathers and daughters.*

And then he wrote: *Talk to her!*

But when did Alma start acting different? He pondered the word *different* and wondered if it was the right one. Was it because of Milla's disappearance? No. Alma had always been… *different*. He had taken secret pride in her uniqueness, as had Siri. Jon was reminded of an incident six years earlier when

Alma was seven and Siri was pregnant with Liv. They were sitting under the blue lamp in the kitchen, it was snowing outside, thick white snowflakes falling on the rough gray stone walls of the house.

"To have an imagination," Siri had said, "means that you like to make up stories, that you have worlds inside of you that you can travel to and live in, either alone or with other people. When Papa writes books, he makes up stories that other people can read and...and...then they become their stories too, just as *Pippi Longstocking* and *Charlie and the Chocolate Factory* are your stories—"

"Papa doesn't write books, he just pretends to," Alma broke in.

"That's not true, Alma," Siri replied. "What makes you say that? Papa has just had a big book published and now he's writing a new one. You know that."

Alma shrugged and said, "But Astrid Lindgren wrote *Pippi Longstocking*, not me."

"Yes, that's right."

"You said that *Pippi Longstocking* and *Charlie and the Chocolate Factory* were *my* stories."

"What I mean," Siri said, "is that to have a good imagination is a valuable thing." She laid her hand over her teacup. "Don't put a lid on your imagination, because your imagination enables you both to make up stories and to identify with stories, identify with other lives, with how other people think and feel, and while the stories may not be true, well we *know* there's no such thing as a girl or boy who's strong enough to lift a horse, we *know* that Roald Dahl used his imagination to make up the story about *Charlie and the Chocolate Factory*, and yet in a way these stories are still true, as all good stories are, I mean."

Alma took a bite of her bread, looked at her mother, and said, "I didn't understand any of that, now let's not talk about it anymore."

"Oh yes, but we will," Siri said, looking to Jon for help. "I'd like to say something about lying," she went on, "I think we lie in order to achieve something, you tell a story that's not true because you don't want to or don't dare to tell the truth, or because you want to trick someone, and it's very important not to lie, the lies you tell become a kind of wall between you and other people. When you lie, you can really hurt other people and you can hurt yourself—"

"Can I have some more chocolate milk?" Alma interrupted.

"It's a bit difficult, from what you're saying, to understand the difference between a lie, which is a bad thing, and having imagination, which is a good thing," Jon muttered, gazing at the ceiling.

"What did Papa say?" Alma asked.

"Papa didn't say anything, really," Siri replied. She took a sip from her teacup and shot Jon a furious look. "Or rather, Papa doesn't think Mama is explaining things very well," Siri went on, "and maybe Papa could explain it much better, although he's not saying anything right now, is he? The thing is, Alma, it's not okay to lie the way you did in school today."

This conversation had been prompted, Jon recalled, by the fact that Alma had told her sweet young teacher, Miss Molly, that she couldn't go out and play with the other children because her mother was dying.

"I want to rest in your arms," Alma had said.

"Are you tired, Alma?"

"No, I'm not tired. But Mama's tired." Alma lowered her voice: "Mama has cancer and she's going to die."

"My God, Alma?" young Molly whispered.

"Mama has cancer, and now she's going to die," Alma continued. "First she's going to lose all her hair. And then she'll die. Very soon, probably. Can I rest in your arms now?"

And Alma had flung her arms around her teacher. "There! I want to stay with you! Don't leave me!"

And Jon recalled Siri's voice that same evening. The despair. The weariness. Had it started to come undone already then, long before the writing became so hard, long before their financial troubles, long before Milla's disappearance, and long before Jenny started drinking again?

"But how do you even know what cancer is?" Siri whispered as they sat there in the kitchen under the blue lamp. "Does someone you know have a mother or father who's ill?"

"Nope!" Alma said.

"But why did you tell Miss Molly that your mother had cancer and was going to die?" Jon interjected.

Alma had only recently learned to shrug. "Don't know," she said.

"I *don't* have cancer, you know," Siri said. "I'm very healthy and I'm not going to die. Not yet. We'll all die someday. But not for a very long time and...and people don't always die of cancer."

"Are you worried that Mama or I will die?" Jon asked. "Was that why you told Molly that story? Because you were worried?"

"Nope," said Alma.

"Well, why then?" Siri asked.

Alma shrugged again, and said, "Can we just not talk about it anymore?"

Soon Siri would come up and tell him that Alma had screamed "FUCK YOU, MAMA" at her, she would repeat that she simply couldn't understand why Alma had picked up a pair of scissors and cut her teacher's hair off, she would say that she dreaded the thought of more newspaper stories, first Milla's disappearance, then Alma attacking her teacher, she would say that it had all started when Milla came to Mailund, the dreariness, no, the sadness, it was Milla's fault, all of it, and then she would flop down onto the floor and say she didn't see why Jenny couldn't just die now. Jenny who could never take anything seriously, Jenny who had taken Alma with her in the car, drinking and driving, on that awful night when Milla disappeared. Jenny who had only laughed when she heard about the cutting-the-teacher's-hair thing.

"I kind of understand why she did it," was all she'd had to say.

"And her drinking," Siri said. "I don't know whether she's drunk all the time now or what's going on down there. Every time I call it's Irma who answers the phone and she always says that Mama's asleep or out or busy."

And Siri would cover her face with her hands and say, "I can't take this. I can't take it. I can't take it anymore."

OCTOBER 23, 2008. To my wife.

What would you say if I told you I had been in the annex that morning after you had gone to sleep, and that I took her diary? I don't know what made me do it. I really don't. It was stupid. She had told me that she had a secret scrapbook—yes, that's what she called it. And I was afraid that there might be something about her and me in there, but there was nothing. There was nothing, because *it was nothing*. I didn't touch her. A kiss on the cheek. A few kind words. She wasn't happy, you know. She wasn't happy staying with us at Mailund. I felt sorry for her. You were angry with her all the time.

Anyway, I tucked the diary into my waistband, under my thick sweater, and took it up to the attic and quickly leafed through it. Lots of photographs. Quotations. Dried flowers. Tufts of grass.

She had faith apparently. There were many prayers and psalms in the book, this little one among them:

Burning in the night
In this world of darkness
So let us shine,
You in your small corner
And I in mine.

Do you remember how we used to sing to Liv and Alma when they were little? It was the only way for them to fall asleep.

I know you lie awake at night, wondering what happened to her. Nobody just disappears, you say. But they do, all the time. It happens all the time. You disappeared. I disappeared. We disappeared from each other. But nobody just *disappears*, you would say again, annoyed at me for belittling this dreadful thing that happened to Milla by comparing it to our own private little hell.

"I'm talking about *literally* disappearing," you'd say. "Not *figuratively* disappearing."

"People disappear all the time, literally and figuratively," I'd reply then. "You know that."

So I leafed through the diary and was relieved. Nothing about her and me. Not that there had been anything to write about. But you never know what's going on in other people's minds.

Here's the thing: The person who appeared on almost every page was you! Did you know that she took pictures of you and stuck them in her book? Including a series of photos of you asleep in a wicker chair in the garden.

And then there were the pictures of the children. And of the house. And one of Irma having a surreptitious smoke behind the annex. Milla had obviously crept up on her and tried to take her picture without her being aware of it (like the pictures of you!), and Irma must have looked around just as Milla clicked the shutter. She looked very angry.

Do you think about Milla's mother? About Amanda? I do all the time. I think about her father too, he was such a quiet man, just standing there, broken, beside his wife when she was shouting at us.

I want us to write that letter.

What do *you* think about when you think about Milla? I keep thinking about Amanda, can't get her out of my mind, all alone, night after night, wandering from room to room, screaming out her grief.

The thing is, Siri: I got rid of the diary. I went into the woods when it was clear she was not coming back and I ripped it up and threw it in the lake.

If I told you all this, if I had let you read this note before I deleted it, would I have lost you then?

"WELL, WHAT IF I write something like this?" Alma said, looking at Jon.

October 29, 2008
Hi, Mrs. Lund,
Sorry about what happened. I didn't mean it.
Yours sincerely,
Alma Dreyer, 8B

Alma was not speaking to her mother or her sister. *Fuck, cunt, shit, prick, cock, stupid, ass, screw.* Alma didn't give a shit about all these people and all the shit that surrounded her wherever she went.

"Try again," Jon said, and Alma wrote:

October 29, 2008
To Eva Lund,
My deepest apologies for the recent incident. I didn't mean it. Best wishes for the rest of the autumn term!
Yours sincerely,
Alma Dreyer

Alma was not attending school at the moment. Expelled. Not wanted. Instead she found herself, along with Siri and Jon, in the office of a psychologist, with a policewoman present, being interrogated, as if Norway were a *bloody dictatorship*, for God's sake. The policewoman and the psychologist looked exactly alike, like sisters, both wore big glasses and had curly hair and tremulous red-wine lips and soppy, school-milk eyes. They both puckered up their faces as a way of expressing concern, frowning so hard that you could crawl into one of the creases in their brows and hide there. The psychologist wore a white blouse and had ice-cream-cone breasts.

Alma found it impossible to answer any of their questions, the psychologist did most of the talking anyway, but sometimes she stopped talking and looked at Alma, as if waiting for her to say something, they all looked at her: the psychologist, the policewoman, her mother, her father. *Why, Alma?* But Alma had no answer. It wasn't that she didn't want to say anything, she just couldn't, couldn't explain what had happened, and in any case she kept getting distracted by those ice-cream-cone breasts.

"Why did you do it, Alma?"

Do what? Cut off the teacher's hair? Well, it was bound to happen, really. They had been planning it for weeks. The whole class had been in on it, so the fact that Alma was sitting here now, having to take all the blame, was unfair and stupid—like everything else in this stupid world. Three thousand kroner she had been promised for doing it. No one believed she would actually dare to. No one else dared to. They all wanted to, though. It wasn't that they didn't like Eva Lund.

Her English classes were actually pretty good. *My name is Alma. I am thirteen years old, I live in Oslo, I attend a very nice Norwegian school, my hobbies are horseback riding and reading, my mother's name is Ms. Brodal, my father's name is Mr. Dreyer. I am a very happy student.*

Alma shrugged, and said, "No idea!"

The psychologist lady's nipples were totally hard, like Alma's nipples after a cold dip in the sea in the summer at Mailund. Like the nipples of a bikini model. And this lady must have been fifty at least. It was crazy. Gravity, grave, the gravity. Did Alma understand the gravity of the situation? Did Alma have anything to say for herself? The breasts were pointing straight at her. Alma said, "Shouldn't you really be wearing a bra when you interrogate children? Shouldn't there be a law about that or something?"

October 29, 2008
Dear Mrs. Lund,
I am very sorry that I cut off your hair.
Sincerely, Alma Dreyer

Alma would never be going back to that school. That had been decided. She was no longer welcome there. That too had been decided. Alma and Jon and Siri would be going for sessions with the psychologist for an *indefinite length of time*. But not now, because now it was almost the end of the semester and the point was to think seriously about what she had done. All these decisions had been made on her behalf. And they wouldn't be going to Mailund either. Milla disappears, everyone goes crazy, and then all of a sudden no one's going to Mailund. Alma wanted to see her grandmother. The only person in the world she could talk to was Jenny. Not because she's her grandmother (she's not like other grandmothers— Jenny wears high heels, never leaves the house without lipstick on, and takes people seriously). And not because she's so old (though she did turn seventy-five the day Milla disappeared). But because she *understands* what Alma says and does and thinks, without asking a whole lot of stupid questions. When Alma called to tell her she'd cut off her teacher's hair, and that she might read about it in the paper the next day, Jenny said, "Well, sometimes you just can't help yourself."

"It's always a good idea to write *Dear so and so*, rather than *Hi*, when you're writing a proper letter," Jon suggested. "Like this: *Dear Eva Lund—*"

"Oh, hello-o! Daddy! Come on! I'm not writing *Dear*. Nobody writes *Dear*. It's not like we're living in the seventeenth century!"

The last image Alma had of Eva Lund, before Alma pulled away, scissors and all, was of her teacher's gaping mouth, from which weird sounds were emanating. Lips distorted, tongue, teeth, and all that soft, pink flesh, the bread crumbs in the corner of her mouth. It had been more of a howl than a scream. It lasted only a second or two. Then Eva Lund's hands flew up to her face, covering her mouth, as if she had to physically stop her own screaming. She stared at Alma—first in disbelief, as if she really couldn't credit what she was actually seeing: little dark-eyed Alma with a pair of scissors in one hand and her own thick, blond plait in the other. And then came the tears. Eva Lund's eyes filled with two lakes that proceeded to flood over her cheeks.

But why? Not for the three thousand kroner.

Not because everybody had said she didn't dare and she was determined to show them.

It was the hair itself, always braided in one long blond plait that dangled down Eva Lund's back; that and the fact that it was indeed doable. That it was mind-bogglingly doable. Day after day, week after week, month after month, year after year she had sat in that classroom, looking at Eva Lund and her long plait. When Eva turned to face the board it was hard to look at anything else. Sometimes with a hair elastic at the tip, sometimes a little blue ribbon. How long would it take to cut it off (one million, two million, three million, four million, five million), five seconds tops, with a decent pair of scissors. She would have to do it when Eva was standing like that, with her back to the class, writing English vocabulary on the board, *my head*, *my face*, *my arms*, *my hands*, *my tummy*, *my legs*, *my feet*, *my body*, she would have to sneak up on her, she would have to grab hold of her, no, not of her but of the plait itself, give it a tug, and then snip, snip, snip. Mind-boggling, overwhelming, beautiful, doable.

As if it was all Alma's fault. As if the whole class hadn't been in on it. As if Theo hadn't been sitting with his phone ready to film the whole thing. As if Nora and Sofie hadn't uploaded the pictures that same day. As if the whole class hadn't bet her that she wouldn't dare.

209

October 29, 2008
Hi, Eva,
Sorry for what I did. I hope your hair will grow back
quickly. ☺ I didn't mean it. It wasn't my idea. You've
always been an incredibly nice teacher. ☺☺☺ Both
in English and Norwegian. Especially Norwegian. It
was fun that time we had to write short stories. ☺ My
sincerest apologies again for what happened. Enjoy the
rest of the school year!
Best wishes, Alma

"Spare me your smiley faces," Siri said. "Have you still not grasped the gravity of the situation, Alma? What's gotten into you?"

"Now we're going to use the rest of this year to think and talk," Jon repeated.

Siri had been very angry after the meeting with the psychologist and the cop. Siri had been angry about Alma's remark about the breasts. She was angry about Eva Lund's plait and she was angry because Alma had become this *strange, baffling child.*

Alma had heard her mother say to her father one evening when they thought she was asleep: "How did she become this strange, baffling child?"

Her mother had been crying. Her father too.

"I've never been so embarrassed! So bloody awful, all of it. What's gotten into you, Alma! You're so goddamned uncouth."

"Couldn't you just make up your mind to be angry about one thing at a time?" Alma said coolly.

Siri opened her mouth and screamed: "I'm angry with you for all of it, Alma! What's gotten into you?"

And for the third time Jon said that everybody should just calm down and take time to think. At that point Siri whirled around and said Jon was a useless idiot who didn't see the gravity of the situation and if he uttered the word *think* one more time she would kick him in the face.

Alma hadn't meant to be uncouth. She had fully intended to be couth. But it had just slipped out of her. Those ice-cream-cone breasts had a life of their own under that thin, white blouse and they had distracted her. Alma hadn't meant to be cheeky. It had, in her opinion, been a perfectly fair question: Isn't there some law that obliges women psychologists to cover their breasts so they don't stick straight out, pointing at people? Isn't the whole idea of going to a shrink to calm the brain so that it will work better? She was a vulnerable child, for God's sake. She was easily distracted. But those present had not considered her questions to be exactly *constructive*.

"I don't see anything constructive coming out of this meeting," the policewoman said, slipping some papers into a folder and slamming it shut. She looked at Jon and Siri.

"I suggest we meet again in January and that we use the next two months to think about things." She looked at Alma. "And I would just remind you again, Alma, of how grave this episode at the school was and how seriously we, the police, are taking it. You have violated another human being in the most brutal way, you have committed a serious crime, do you know what that means? It means that if you were older we would have been looking at a sentence of anything up to two years.

We're talking prison here, Alma. And it's really disheartening to have you coming here *railing* at everything. I'm disappointed and saddened by the outcome of this meeting."

Alma didn't know what *railing* meant. But she liked the word.

The lady psychologist had clammed up completely. Which was why the lady cop had had to step in and be disappointed and saddened and talk about what the correct outcome of constructive meetings ought to be. But the lady psychologist (who had talked and talked and talked and talked and talked and talked) had been turned princess-silent by Alma's mention of the ice-cream-cone breasts.

There, now I've got you tongue-tied, Alma thought, but didn't say.

Alma Ash-lad rails and rails anywhere else but Albury, Australia.

To tongue-tie means to render speechless, make inarticulate, leave at a loss for words. They had read a folktale in Norwegian class about a princess who was never lost for words until the Ash-lad came along and shut her up, and Eva Lund had opened the dictionary and read out loud the definition of tongue-tie— render speechless, make inarticulate, leave at a loss for words— and Alma thought they were lovely words, even if she didn't completely understand them, render speechless, make inarticulate, leave at a loss for words. And then Eva Lund had split the class into groups of twos and threes and got them to play a game in which they all had to try to tongue-tie one another.

The story about the scissors incident appeared in the tabloids, it was on TV and all over the Internet. One newspaper,

Dagbladet, had it splashed across the front page, as part of a series on violence in Norwegian schools: THIRTEEN-YEAR-OLD GIRL ATTACKS ENGLISH TEACHER, it said in huge letters and inside the newspaper it said:

The plait was the 52-year-old teacher's pride and joy. But the work of a lifetime was cut short when a 13-year-old student attacked her during an English class and hacked off a 42-centimeter chunk of her hair.

October 29, 2008
Hi Eva Leva Lund,
My mother and father, the police and the shrink, the principal, the teachers, the students, and all the people of Norway say that I have to write a letter to apologize. I hereby apologize. It said in the paper that your plait was 42 cm. long.
Best wishes from rolling, rounding, railing Alma Dreyer, 8B

Siri and Jon had gone to the school to collect Alma at the principal's office. Nothing was said. Alma had noticed that Siri seemed unsure of herself. There was the principal and there was Mama, unsure of herself. Mama, who always knew what to say and do in any situation, who always had a smile for everyone. That was what people said about Siri.

But when Siri and Jon arrived to collect Alma after the scissors incident, Siri had no smiles for anyone. Siri was confused. Alma wasn't to know that Siri had been inundated by memories and that when she saw the principal's lowered brows and Alma's averted face she recalled Alma's first day of school.

Siri, Jon, and Alma, who had been six at the time, had been in the school yard, waiting for Alma's name to be called out. Alma, in a red-and-white gingham dress over blue jeans, with her short dark hair and shining dark eyes, a new schoolbag hanging down her slender, violin-shaped back. Siri remembered Alma's hand clutching hers. And when Alma's name was called and it was her turn to cross the school yard and meet her teacher, the child reached for her mother and whispered in her ear: "I can do it, Mama. Let go of my hand." And she had walked alone, across the school yard over to her teacher, shaken hands politely, and quietly lined up with the other children.

And now here we are, Siri thought, glancing over at her daughter, sitting in the wicker chair in the kitchen and refusing to speak to her. *This strange child. When did it happen? When did we lose her?*

October 29, 2008
Hi Mrs. Lund,
I'm sorry I cut off your hair. I hope it'll grow back soon and that you'll enjoy the rest of the semester.
Best wishes,
Alma Dreyer, 8B

Jon and Siri circled each other, each of them alone, each on their own planet, so it seemed, both loving that strange child.

And little Liv with her flaxen locks hopped from planet to planet, singing and singing a song she had made up herself.

Siri sat down on the kitchen chair and wept and shouted at her daughter: "Don't you realize, we can't send that letter until you show that you're sorry, and that you really mean it?"

HE TRIED WITH words.

Jon told Alma she was the apple of his eye, although he didn't know exactly what that meant, *apple of my eye*, or why he had chosen that particular expression.

Thirteen years old. Small and chubby. Short black hair. It was now the beginning of March, still very cold, and Jon had picked her up at school (yet another school) and taken her to a bakery for hot chocolate and cupcakes. They passed a table where a young woman was drinking coffee, with her baby on her lap. Jon looked at her, but the woman didn't look at him. He noticed things like that. At another table some young girls giggled and dropped their eyes as he and Alma walked past them.

"This is our new tradition," he said jauntily. "A father-daughter tradition."

Alma said nothing.

"Do you know those girls over there?" he asked.

"They're in my class," she said.

Two enormous cupcakes sat between them on the table. His voice was a little too loud (oh, how he floundered, but he hadn't the faintest idea what to talk to her about) and the elderly couple drinking coffee not far from them looked across and the old lady smiled.

"Oh, isn't that nice, being out with your father," she said. Alma looked down and the old lady smiled knowingly at Jon. He found this—all of this—annoying. Alma's sullenness, his own loud, jolly voice, the people looking at them, the old lady's smile. It wasn't a damned performance! And then he leaned across the table and uttered those words that he normally never used: "You are the *apple of my eye* you know."

He spoke them softly. He wanted her to understand that she was loved and seen and that there was nothing to worry about. She reached a hand across the table, twined her still-chubby fingers with his, and said, "You don't have to make such an effort, Papa."

He wanted to defend himself.

"No, Alma, I'm doing this because I want to, I'd so like for us to find things to do together and create our own traditions—and you really are the *apple of my eye*."

Alma took a sip of her hot cocoa and then she said, "You still feel bad about Milla disappearing?"

The question came out of nowhere and he had no idea how to answer it. He looked at her.

"Yes," he said finally, "I feel bad."

"It's been eight months," she said. "They might never find her."

"They will," he said. "Probably...I'm sure they will."

She fell silent, drew her hand back and picked at the cupcake, got pink frosting on her fingers, and wiped them on a napkin. She looked down. Her short black hair was brushed back and her cowlick was sticking straight up, like a cartoon character's, lending a droll touch to her otherwise solemn face. When she was little they had called her Lull.

"I don't even like cupcakes," she said, spreading her hands resignedly. "They're so gloppy."

He felt like getting up and leaving, or crying, he wasn't going to be able to fix this, she wanted too much from him, and at the same time he wished that she would understand him, *that she would understand him*, and not just need him all the time, even though he knew, of course, how unreasonable this was, this desire for her to understand him.

Alma was a child, he was the parent.

He said she could have something else if she liked, the glass display case was full of cakes and filled rolls and buns and chocolate tarts, and while he was talking he realized, or maybe he didn't realize it right then and there but later, that they had reached the point where he couldn't just tell her that he loved her, because if he did she would drop everything she had in her hands (hot chocolate, cupcake, a glass of lemonade, whatever!) and throw herself into his arms, or onto his lap. Her movements were so fierce that something was always getting knocked over—chairs, tables, piles of paper, glass vases. In her eagerness to hug him she was totally heedless of everything around her.

Alma had grown up, as all girls do, and she was too big now to sit on his lap, with her rather broad plump behind, her long skinny arms, her long skinny legs, her clumsy hands, the bone-hard bumps under her T-shirt, where her breasts would appear. Her daughter-body no longer had the weight and warmth of his little girl, his baby, now there was something else, something alien and invasive about her.

"Or we could just leave right now," he said. "We can make up another tradition."

He scanned the surrounding tables, caught sight of an attractive woman in a red dress and thought of the scarlet poppies he had seen years before, when he was in Gotland with Siri. He smiled at the woman and she smiled back.

Alma nodded.

"Another father-daughter tradition," he said.

He had already put on his coat and hat and gloves. She nodded again. The dark eyes under her bangs.

"We could go and look at the sea," he said. "Not today, but some other day. Soon. We could go and look at the sea and celebrate the coming of spring."

He couldn't get out of there quickly enough now, but Alma took forever to put on her mittens, hat, scarf, and down jacket, while Jon stood there breathing and exercising self-control. He mustn't get impatient. He inhaled. *I will not be impatient. I will not be impatient.* When Alma was younger, about six or seven, her response to Siri's and Jon's impatience had been to reserve the right to take exactly as long as she needed to do whatever it was she had to do—whether she was getting dressed in the morning, eating, going to the bathroom, playing with her stuff. Taking forever to put on her clothes, especially her outdoor clothes. Because everything had to be done in a particular way and in a particular sequence. Her clothes had to sit just *so* if she was to feel comfortable in them. Gaps and bumps had to be avoided, her socks had to be pulled well up her calves so that they sat snugly around the feet of her wool tights, and the cuffs of her mittens had to be tucked into the sleeves of her down jacket. All of this took time and both Siri and Jon knew that there was no point in saying that maybe getting dressed didn't need to take so long, that maybe it didn't matter too much whether the mittens went on before or after the down jacket.

When Alma was younger, reproofs of this nature would only result in her taking off all her clothes, stripping completely to then start all over again. And there was no point in nagging at her now either. Siri's and Jon's impatience had the same effect on Alma as the mountain troll on the traveling sons of kings—she turned to stone and would not budge.

Alma, you'll be late for school.

Alma, everybody's waiting for you.

Alma, it doesn't matter whether your mitten cuffs are inside or outside your jacket.

Alma brushed some invisible cupcake crumbs off her woolly hat, she wouldn't put it on until she had brushed away those crumbs, she brushed and brushed, then she shook it, laid it on the table, and brushed it again.

Jon closed his eyes and took a deep breath. He opened his eyes and said as softly and as tenderly as he could: "Do you think you're about ready, or shall I wait for you outside?"

Alma inspected her hat, ran a hand over it. "Can't you wait here for me? I want to leave with you!"

The old lady at the other table looked at them. She said, "Are you leaving already? Didn't you like your cupcakes?"

Jon smiled at her, wondering what benevolent forces prevented him from lunging at her and knocking her off her chair.

ALMA BRUSHED SOME cupcake crumbs off her hat, you simply could not go around with crumbs on your hat, it was just the sort of thing the girls in her class would comment on and in her mind she saw herself raising her eyes and staring them all to death, and how the whole bakery would be transformed into an inferno of upturned tables and chairs with plates and cutlery and glasses and cupcakes and pastries and sandwiches garnished with little sprigs of parsley strewn all over the floor. The sound of people trying not to make a sound because they were so afraid of what she might do to them—just by staring at them. Standing, crouching, lying down, curled up, and half hidden behind overturned tables or chairs. She pictured her gaze passing from face to face. The woman in the poppy-red dress. The old lady with the coffee cup who wouldn't leave other people alone. The girls from her class. Papa on his way out. *Can't be bothered waiting here. I'll wait for you outside.* The mother with the baby. The tiny baby who didn't understand what everyone else thought they understood, namely that a deafening silence was their only hope of survival. The baby wailed because it was hungry and because its mother wouldn't open her blouse and give it the breast. Alma imagined what it would be like to open her mouth and let them all, the living and the dead, hear her voice. "MAKE THAT FUCKING BABY SHUT UP!"

The woman in the poppy-red dress got up and walked toward Alma. She pointed to the empty chair, the one her father had been sitting on. She said, "Is it okay if I take it?"

Alma nodded.

The woman thanked her, took the chair, and carried it over to her own table. And then it was as if it happened again. The woman in the poppy-red dress got up and walked toward her, saying "Is it okay if I take it?" but adding in a quiet voice, "You know that little baby girl can't help it if she cries. She's just a baby. And no one can do anything about it one way or the other. But I'll help you. Give me your hand!"

And Alma gave the woman her hand and the woman drew her into her arms and held her close.

"It will be fine," the woman whispered. "You will be fine. Everything will be okay."

All the crumbs were gone from her hat now. Not a single crumb left.

"Bye-bye then," said the old lady who couldn't leave other people alone.

Alma didn't reply and she didn't look back as she walked toward the exit. It was Milla who had said you should never look back. No good came of looking back. But Alma had looked back that time in Grandma's car, Alma had seen Milla sitting there at the side of the road, and Alma had said *Stop!* She clearly remembered saying *Stop!* And then she said

Shouldn't we take her with us, and Grandma said, *Take who with us?* and Alma said *Nobody, I thought I saw somebody, but I didn't, forget it,* and Grandma said, *Let's go home, then,* and they drove the last bit of the way up to Mailund, and that night Alma had actually thought that Grandma wasn't quite herself, that she might have had too much to drink.

The girls from her class giggled, but Alma walked past them and didn't look back.

SIRI HAD KNOWN for many years that her husband was cheating on her.

He cheated on her long before Milla came into their lives, but that was a time when Siri more often than not made the choice to forget—she thought of this, her habitual ability to forget, draw a blank, leave well enough alone, as acts of tenderness, a way to ward off fear.

But now it seemed Milla wouldn't let her. Milla wouldn't let her forget about anything.

The pretty lost girl in the photograph looked at her from everywhere and didn't care if what Siri remembered (and would rather forget) had happened before she came into their lives.

Siri remembered that it was a Sunday, that it was raining, that she had been out for a long walk, that she came into the living room, her hair still dripping, and how a few drops of water had fallen on Jon's laptop (had she ruined it?) and how she thought that the laptop had been left there on the dining table on purpose, open, blatantly flaunting itself, shamelessly inviting.

She remembered sitting down, tying her hair in a knot so it would stop dripping, and reading.

It was an e-mail from Jon to a woman called Paula: *I think of how it would have been, just you and me, morning, afternoon,*

evening, night, and I think of everything you are and everything
you can show me and all the things I want to do with you. You
ask if I'm unhappy, if the thought of you makes me unhappy,
but just knowing you exist makes me happy. I picture your face,
your hair, your eyes, your light shining. But you know my situ-
ation—maybe that's what's making me unhappy. I think of you
morning, afternoon, evening, and night, but I can't be with you
except in my thoughts, because, well, you know. Because...

First, relief. *I'm not crazy.* Everything fell into place. All
suspicions confirmed. She had been right, although time and
again he had told her she was wrong.

During their first years of marriage, when she was still con-
fronting him about those inconsistensies that kept popping up
in his stories (not the stories he told her at night, out of love,
to help her fall sleep, or the stories he wrote in his books, but
the other ones—about where he had been, whom he had seen,
what he had done), he had told her that she was just imagining
things, that she needed to see someone about her paranoia and
insecurities, that he was fed up with her accusations.

Siri read the e-mail again: *But I can't be with you except in*
my thoughts, because, well, you know. Because...

Because... what?

Because he was married to Siri? Because Siri was a burden so
heavy that words could not describe it? Or because Siri was so
utterly light—insignificant, weightless, transient, forgettable—
that she wasn't worth a single letter of the alphabet?

Because, well, you know. Because...

She read it again.

Why didn't he write "I can't be with you except in my

225

thoughts, because I'm married to Siri"? It was very simple, no need for pregnant pauses and meaningful silences. No need for *dot dot dot*. And what was up with that anyway? Does any self-respecting person, let alone a highly acclaimed novelist, indicate significance by writing dot dot dot to finish off an unfinished sentence? Is that even allowed?

It's really very fucking simple, Paula.

Siri trembled, but said nothing to Jon. Not the first evening, not the second, not the third.

"What's the matter? You're very quiet. Is something wrong?"

"No, nothing," Siri said.

The next time she checked his inbox he had deleted the letter.

I picture your face.

But Siri knew the words by heart and for a while she started her day by quoting the e-mail to herself, as if it were a difficult text that she had to learn by heart so as not to forget it (until she chose to do so), she examined the letters from every angle, pictured Jon writing, and Paula reading, and the words dissolved and re-formed, giving rise to new meanings and associations, depending on the point at which she chose to enter the text and the point at which she chose to exit it.

I think of how it would have been, just you and me.

If Siri had said anything to Jon, she might have said: You make dates with another woman, you walk around looking forward to those dates and lie to me and go off with the dog, *going to get bread, going to get milk.* And there was me thinking that we were the exception, that you were my one and only, and I was your one and only, and that the disaster that strikes everyone else,

the most embarrassing of all thinkable disasters, the most humiliating and the most banal, the kind of disaster that we laugh
about when it strikes others, would never strike us. I wanted to
be your one and only, Jon, not one body among other bodies.
Your hair, your eyes, your light shining.

Once he'd said to Siri: *Your light shines more.* She'd thought
it was a lame line, but she'd let him get away with it. She was
light. She shone. He needed her. She was his one and only.

But now he had taken their words, their silly little secret
passwords, and given them to someone else. To a woman
named Paula. Words which, when put together in one way or
another, or rather in one very specific way, constituted the sum
of Siri and Jon's story. Siri was no longer the one and only. She
wasn't even the only one who shone.

Now the story went like this—*and this is not a particularly
original story. In fact, Jon, it's an extremely banal and embarrassing story and I hate that you made me a part of it*—first
there was Siri who had light. Then there was Paula who had
light. *Your light shines.*

(In Jon's, the unfaithful husband's, defense it should be added
that he is a writer suffering from writer's block. It's years since
he was supposed to have finished the third part of what was
to have been the trilogy of the millennium, but he can't seem
to find the words, the only thing he has come up with so far is
that he wants to write "a hymn to everything that endures and
everything that falls apart" and that, as he has painfully had
to acknowledge, won't get him very far, a hymn to everything

227

that endures and everything that falls apart is a crock of shit. In other words, you could not expect—it's unreasonable to expect or demand—that Jon, a writer who can no longer write, should invent an entirely new language every time he becomes enamored of a new woman.)

But the bit about the *light shining*—that she couldn't forgive. *Your hair, your eyes, your light shining.* That the other woman had hair and eyes was reasonable. Siri too had hair and eyes, most women had hair and eyes, but Jon hadn't made special mention of the hair and eyes simply to confirm the obvious: that Paula had hair and eyes. No, Jon made special mention of the hair and eyes in order to assure her that: *I see you. Your particular hair. Your particular eyes. You are not one body among other bodies. You are the one and only.*

Whether he actually meant that Paula was the one and only is not important here. Whatever was going on in Jon's mind when he was writing this letter is very different from what went on in Siri's mind when she read it. Jon's love letter was most probably a manifestation of a perfectly ordinary instance of barter in which the rules governing supply and demand were clear and unambiguous: *You have been seen and described by me. Now it is my turn to be seen and described by you.* But the other woman didn't only have eyes and hair, she also had *light*—screw him.

And if Siri had told Jon that she had read the letter, that she was about to collapse and wouldn't be able to get up again, that the pain was cold, like being force-fed icicles, then she might have asked: "Do we both shine at the same time, Paula and I, like the twin lights on Thacher Island? Or did I stop shining the moment Paula started? And how many shining lights are we actually talking about?"

Siri broke a glass, but she didn't cut herself. That sort of drama wasn't her, it would only make the banality complete. The banal story of a banal woman who slashed herself because her husband had cheated on her. No, she wouldn't say anything.

But if she had, she might have said:

"Why did you put me in harm's way like that?"

Out with the dog, going to get bread, going to get milk.

During the weeks and months and years after Siri had read the letter, Paula was everywhere. Siri googled her and learned that she was thirty-four years old, *younger than me*, worked in an art gallery, and lived on Oslo's trendy east side. She had 567 friends on Facebook. Her profile picture was indistinct, slightly out of focus in an interesting sort of way, she had a teasing look in her eye and long fair hair. Paula's picture said: *I'm beautiful in an interesting kind of way, my picture is not like all the other pictures, I have a teasing look and long fair hair.* Oh, all those beautiful women, and even women who weren't quite so beautiful but whom Siri imagined could be Jon's type, were everywhere. The long fair hair, the slender shoulders, the small breasts, the teasing look in the eye. *Everywhere.* In every café, in every shop, on every street corner, at the gym dancing and spinning and lifting weights and taking their clothes off in locker rooms, and in the pool where she occasionally went swimming. And each one was the one and only, and Siri a body among other bodies. And Siri let her gaze pass over their faces and their bodies, at first shattered (betrayed, tricked, supplanted, painted out, debarred), and then curious (if he can look at them, so can I), and eventually greedy.

And if she had said anything to Jon, she might have said, "I want to see what you see, unearth whatever it is that you unearth, I want to understand that thing that makes them special. I want to share them with you, undress them, rend them apart, make love to them, and hear them say my name, *and I think of everything you are and everything you can show me and all the things I want to do with you*, see them fall, feel what you feel when they look at you, you look at them, look at me."

But she didn't say anything to Jon. She let it go, because she chose to. *These were acts of tenderness.* But now, with Milla, it all came crashing back.

AND IF HE were to think about it, something he preferred not to do, he couldn't pinpoint exactly when he and Siri had started sleeping apart. She in the bedroom and he in whatever attic was available. When did the unraveling of their marriage begin? It was long before Milla. But *when*? It had been years now.

They said to each other: "Oh it's been months, we should go away somewhere and be together." But the fact was that it had been years.

These were all things he preferred not to think about, so instead he thought and did other things. Drank cheap wine, which tasted better than expensive wine, and texted whoever was up, listened to music, and talked with the dog. They told each other it was because of the children—which, to some extent, it was. Alma still came to their room every night, she had done so for years, and when he was still sleeping in the master bedroom, she climbed into their bed next to him. *Hold me! Stroke my hair!*

"We can't rule out the possibility," Jon remembered saying, "that the reason I'm not writing is that I'm not getting any sleep now that Alma's in our bed every night."

Siri turned to him and said, "She doesn't just keep *you* awake, Jon! Last night she nearly pushed me out of bed and you snored."

Her voice was shrill.

"Oh, just listen to yourself," he said.

"No, you listen, you bastard! Have you given any thought to the fact that of the two of us I'm the one working and earning money so that you can write that bloody book of yours? Or rather, not write it."

And so they went on.

There was a time she couldn't even consider falling asleep unless he was right next to her, holding her hand, telling her stories.

Not long after Liv had learned to walk, she too started coming into their bed at night. She wandered through in the dark, climbed over Siri and Alma and Jon, and stretched out across the mattress, shoving everyone else over to one side. She didn't ask for permission and she didn't want to be held or stroked. She just wanted to sleep, but she took up more room in the bed than anyone else. And so their nights went. Everyone—apart from Liv, who slept undisturbed—waking and sleeping and waking and sleeping. Jon detached Alma's arm, laid it down along her side, and she promptly snuggled into him again and put her arm around his neck, and Siri put Liv's head on the pillow, gently shifted her legs until they were pointing straight down to the foot of the bed, but she merely drew them up again, squirmed, and stretched out across the bed as before.

On those few occasions when they had the bed to themselves, those miraculous nights when the children slept in their own beds, he tried to hold Siri, but his arms weren't long enough and she didn't budge and so they lay there, each teetering on their own edge of the bed. And Siri said, "I really need to sleep. Please, just leave me alone."

They reminded each other on a regular basis that sleeping apart was merely a temporary solution, and they often talked about when they would sleep in the same bed again.

"I've so much to do," he remembered her saying. "I feel so inadequate, on all fronts."

In the beginning, when this arrangement of sleeping in separate rooms began, as a very temporary thing, she would carry his blanket to him in the attic and make up his bed for him on the mattress on the floor, then Jon would carry the blanket downstairs the following morning and put it back on the double bed. After a while, though, she stopped making up his bed for him and merely laid his blanket on the stairs so that he could carry it to the attic himself.

And now it was April. Nine months gone. Siri and Jon had started sending text messages to each other at night. She in the bedroom, he up there in the attic. Not about what might have happened to Milla or what had happened to their marriage or what had happened to Alma. Just little things.

Thinking of you.
I miss you.
Don't leave me.
Sweet dreams.
Kisses.

And one evening she took a picture of the water glass on her bedside table and sent the photo to him.

It was a very long time since Jon had touched his wife, and he sent her a picture of a corner of his pillowcase. The following evening she sent him a picture of a detail from a child's drawing (Alma's? Liv's?) that was lying in the drawer of her bedside table, and then he sent her a picture of the knot at the end of the cord for adjusting the blinds in the attic. Siri sent him a picture of Liv's flaxen curls on her Peter Rabbit pillow, and then he sent her a photograph of the two of them when they were young and in love. She was wearing her corn-yellow boots and he was Giacometti thin and had big curly hair. She sent him a picture of her left hand without her wedding ring—at some point during the evening she always took her wedding ring off and would spend the next morning trying to find it. He snapped a picture of her wedding ring, lying next to his on a stack of books by his mattress. She sent him a picture of the rusty window hinges, he sent her a picture of a wine cork, she didn't know that he had opened the evening's second bottle of Barolo, she didn't know that she wasn't the only one he sent text messages to at night, she didn't know that he had to keep a firm grip on himself the next morning, so as not to scream at her, scream at the children, thus arousing the suspicion that he was drinking too much, the hangovers were the worst, she didn't even know that it was a picture of a wine cork, it could have been anything, and during the short month of April when they were sending each other pictures at night certain unspoken rules evolved, one being that they should not ask what the pictures actually depicted.

And Siri sent him a picture of a tiny brown spot, no bigger than a pinprick, surrounded by what might have been skin. At first he thought the brown spot was a freckle and this made him happy. Siri had freckles on her shoulders, or at least she used to have freckles on her shoulders and he had always loved that about her. He looked at the picture. Something brown. Something that looked like skin. Maybe a freckle.

And Jon sent her a picture of the cover of the VHS of *Manhattan* with a picture of the silhouettes of Diane Keaton and Woody Allen against the New York skyline. There were stacks of VHS tapes in the attic. They couldn't bring themselves to get rid of them, even after DVDs came along, even after they started downloading all their films off the Internet, they had been proud of their collection, and Jon had once suggested that they could make a huge library in the basement at Mailund and fill it with only ghostly things—all their LPs and VHSs and DVDs and letters and books and actual photo albums.

Siri sent him a picture of her right hand, she sometimes fretted about her hands, over the fact that they were dry and bluish, that her cuticles were split and tender and that they hurt. On her bedside table she kept a jar of expensive, fragrant hand cream that she rubbed into her hands every evening. He sometimes missed the scent of her hands in the evening, and one night she sent him a picture of the jar of hand cream.

And Jon took a picture of his own face and sent her the picture and under it he wrote: *Can I come and lie next to you?*

I miss you.

I can tell you stories.

BUT THERE WAS no response. After waiting awhile and drinking some more whiskey—Jon had switched to whiskey, red wine gave him a headache—after searching for and finding Klaus Nomi on YouTube and watching Klaus Nomi do his weird and shattering rendition of Purcell's aria from *King Arthur* and after drinking still more whiskey, Jon picked up his phone and sent another text.

Hey, answer, why don't you? I want to be with you. I don't want to lie here in the attic anymore.

He stared at the ceiling. No reply. Fuck her. Why couldn't it just be simple? Why did he have to lie here in the attic, banished? Why couldn't they just lie in the same bed and have sex? Was it so unreasonable to want a little normal, everyday physical contact? Why did the conversation have to be about everything but sex, everything that had to happen *before* sex, when they talked about sex? Housework, for example. Responsibility. He had to take more responsibility. Feelings. He lacked empathy. She couldn't trust him. He didn't see the bigger picture. Children. They wore her out. Work. She was worked off her feet. Money. He was never going to get that book finished. They couldn't live on her income alone. He would have to find a real job. Only the other day she had actually said, "We need to work toward an even distribution of chores and privileges."

"Okay," he had replied, and then he had started yelling: "How much is a fuck with you worth? Tell me and I'll pay. Do you want me to vacuum the whole house? Cook dinner every day? Get a nine-to-five job? Write a best seller? Separate the trash? Vote Labour? Just say! How much to fuck you?"

He looked at his phone. No reply. Damn her. He wrote another text. To Karoline this time.

I'm going away for a few days, to write, have borrowed a house in Sandefjord. Can you come? I want to see you.

The response was swift.

When?

He hadn't actually been planning on going anywhere to write, not right now, after Easter sometime, maybe, and he certainly hadn't been planning on taking Karoline with him, she was humorless, she bored him, he had been planning to end the whole thing, it had been going on for years and he was fed up, and it wasn't entirely unproblematic that Karoline was married to Kurt and that all four of them—the Dreyer-Brodals and the Mandls—were friends.

What he had thought when he was offered the chance to borrow a house in Sandefjord was that it would be good to be on his own, that he needed some time on his own. To shut himself away. With no interruptions. And enough whiskey. Alone. No wife. No children. No dog. Or maybe the dog. He took a swig of whiskey and wrote: *In two weeks. Can you get away?*

She replied right away. They all did. (Apart from Siri, who shut him out.) He pictured an entire city of lonely, sleepless women sitting up at night with their cell phones, writing to him. The thought was amusing and at the same time depressing. His cell chirruped.

Kurt going to U.S. in two wks ☺ so shld be possible. Will check with my mother if Gunnar can stay with her...Kisses ☺

Jon looked at Karoline's message. How old was this woman? He counted on his fingers. Two years younger than him. Forty-nine? So what the hell was going on with the little smiley faces? Did she think of herself as a little girl having her first love affair? A little Lolita. A little dish. He laughed out loud. How awful. A *smiley face.* She wasn't just humorless, she was stupid too. And just the mention of that son of hers. Gunnar.

I don't want us to be with these people, Dad.

Alma is weird...She's a freak, you know.

He wrote: *I don't ever want to go anywhere with you or talk to you again or hear about your son. You're humorless, pathetic, ridiculous, ugly, and boring, I hate fucking you, I hate your shriveled-up cunt, you stink, you remind me of everything that's despicable about myself and the whole fucking world. ☺ Jon*

He read it over. Yes, that was it, exactly! Then he pressed DELETE. What difference did it make, anyway? Why not go to Sandefjord with Karoline? He might just as well go to Sandefjord with Karoline as not go. Karoline would at least want to fuck. His phone chirruped again. He read the text.

Jon—has it ever occurred to you that everything you do has consequences. Always.

Jon started. What the hell? Had he sent that shriveled-cunt message to Karoline after all? He eyed the whiskey bottle. What

the hell had he done now? He broke out in a sweat. He checked
DELETED MESSAGES—and there it was. He hadn't sent it. He deleted it again. He looked at the message he had just received.

*Jon—has it ever occurred to you that everything you do has
consequences. Always.*

He looked at the number from which the message had
been sent. He didn't recognize it. Was Siri sending him messages from a secret phone? Was this a new kind of game? Had
she found out about the other women? He felt the whiskey
coming back on him and had to put his hand to his mouth to
keep from being sick. He took a deep breath. It was all right.
He wasn't going to be sick. He wasn't going to die. This was
nothing. There was nothing to worry about. He was here in
his own home. Everything was all right.

But could Siri have somehow hacked into the night's exchange of text messages and sent him a message from a cell
phone he didn't know about—and why did she have a cell
phone he didn't know about? Jon keyed in the number for
directory inquiries but drew a blank there. And then came
another message, repeating the words from the last one.

Everything you do has consequences. Always.

He poured another drink and wrote: *Who are you?*

He did not have long to wait.

You haven't told all you know about why she disappeared.

Then came another message.

I'm Amanda, Milla's mother, but you knew that, didn't you?

IN THE SUMMER of 2009 Jon and Siri and the children spent precisely four days at Mailund before packing up all their stuff and heading back to Oslo. Jenny and Irma had sat up every night drinking Cabernet and wanted nothing to do with the rest of the family, and when Liv wouldn't stop crying after having run into her grandmother drunk in the kitchen early one morning at the end of June, Siri announced that she wasn't staying there another minute. And there was nothing for it but to leave.

And anyway, the whole house was a reminder of Milla. Siri imagined finding strands of dark hair along the baseboards and around the doorframes, in the annex, in the meadow behind the house, in the vegetable plot, under the maple tree, and in her white flower bed.

That white peony in your hair—that's from one of my beds. You wreck things.

Siri left the running of Gloucester in the hands of one of her young and talented chefs and hurried back to Oslo.

Amanda's voice was everywhere.

But surely, you must know something? You can't just stand there and not know. It's not good enough! Please! She lived in your house! You were supposed to watch over her! Where is she? Where is she goddamn it? Tell me where she is!

It would soon be July and then she would have been gone a year.

A few weeks earlier that summer, Jon had had an excellent meeting with his editor, Gerda, and Julian, the publisher. They had split a bottle of wine. Everyone had agreed that the third part of the trilogy should be published in mid-November, which meant that he would have to deliver the manuscript by mid-August at the latest.

"Writer's block or no writer's block, this book will be published," Jon had said with a loud laugh. Much louder than Gerda's and Julian's. He had wanted to show them that he could actually joke about this whole awkward situation that had arisen over the past few years, namely that he 1) owed the publishing house a lot of money, and 2) had never produced a manuscript.

It so happened, though, that the writing had been coming easier over the past couple of months. He'd had two good weeks in Sandefjord in April and May, except during that first weekend, when Karoline joined him and was all set on "defining their relationship." She thought it might be better if she just told her husband, to which Jon had replied that he really didn't think she should. Jon had Siri and Karoline had Kurt and they were all good friends and she mustn't go messing things up or muddling things up or whatever the right expression was. "Let's think about the kids, Karoline," Jon said. "And besides, what good would it do telling Kurt about us?" And when she didn't answer, he repeated: "Let's think about the kids."

Really, he just wanted to end the whole thing, but somehow he couldn't bring himself to do it.

And the text messages from Milla's mother kept on coming, sometimes with weeks in between them, sometimes days. More often than not they came just when he had managed to put the whole thing to the back of his mind.

Her birthday today. She's twenty. Walking around the flat searching for her. A.

We find it almost impossible to talk about her. A.

Is there something you're not telling, Jon? Is there something you and Siri aren't telling? A.

July 15. She's been gone a year. These are the anniversaries we will be observing from now on. A.

On one occasion (when she had written "we find it almost impossible to talk about her") he replied, asking if they should meet for coffee, and was relieved when he didn't hear back from her.

Jon had imagined finishing the book at Mailund, Alma could watch Liv for a few hours outside while he wrote, but when, typically, Siri changed all their plans and moved everyone back to Oslo, he realized there would be nothing written this summer either. Siri immersed herself in work at the Oslo restaurant and it was up to him to figure out what to do all day with the children in the city.

When August came along, he tried to explain to Gerda why he didn't have that many new pages to show her, why he would probably have to ask for a new deadline. Gerda said she would speak to Julian, but Jon sensed that she didn't really have time to listen to his explanations. Gerda had actually been quite brusque on the phone.

In October, Jon drove down to Mailund alone—to clean the gutters. He had never cleaned gutters before, but the strangest thing had happened: Irma had called him on his cell to ask if by any chance he had time to come down to Mailund and clean the gutters. Naturally Jon had been surprised that Irma should be calling him about anything. They had never spoken on the phone, or exchanged many words at all, despite having shared a house every summer for years, she living in the basement and he up in the attic, and neither of them needing to have anything to do with the other. But now: the gutters.

"Why are you calling *me* about this?" Jon asked.

"Well, because Ola was here and he said it was time we got the gutters cleaned," Irma said.

"Can't Ola do it?" Jon asked. "Or you, for that matter?"

"Ola's too old," Irma said, "and I'm too big and heavy, I'm afraid of heights. I don't know anything about gutters."

"Well, neither do I," Jon said.

"Ola says the gutters are full of leaves and twigs, and something about if they freeze they could burst in the spring when it thaws."

Siri said Jon *had* to go. This was an overture from Jenny and Irma. And such an overture had to be accepted. Siri was afraid that suddenly one day Jenny would be on her deathbed and that she wouldn't be there.

"You know...*be there* for her," she said. "And it could happen anytime, the way she's drinking and going on. It's not like

Irma is taking care of her. Not really. And anyway, I should be
the one taking care of my mother."

So Jon googled "cleaning gutters," then drove down to
Mailund, spent the night in the attic, and cleaned the gutters
as well as he could, and since he was there anyway, Irma wondered whether he could do a couple of other little chores. He
stayed for three days, but didn't see much of Jenny or Irma,
which suited him fine. He actually wrote a few pages too, in
between the odd jobs, and he found himself thinking that
it was nice to get away for a little while. Now and again he
would get up from his desk and look out the attic window
at the meadow, which was covered with frost in the mornings, and sometimes when he did that he thought of Milla.
But he didn't want to think about Milla and he didn't want to
think about the letter he had never gotten around to writing to
Milla's parents and he certainly did not want to think of how
he might have been able to save her that evening, had he gone
to meet her as she suggested.

*I'll be around this evening if you feel like getting away from
the party and having a glass of wine with me, at the Bellini,
maybe?*

On his last evening at Mailund, Jon took a walk with Leopold
down the long road to the jetties and the shop. They normally
went for a walk in the woods, but Jon wanted to pick up a
couple of beers and some peanuts. The evenings were dark
now and he and Leopold barely missed bumping into a boy of
about ten who came tearing toward them on his bike.

"Hey, you," Jon cried. "Watch where you're going."

Simen stopped and looked back.

"You're Jon Dreyer," he said, unfazed by Jon's attempt at a stern voice. "You're a writer, aren't you?"

"That's right, yes," Jon said with a little laugh. "But how did you know that? I don't expect you read my books?"

"No, I don't," said Simen. "Neither does my father, he tried to read one of your books, but he thought it was boring. My father likes books based on real life. But my mother likes you. She's read all your books. But it's a long time since you wrote anything new, my mother says. She's in this book group in Oslo, with five other women, and I think they once read something by you. She's talked about you because you stay at Mailund in the summer. You're kind of like a neighbor, she says. You're Alma's father, aren't you?"

Jon nodded.

"Alma used to look after me sometimes when I was younger. That was a long time ago."

"Oh, yes," Jon said. "I think I remember you now."

"But you weren't there this summer," Simen said.

"No," Jon said.

"That girl Milla, she lived in your house a year ago, when she disappeared?" Simen went on.

"Yes, she did," Jon said.

"Was it because she couldn't be found? Was that why you weren't here this summer?"

"No," Jon said. "We were here for four days, but then we went back to Oslo to work."

He checked himself. He did not have to explain himself to this boy. His cell phone trilled and Jon pulled it out.

She had so many plans. A.

"I'm a Liverpool supporter," Simen said. "Who do you support?"

Jon stuffed his phone back into his pocket and said, "I'm a Liverpool supporter too, but I haven't really kept up with them lately."

Simen had been cycling around him during this conversation. Round and round and round. His cycling was as effortless as his speech, as instinctive, or more so: The turn of the pedals, the whir of the wheels, the hum of his voice, it was as if, Jon thought, he were actually talking through the bike, breathing through the bike, as if he and the bike were one. Jon walked ahead and Simen and the bike circled around him as they carried on down the road.

"You must know Irma, too, then," Simen said.

Jon confirmed that yes, he did know Irma, seeing that she lived with Jenny at Mailund.

"She hissed at me once," Simen said. "I hadn't done anything wrong, nothing at all. Was just cycling around the way I am now. Wasn't even anywhere near her with my bike and suddenly she grabbed my handlebars and hissed at me."

Simen reached his hand out to Jon and grabbed his arm, opened his mouth and let out a hissing sound, to show him what had happened.

Jon nodded slowly.

"I mean, I could have fallen off my bike," Simen said.

"Maybe you scared her," Jon suggested. "Maybe she thought you were going to run into her?"

Simen shook his head. "No, she didn't look very scared."

Simen and the bike reared up slightly, possibly in an effort to regain Jon's full attention.

"Have you noticed that she glows?"

"Glows?" Jon said. "How do you mean?"

"That she shines in the dark," Simen said. "I don't know how to explain it." He executed a perfect circle around Jon. "You're the writer," he added. "You explain it!"

"I've sometimes thought that she has the face of an angel," Jon said. "Maybe that's why she glows, if that's what she does. I think she looks like the angel Uriel in that painting by Leonardo da Vinci, the one called *The Virgin of the Rocks*. You've heard of Leonardo da Vinci, right?"

"Irma doesn't look anything like an angel," Simen interjected, clearly annoyed with Jon for making such an inaccurate comparison. "I mean, she's huge. She must be the biggest woman in the world. She's even taller than Peter Crouch."

"Who's Peter Crouch?" Jon asked.

Simen slammed on his brakes and stared at Jon.

"I thought you said you were a Liverpool supporter."

"What I said was that I used to root for Liverpool, but that I haven't really kept up with them lately. Does Peter Crouch play for Liverpool?"

"No." Simen sighed. "He's with the Spurs now, but he *used to* play for Liverpool. *He's big, he's red, his feet stick out of the bed.* You know?"

Jon shook his head.

"He's REALLY tall. Just like Irma."

"Yeah, so you said," Jon replied. "And you're right, she is really tall. But I still think she has the face of an angel, and there's no saying that all angels have to be small and sweet. Like the angels on Christmas trees—"

"The point," said Simen, interrupting, "is that she glows. And I was wondering whether you'd noticed this."

"That she has a kind of inner glow, you mean?" Jon asked uncertainly.

"No, that's not what I mean," Simen said. He thought for a moment. "She glows in the dark. I know she does. I saw it. It was like she'd just swallowed a fireball."

"Like she'd just swallowed a fireball," Jon repeated.

"Yes, exactly," Simen said. "That's exactly what it was like."

V

JENNY

OLD AGE STRUCK quickly. Who would have thought that in the prime of her life Jenny Brodal the bookseller would get sick and then go lose her mind?

One day in the early spring of 2010, on her way to the hairdresser, Jenny slipped on a patch of ice (or was she, in fact, drunk?) and broke her hip. From then on she was confined to a wheelchair and began to tell the same stories over and over again; people stopped coming to visit her and after a while they also stopped calling. Eventually her wits deserted her and she just sat in her wheelchair or lay in bed, rambling. She wasn't suffering from dementia, the doctor said, as he endeavored, with a few carefully chosen words, to explain to Siri why, at the age of seventy-six, her mother had become this way. Jenny's condition was the result of many little aneurisms.

Irma the giantess appointed herself deathbed nurse and decided that it was time to bolt the doors, shut everyone out, including Siri. The story of Jenny Brodal as helpless old loony was not one to spread around, she said. "Certain stories have to be kept under wraps."

Siri stood in the garden, looking up at the big white house. The tall maple tree in the yard had started to rot and whenever it was windy large branches fell off and crashed to the ground.

"She doesn't want you here!" Irma said. Then she said it again, more softly: "She doesn't want you here, Siri."

Siri pushed Irma aside and walked into the kitchen. She sank down onto a chair.

"This is my home too, Irma. She's my mother."

In the middle of the kitchen table Irma had placed a pink baby monitor. It was switched on, crackling. Siri pointed to the device.

"What's that?"

"That's so I can hear her," Irma replied. "If she needs anything. I carry it around the house with me."

Siri nodded.

"It's a big house," Irma added.

Siri nodded again.

The baby monitor emitted a wail. It was Jenny squealing. A frail scream.

"I think I'll go up and check on her," Siri said. "I mean, she's lying there screaming."

"Oh, she makes noises all the time," Irma said. "She can't figure it out."

"What exactly can't she figure out?"

"I don't know. But whatever it is, she can't seem to figure it out. So she gets frustrated. She doesn't want to be disturbed, though. And you're not going up. She doesn't want to see you."

Siri rose from the chair.

"She doesn't want to see you, Siri!" Irma repeated. "I promised to keep you out. Go home."

Irma marched up the stairs with Siri behind her. That interminable stairway. Irma turned to face her.

"Go home, Siri. I'm sorry, but you're not wanted here."

Irma opened the door to Jenny's room and Siri caught a glimpse of her mother in the bed, saw the withered gray hair on the pillow, and then the door was slammed in her face and the key turned on the inside. Siri froze. She should probably have banged on the door, she should have screamed and shouted. *She* should be in there with her mother, not Irma. But she didn't scream and she didn't shout. She turned and walked down the stairs. She'd come back another day.

SHE DID COME back, once, twice, three times, four times, as often as she could, and gradually she learned the routines that Irma had established. The new rules of the house. At a quarter to one every day Irma lifted Jenny out of her bed. Her old nightdress was pulled over her head, her blue-tinged body was washed with a warm, wet cloth, and afterward she was dressed in a freshly washed nightdress and her regular light blue terry-cloth robe. Then Irma would pick her up and carry her down the stairs, sit her in her wheelchair, and take her into the kitchen. Her wheelchair was parked at the kitchen table and a plate with an omelet on it placed in front of her. Always the same thing: plain omelet, ketchup, and a large glass of red wine.

"One o'clock is omelet time," Jenny would say, grinning at Siri.

Siri wouldn't give up on *being there* for her mother, not without a fight. She made the two-hour drive from Oslo as often as she could. It was spring. Alma would be fifteen soon, Liv would be going into second grade in the autumn. Both her restaurants needed attention. There were a thousand things that Siri would rather be doing. But she wouldn't give up on this. It was always the same story: Irma refusing to let her in and Siri pushing her aside. There was no way Irma was going to take her mother away from her. Several times Siri had made an effort to befriend Irma. On one occasion she baked banana muffins, one of the brunch specialties at the restaurant, and took them down to Mailund. And when Irma opened the door, Siri smiled and said, "Muffins, here!"

As if the word *muffins* would make everything all right.

Siri held out the box of banana muffins. But Irma merely told her she could have saved herself the trouble.

"Always showing up here, interfering, making a nuisance of yourself, upsetting things. Jenny doesn't want to see you, and you know why."

Siri thrust the box at her and said, "Yes, well I baked them for you and I want to come in. You can't shut me out. And no—I don't know why. I think *you* don't want to see me. I think you speak for yourself, not my mother." And then she pushed Irma aside again and strode through to the kitchen.

Jenny was in her wheelchair, eating. She looked pale and thin. Indistinct, disjointed words dripped from her lips and occasionally bubbles instead of words—as if she were under water, speaking the water language, at long last reunited with the child she loved. Jenny eyed her daughter dully.

"Are you the lady that's brought Syver?" she asked.

"No, Mama. I'm Siri," Siri said, sitting down at the table.

Jenny shrugged. "Well," she said, "are you the lady who's come to take me to the palace?"

Siri started to laugh. Irma glared at her. Siri said, "Why are you going to the palace, Mama? Planning to return your medals?"

Jenny did not reply, instead she began to eat her omelet. She ate slowly, spilling egg down her nightdress. After a little while she pointed her fork at Siri.

"Want some?"

Siri shook her head.

"Ketchup," Jenny said. "Ever taste ketchup?" She chewed with her mouth open. "Ketchup's good. Are you sure you don't want some?"

Irma had settled herself on a chair by the open window. She lit a cigarette.

"You shouldn't be smoking in here," Siri said. "You know cigarette smoke's not good for her."

"Why don't you just mind your own business?" Irma retorted.

"I can't believe I could have lived for nigh on a hundred years and never tasted ketchup," Jenny broke in. "Are you quite, quite, quite sure you don't want a taste?"

"No, thanks," Siri said. "And you haven't lived for nigh on a hundred years. You're seventy-six."

Jenny shook her head, then she lunged at Siri, shoving the fork with the omelet and ketchup into her mouth.

Siri flinched. The fork stabbed her lip and she caught the taste of blood and the nauseating taste of egg and ketchup.

"Good, isn't it?" Jenny said. "I told you it was good."

"No thanks, Mama," Siri said. "I don't want it."

"Have some more," Jenny said, lunging forward again and pushing another chunk into Siri's mouth.

Irma stubbed out her cigarette in the ashtray and lit another. She looked at Siri and Jenny and laughed.

"And here's more," Jenny said, offering her daughter yet another bite while glancing proudly at Irma.

IT WAS NEARING the end of April and Siri had carried a chair out to the garden at Mailund and settled herself under the tall, rotten maple tree. Jon was in Oslo. He had called her immediately after his meeting with his editor.

"Mortifying," he said, "to hell with her, to hell with that whole bloody publishing house, I'm going to call Erlend at Gyldendal right now, you remember he said I'd always be welcome at Gyldendal."

"That was five years ago," Siri murmured.

"Jesus Christ, Siri, don't *you* start!"

"All I said was it's a while since you and Erlend talked about you switching to Gyldendal—and what matters most now is not to switch publishers but to write."

"You don't understand," Jon said. "You just don't get it!"

"So what did Gerda say?" Siri asked.

She gazed over at her white flower bed. It was dormant still, after the winter. It didn't shine. It didn't come surging toward her. She wondered what would happen to Mailund after her mother died. Should she sell it? Or should she and the children and Jon carry on using it as a summer house?

There was silence at the other end.

"Jon? Are you there?"

She thought of how much he had been dreading this meeting with Gerda, dreaded telling her that he was stuck again. Dreaded asking if she could agree to a new deadline and maybe a very small advance—or even a short-term loan. They could no longer manage on the income from the restaurant, their mortgage was astronomical, and this year all of his applications for grants had been turned down. Siri had told him he would have to find other ways of earning money.

"Jon, what did Gerda say?"

"Gerda said I would have to work for my living like other people. That I could no longer rely on the publishing house supporting me. She said the book would just have to be published when it was ready, but that they would not be including it on their autumn list. She said: 'I haven't seen any new material for a year.' She said: 'Face it, Jon. This is it.' So, anyway. It won't be September, it won't be November, I'm no longer a part of the plan. Oh, yeah. And then she had to go. She had a lunch date. And here was me thinking I was her lunch date. And she got up and told me again that it was time to face the truth."

"And what did you say to that?"

"I said: 'What the hell does that mean?' And then I cried."

"How much money do you owe, Jon?"

"More than a million. More, maybe. I don't know. Gerda was going to send me a statement."

"But she... Gerda said they would publish the book as soon as you finished it, didn't she—"

"For Christ's sake, Siri, it's all falling apart."

His voice cracked. She wanted to touch the back of his neck. She also wanted to tell him that she couldn't take it anymore.

"I don't know what to do, Siri." He sighed.

"I'll be home this evening," she answered. She cast a glance at the white flower bed. "And then we'll sort it all out. Okay?"

MOST OF THE time now, Jenny was silent. Siri removed a long dark strand of hair from her mother's robe and was reminded of Milla, she looked around, startled, as if the girl would suddenly appear in the room, but then she realized it must have come from Irma.

Her mother's hair was very beautiful before all this happened— the aneurisms, the wheelchair, the half madness. Now it was thin and stringy and not quite clean. Apparently Irma didn't care about such things as hair, perfume, dresses, although to her credit she had made proper carpentry adjustments in parts of the house so that Jenny could be wheeled from one room to another without being knocked around by thresholds and narrow doorways.

Siri rolled Jenny's wheelchair to the bathroom. She filled the bathtub with hot water, wrapped her mother's thin terry-cloth-robed body in fresh towels, and carefully began washing her hair. Jenny still had bottles of expensive shampoo and conditioner on the shelf and soon they were both enveloped by the smell of cardamom.

And while Siri lathered up her mother's hair, Jenny rambled on.

"I've shrunk, I'm much thinner and wispier than I used to be. I've always been a thin woman, though never wispy, but now I'm both thin and wispy and I have to tie a cord around my waist to hold my skirt up. Look at this, Siri! You're Siri, right? My skirt has to be tied with a cord.

"Look around you. I know this house. I know these walls and the room we were just in and this bathroom here. I recognize the smell of cardamom. But sometimes I ask myself: Who lives here? Who owns this house? And that big woman you hired to take care of me answers: Why you do, Jenny Brodal.

"What you'll discover when you get older is that the words disappear. And your memories, of course. And big parts of your body. I have to hold mine up with a cord.

"What I'd most like to do is to leave. I don't want to be here anymore. I don't like that big woman. Do you know who she is? Was it you who asked her to come here? Do you think I can't look after myself? Are you here to check on me? You're Siri, right? Couldn't you go and find my shoes? I've a pair of white sneakers in the cupboard, size thirty-eight. Very good shoes! Do you know where they are? Could you get them for me so that I can get the hell out of here?

"In one of my cabinet drawers I have a photograph of the Olympic champion Abebe Bikila and do you know, in it he is wearing exactly the same kind of shoes as I—in my nigh on a hundredth year—have in my posession? The first time Abebe Bikila won the Olympic gold medal he ran barefoot. That was in 1960. The next time he ran with shoes on. *My* shoes. He won that time too. That was in the summer of 1964, in Tokyo. He won the Olympic gold medal twice! Once barefoot. Once with shoes on.

"That's the sort of thing I remember."

Siri let her talk, while at the same time gently pushing her mother's head over the rim of the bathtub, rinsing the shampoo out of her hair.

"I wanted to tell you about your little brother," Jenny continued when she sat upright again, with a towel around her head. "His name was Syver and he lived for four years. Each morning I wake up and there is a brief moment when I don't remember that he is dead. And then it all comes back to me like sheets of hail. With age, you'll discover that everything disappears. Words, images, days, months, years of your life. And you'd think there would be relief in that. But there isn't. Because there's one thing that never goes away, and that is waking up every morning to a world without him."

"I'm sorry," Siri said, kneeling down in front of her on the blue tiled bathroom floor, patting her mother's dripping face with a dry towel. "I am so sorry."

"Oh, it isn't your fault," said Jenny. "Some years ago I wrote a speech that I meant to make to you. There was a party in the garden and charming people strolled around, raising their glasses and chatting pleasantly to one another. I don't know what happened to it. The speech, I mean. But I know it must be around here somewhere. I think you had arranged the party for me and that things didn't go as planned. Something happened, but this I can't remember."

But most of the time Jenny just sat silently in her wheelchair, slumped, with her big head lolling, her chin resting in the hollow of her throat, her mouth half open. She was liable to fall apart at any moment, thought Siri, snap in two.

The first time she saw her like that, slumped over in her wheelchair, Siri sat down in front of her and whispered, "Are you even there, Mama?"

She received no answer.

Then she leaned in, as if her mother were a sleeping baby, to check whether she was still breathing.

JON WENT DOWN to Mailund with Siri for a couple of days in June 2010, to help her clear out the annex. Irma refused to see either of them and locked the door.

"Jenny doesn't want the two of you here," she hissed. "You upset things."

And so it went. Sometimes Siri made it over the doorstep, sometimes she didn't. The main thing was not to give up, it was important to *be there*, Siri said, so they retreated to the annex and hoped for a change of mood. Irma had evidently turned the little house into a storage room of sorts: two bikes, a couple of boxes of books, and three wicker chairs occupied the center of the room, and a ceiling lamp shaped like a huge, smiling moon lay on the narrow bed. Jon carried the whole lot over to the garage, where Jenny's gray Opel sat under its tarpaulin. Covering the car with a tarpaulin when it was already in the garage, it seemed so old-fashioned, so touching, somehow. The lost art of taking care of one's belongings. His phone gave its text-message trill, Jon checked it, and the green display glowed in the half-light of the garage.

She was irreplaceable, Jon. I don't know if you can imagine what it feels like to have lost her. A.

Fuck!

By the time Jon returned to the annex, Siri had lit candles and was fiddling with the tuner on the little portable radio, searching for some suitable music. He went to sit on the bed. He dreaded the moment when they would have to go to bed, couldn't stop thinking about the slug he had found on the sheet of Milla's mattress the night she disappeared, and the bed was so narrow, it was a long time since Siri and he had slept together. Maybe he should offer to sleep on the floor. He felt in his pocket to check whether his cell was in silent mode, he couldn't have another text from Amanda coming in right now. He couldn't tell Siri, what would he say? *Amanda Browne thinks I know something about Milla that I'm not telling, she sends text messages all the time, I think she's lost her mind.*

Siri abandoned the radio and straightened up. Jon tried to think of something to say, something harmless and confidence-inspiring, but Siri beat him to it: "No one has stayed here since Milla. You think about that?"

He felt a prickling on the roof of his mouth. "No."

"Were you by any chance in the annex, in here I mean, on the night she disappeared?"

"Why do you ask?"

"I don't know."

"No, I wasn't in the annex. I knew she hadn't come back, that she wasn't here, so why would I be in the annex?"

Siri regarded him.

"Sometimes I wonder whether you lie about everything, Jon. You can't help it. It just happens."

Jon sighed. "What brought that on? What have I done now? Do you want to fight, is that it?"

"I only asked if you'd been here in the annex that night when she disappeared."

"No, of course I wasn't."

"Was there something going on between you?"

Jon got to his feet and yelled. "No, damn it, now will you give it a fucking rest. What's gotten into you?"

"I just thought you might have been a little besotted with her, little moon-pretty Milla, I mean, you like them young, don't you?"

Jon stared at his wife and said quietly, "What do you want, Siri? Where are you going with this?"

Her cheeks were pink. She spoke softly, and what she said came from somewhere deep inside: "So I suppose you weren't besotted with Paula either?"

Jon dropped down onto the bed. *Paula.* What was she talking about? Who the fuck is Paula? Did she mean *Paula...*? But that was such a long time ago.

"What?" he stammered. "Okay, now you've lost me."

"Ah, I bet I lost you," Siri said. Her hand was shaking. "Maybe you thought I didn't know about Paula?"

"But," he broke in, "but...Christ."

Siri took a step closer, planted herself in front of him, and with pink cheeks and pink-tipped nose proceeded to recite some words, he didn't know what it was, a letter, something he had written and she had learned by heart, he wanted to get up and put his hand over her mouth and make her stop. This was just a huge misunderstanding. He scarcely remembered that letter. He scarcely remembered Paula. Fair-haired. Nice-looking. A bit on the plump side, though. And a bit fumbly when it came to the actual fucking. She was all talk, really.

But this he obviously couldn't say to his wife.

He and Paula had had a couple of unsuccessful sexual encounters after Siri and Jon's trip to Gotland. First that night at a hotel in Örebro and then a couple of times after that, one of these at Paula's house, in a child's bedroom, he remembered lying on a narrow IKEA bed with her writhing on top of him. He remembered staring straight at three blue cardboard crowns decorated with glitter and fancy writing. Three crowns marking three birthdays of a certain Benjamin, ranged on a shelf over by the window. Benjamin age three, it said on one crown, Benjamin age four, it said on the second, Benjamin age five, it said on the third, and he wondered why she would want to fuck him in her child's bedroom, why not in the marital bed—this woman who had boasted about living in an open marriage (he had found that exciting)—or on the sofa, or any fucking where but here, in Benjamin's room, oh, it was awful.

But the first time they'd been together was at a hotel in Örebro. It had been difficult right from the start. With Paula everything had been difficult, that was why he had ended it. Or was it Paula who had ended it? At any rate he had been relieved to have her out of his life. He remembered how Leopold had rested his head on the edge of the bed and gazed up at him as he entered her from behind. He remembered how he pressed her head down hard into the pillow so she wouldn't be distracted by the staring dog, and how he had motioned as discreetly as he could to Leopold, man to man as it were, to go away, but Leopold wasn't a man, Leopold was a dog, and

Leopold would neither go away nor stop staring, he just stood there, with his head on the edge of the bed, his ears pricked up and that doleful doggy look in his eyes, and in the end Jon'd had to pull out of her, apologize profusely, and shut Leopold firmly in the bathroom.

Jon looked at Siri. She reminded him of a child who had just learned to read, flushed from excitement and exhaustion and without the ability to recognize punctuation marks yet.

She stood there bolt upright reciting the words he had written.

I think of how it would have been just you and me morning afternoon evening night and I think of everything you are and everything you can show me and all the things I want to do with you you ask if I'm unhappy if the thought of you makes me unhappy but just knowing you exist makes me happy I picture your face your hair your eyes your light shining but you know my situation maybe that's what's making me unhappy I think of you morning afternoon evening and night but I can't be with you except in my thoughts because well you know. Because *dot dot dot.*

Siri was trembling. "Okay," she said. "Who is she?"

Paula Krohn liked his books, she was a *reader.* But he couldn't tell Siri that either. It would sound too stupid. An enraptured reader. She had come up to him in a bar and said something about how wonderful his books were, and then she had whispered, "Do you know that you have an exceptional effect on women?"

Well, for God's sake, what was he supposed to do? He had been on his way out but stayed awhile longer. They drank a bottle of wine. Two maybe. She drank more than he did. The next day she sent him an e-mail in which she wrote that she had been *struck by their meeting*. She'd been *struck*. Those were her exact words. She had told him that she lived in an open marriage, she was, in other words, available, not to mention *struck* and quite pretty. Or at least he had thought she was quite pretty that first evening, and the more red wine he drank the prettier she became. And they had started exchanging e-mails and after a few weeks he and Leopold drove to Slite in Gotland to meet Siri and on the way down he called Paula and suggested that they meet in Örebro in a few days, when he and the dog would be on their way back to Oslo.

"Now maybe you could tell the truth," Siri said.

She sat down on the bed and wrapped her arms around herself to stop the trembling.

Jon chose his words with care, but couldn't help noticing that, despite "choosing his words with care," he sounded like a Linguaphone tape. And that Siri, too, sounded like a Linguaphone tape. *Hello, my name is Jon. What is your name? My name is Siri. Would you like something to drink? Yes, please, I would like a glass of cold water.*

"It didn't mean anything."

"What didn't mean anything?"

"Paula. She didn't mean anything."

"Are you still seeing her?"

"No, no, no, Siri, it was one night, one single night, it was a long time ago. Years ago. That's all it was. It didn't mean anything. It was awful."

"When?"

"You remember," he said hesitantly, "when we went to Slite to see Sofia? We took Leopold with us, remember? So we decided that I would drive back and you would fly. You remember I stayed overnight in Örebro. I met her there. At the hotel in Örebro. She came down. We spent the night together. It was awful. The minute I saw her I knew it was a mistake. She was fat and she had a mustache."

"How many times?"

"Once, I told you. It was a disaster."

"And you had Leopold with you. He saw the whole thing?"

Jon sighed. "It didn't mean anything."

"And you had sex just one time that whole long night? Is that what you're saying? Lying next to each other all night in the same bed and you did it just once? You expect me to believe that?"

"Twice, maybe. I don't know."

"Why twice, if the first time was so awful? What was the point of doing it again?"

"It just happened. Siri, please. It didn't mean anything."

"And then?"

"And then what?"

"Did you fall asleep? Did you sleep there with her? Did you drive her back to Oslo the next day? Have you seen her again?"

"I didn't sleep much. I drove her back. I wanted her to take the train, but she insisted on coming in the car with me. And no, I haven't been with her since. She wanted to, but I wouldn't."

"So she sat next to you in the front seat, of our car, she sat in the front seat, with her fat ass and her mustache, in our car?"

"Yes, but it didn't mean anything."

"And when you wrote that letter?"

"What letter?"

"The letter I just read for you, the one I fucking know by heart, the one you were so careful to delete, like five years ago, the way you delete everything."

"Oh, right, that letter."

"Why did you write it?"

"I'm trying to remember...but I simply can't...I can't remember."

"You wrote a love letter to another woman and you don't remember why you did it. *Your hair your eyes your light shining*." She screamed and flew at him. "*Light shining*, Jon! *Your light shines more!*"

He grabbed her wrists, shook his head. "Siri, please."

She pulled away, *don't touch me*, and said under her breath, "Did you write the letter before or after you met her in Örebro?"

"I don't remember, Siri, I guess I just wanted to—"

"You just wanted to fuck her one more time?"

"No! Not that! I don't remember."

"*Your light?*"

"Light...what?"

"You wrote *your light*. You wrote *your hair, your eyes, your light*. Just to be sure I'm understanding you correctly: first I shone, then she shone, how much light are we actually talking about, Jon?"

"Cut it out, Siri!"

"I don't ever want to hear you say the word *light* again."

"Cut it out!"

"Her light, my light, can't you be just a little more original?"

"It didn't mean anything, Siri."

"What didn't mean anything?"

"None of it."

"And where was I?"

"Where were you?"

"Yes, where was I?"

"Weren't you in Oslo?"

"I mean, where was I in that letter?"

"Sorry, I'm not following you."

"You wrote a letter to this Paula *as if I didn't exist.*"

"It wasn't that you didn't exist. I . . . It didn't mean anything!"

Siri started reciting again: "*I think of you morning afternoon evening and night but I can't be with you except in my thoughts because well you know. Because dot dot dot.*" She edged up close to him and whispered, "What does *dot dot dot* mean? What comes after *dot dot dot? Because* what?"

"It was just something I wrote, Siri. Meaningless words."

"Meaningless words?"

"Meaningless words."

"How many women have you actually fucked Jon?"

"Just her. Just that once."

"Five years ago?"

"That's all."

"Anybody else?"

"Absolutely not! Nobody else. That was the only time."

"I don't believe you. I believe there are others."

"Please, Siri. Please."

"And Milla?"

"What about Milla?"

"You didn't go into the annex that night?"

"No."

"Maybe just to check whether she had come back?"

"No."

"To fuck her maybe?"

"No! Absolutely not!"

"And that's all? Nothing more?"

"More?"

"More to tell?"

"That thing with Paula—that was in another life."

"Another life? What the hell does that mean?"

"It means I wasn't myself. I've told you everything. All I want is to be with you."

AND YET AGAIN Siri was at Mailund and yet again Jenny said, "I know this house. I know these walls and this room and the meadow and the woods behind the house. But sometimes I ask: Who lives here, and that big woman replies: Why you do, Jenny Brodal."

Siri leaned over her mother and said, "Alma asked me to say hello!"

They were in the kitchen and Jenny fiddled with the food on her plate. She had eaten almost all of her omelet.

"Who's Alma?" she said.

"You have two grandchildren," Siri said. "Alma and Liv. And Alma asked me to say hello."

Jenny nodded.

"And Liv says she's going to draw you a picture."

Jenny nodded and opened her mouth.

"Shall I say hello to Alma and Liv from you?"

Jenny picked up her plate. "Empty!" she said. And then she raised her eyes, looked at Siri, and lowered her voice. "I ate it all up."

SIRI WALKED ACROSS the meadow and through the woods to the lake. She sat on the shore. She tried to pray but got distracted, thought of other things, thought, *I'm not praying right.*

She was six and he was four. She was following him—they were on the forest path on their way to the lake—trying to keep up and shouting *Syver, Syver, you've got to stay here* and he skipped on ahead of her, in and out of the tree trunks, one minute he was there, the next he wasn't. Big gray woolly hat, blue sweater that had been hers the year before, brown dungarees. It was early spring, Siri would be starting school in the fall.

She doesn't remember the sound of water trickling and purling although it must have been there. What she remembers is the silence, as if someone had turned off all sound apart from her voice. *Syver! You've got to stay here beside me! I can't be bothered running after you all the time!* They were both wearing thick sweaters, not their regular winter jackets. It was their first day with sweaters instead of winter jackets and she felt light.

Jenny was inside, at the kitchen table, writing a letter to their father, to Bo Anders Wallin, and in this letter she cursed him for being on the island of Gotland while she was trapped at Mailund with two young children.

And what am I? Where has this endless child rearing gotten me?

And: *Syver was crying again last night, water doesn't help, milk doesn't help, singing doesn't help, being held in my arms and looking out the window at the snow falling through the night doesn't help, nothing would quiet him, so in the end I took him into bed with me (where you are not), and there he slept, cuddled up close.*

It was a big day, the day that Jenny allowed them to leave off their winter jackets, the day when they could go out wearing just woolen sweaters and thick dungarees. Siri's sweater was too big for her, it was red and white and only a little bit itchy around the collar; it had belonged to the pretty thirteen-year-old daughter of one of Jenny's friends. The smell of the girl still permeated the sweater, even though it had been hand-washed in warm, soapy water. A faint whiff of perfume, of sweat, of milk. Siri didn't smell of sweat yet, she was too young, the sweater was a bit itchy, but not as itchy as her blue woolly knit now handed down to Syver. She had on a scarf and a woolly hat and winter trousers and winter boots and she walked through the woods, calling to Syver who would sometimes disappear from view and then show up again and it was up to her to look after him. Jenny had told her so. *Now, you look after your little brother,* she said every time she opened the door and shooed them out into the winter day. Outside time. You weren't allowed inside the house when it was outside time, not even if you had to go to the bathroom (you went to the bathroom before you got dressed and went outside). You weren't allowed to go in and get something to drink (you had a glass of water or milk before you went outside and—most important!—before you went to the bathroom). You weren't allowed to ring the doorbell even if you had something really, really important to say. Outside time was from noon to two o'clock. And Siri called to Syver, and Syver popped up behind her, grabbed her legs, and heaved, sending them both tumbling over into the snow, and she said, *Oh, shoot, Syver, now we're both going to be soaking wet, don't do that*, and she scrambled up onto her knees in the snow and at this point, for a brief moment, the sound was switched on and the wind sighed in the trees and the birds twittered and spring was everywhere and Syver blew in her ear and wet snow slid between her scarf and the neck of her sweater, into the gap just there, and trickled icily down her back and Syver started to cry and wrapped his woolly-sweater arms around her and said, *Don't be mad at me, Siri.* And they both got up and she said, *I'm not mad,* but now he had to stay beside her, she was in charge, she was the oldest and they weren't really allowed to wander as far away from home as they had done, but the yard around the house, where they were supposed to stay when it was outside time, had its limitations. And Siri remembered that the biggest problem was *time,* because she didn't know when it was two o'clock and when outside time was supposed to end. When were the two hours actually up? One day she had come back from the woods with Syver in tow and banged and banged on the door because they had been out for ages, and Jenny had opened the door, flung the door open, with a towel wrapped around her head, and said, *What have I said about coming to the door when it's outside time?* Jenny had said a great deal on this subject. Among other things, how important it was for children to get fresh air every day. And how important it was not to disturb their mother when she was working. And how important it was that they respect the rules laid down by her. And Jenny stared at Syver and Siri (he had hidden behind his sister and peeked around her, giggling, and Jenny almost, but only almost, smiled) and said, *Twenty minutes, Siri! You've been out for twenty minutes! It's twenty minutes past twelve. I want the two of you back here at two o'clock. That's in an hour and forty minutes from now, for heaven's sake! Not a minute before,* Jenny said, *not a minute later.*

And the strange thing was, Siri thinks now, and in fact she had thought the same thing then too, at the age of six, that it never occurred to Jenny that Siri hadn't yet learned to tell time. *I wonder, I wonder how much longer we've got to stay out,* she said to Syver, who wasn't even old enough to understand the problem.

Siri was old enough to understand the problem, she just didn't know how to solve it. Usually, though, she got it right. Siri had a rough idea of when they ought to turn and head for home so that they would be in the yard when Jenny opened the door and said, *Come on, come on, you two, there's cocoa and sandwiches on the kitchen table.* And it was about time to turn around now, but Syver had disappeared again. He was nowhere to be found. She called to him. But Syver was nowhere to be found.

Syver!

She turned and turned and turned and finally faced the lake.

Syver! We're turning around now! We're going home!

And now the woods were silent again and Siri knew in herself, even before she knew for sure, that Syver had gone and died.

JENNY'S SEVENTY-SEVENTH BIRTHDAY was coming up. Irma had agreed that Siri, who never gave up trying to celebrate her mother's birthday, could organize a small birthday party in the garden at Mailund. For the children's sake, Irma said, "I want no one else there, though, just Jon and you and the children.

Liv made a drawing of a house and a garden and a tree and a blue sky and a sun, and on the drawing she had written: HOY HOY HOY! TO GRANDMA FROM LIV.

"HOY HOY HOY doesn't mean anything," Alma said, looking at her little sister's drawing.

"Yes, it does," Liv insisted. "You just don't get it."

Alma wanted to buy her grandmother a bottle of perfume, it was a few days before the birthday and Siri and Alma were out buying their presents... Siri suggested that she might rather buy a scarf to lay over Jenny's feet. "Grandma's feet are really very cold," she said. But Alma had shaken her head, asked to have the bottle of perfume gift-wrapped, turned to her mother and said, "Fuck you, Mama!"

Siri gripped Alma's arm and said, as steadily as she could, "Please don't speak to me like that. I don't ever want to hear you say that to me again. Never again, okay?"

Alma smiled and said, "Okay, if you say so!"

The big day arrived, only it wasn't a big day at all, but a very little day, and on this day that Jenny turned seventy-seven years old, Alma had gotten all dressed up. She had opted for a figure-hugging black dress, thick black tights, and black high-heeled ankle boots. Jon made the effort, and said, "Alma, you look very nice. What a good idea, to dress up for Grandma. Jenny was a very stylish lady. Think of all those beautiful dresses and shoes. And you do her honor by getting dressed up."

Alma threw her arms around her father and wouldn't let go. Jon was still subjected to these tight, needy hugs from his eldest daughter, and didn't quite know how to respond to them. He didn't want to hug her too tightly in return, so he often ended up patting her deprecatorily on the back. And he was always the first to end these hugs, except this time. She broke free and looked at him. "Why are you talking about Grandma in the past tense?" she said. "Like, she *was* a stylish lady. She *had* style? She's not dead. She's not dead, you know. You and Mama talk about her as if she were dead. You've got no morals, you two! I bet you're both just waiting for her to die!"

Jon took a deep breath and looked over at Siri, who was in the middle of packing one picnic basket with cake, candles, and a coffee thermos and the other with croissants, scones, rolls, jam, and honey. She just shook her head and turned away.

"I didn't mean it like that, Alma," Jon said. "I only meant to say something nice and it came out wrong."

Liv looked from one to the other. She was wearing Alma's old sweater, it was pale blue, full of holes, and came down to just below her bottom. She wore it as a dress. Her knees were covered in summer scrapes and grazes. Liv had just learned to ride a bike. Her flaxen hair was tousled. She was as thin as rain. She sighed, fixed her eyes on her parents and her sister, made a decisive little gesture with both hands, and said, "Everybody's fine. And nobody's dead. Can we please just go?"

They found Irma waiting for them on the front steps. She told them they could put their party stuff in the garden and she would carry Jenny down the stairs and get her into her wheelchair, which was already set out under the tall maple tree. Jon asked if he could help her; Irma snapped that if Jenny was to be moved from one place to another, she would do it herself. Siri fetched a blanket from the living room and spread it on the grass.

Once Jenny—who was tiny and brittle as a bird's breast—had been installed in the wheelchair, Irma positioned herself over by the wall of the house, some distance away from the others. She wanted neither coffee nor rolls nor croissants nor scones nor cake, even though Siri had made a proper birthday cake, with vanilla custard and fresh berries, hastily decorated with seven candles since there wouldn't have been enough room for seventy-seven.

Jon sat on the blanket in the sunshine, still trying to shake off the memory of the scene with Alma earlier in the day. His daughter was still small and rather chubby, but the shining, black-lined eyes, the full red lips, and the coal-black hair belonged to a girl he didn't quite know, couldn't reach.

It wasn't that he didn't try, that he didn't want to. When it came to Alma he never looked the other way, he looked her straight in the eye, *I'm here for you*, but he didn't get her. Siri didn't get her either. But they refused to give up. Jon tried to understand, but it was like in that dream, the nightmare in which you're a child again, standing in front of the whole class, and the equation you have to solve is totally incomprehensible, made up of numbers and symbols you have no idea how to make sense of. Day after day and night after night— don't give up! But where had they gone wrong?

With Liv it was a completely different story. He had never considered it *hard* to love Liv. *Hard* to reach her.

"Right, dig in everyone," Siri said, unpacking the baskets.

She glanced over at Irma, who was leaning against the wall of the house.

"Are you sure you won't have some?"

Irma lit a cigarette and shook her head.

"Well, in any case, I'll make up a lovely plate for Mama," Siri said, her voice sounding false even to her own ears.

"Oh, no you won't," Irma retorted from her position against the wall. "Jenny has a delicate stomach. Jenny can't eat cake. Jenny already ate."

"A tasty omelet, I presume?" Siri snapped.

Irma didn't reply.

Liv stood up and reminded them all that before they ate they had to sing "Happy Birthday," and so Jon and Alma and Siri got up from the blanket and raised their glasses.

"You too, Irma," Liv chimed. "You sing too."

Irma looked somewhat taken aback by the child addressing her, but stubbed out her cigarette, came over, and stood giant-like next to little Liv.

And then they all sang:

Happy birthday to you,
Happy birthday to you,
Happy birthday dear Jeee-nny,
Happy birthday to you!

Jenny, who was dressed for the occasion in a pale blue, egg-stained dressing gown, was slumped in the wheelchair under the maple tree, already half asleep.

Everybody looked at her.

"Hmm," Jenny said, opening her eyes.

She pointed to something.

Six, no, seven ducks were swimming around in the overgrown pond at the bottom of the garden, including four ducklings.

"They're mine," Irma said by way of explanation. "They showed up in the pond one day and now I feed them."

"Hmm," Jenny said again.

Jenny had almost ceased speaking altogether, but when she did say something, she had to work to push every word out of her, as if the words were physical objects, each with its own particular size, shape, structure—soft, fuzzy, smooth, angular, pointed. She often strayed down sidetracks that ended in nothing but breath and silence. An abscess in her mouth further prevented her from speaking clearly. Sometimes it was impossible to understand what she was saying, but everyone tried, and Jon remembered (he wrote this down later that day) that she was in her wheelchair under the tree and that she said, "I wonder who lives in this house and who laid out this garden."

And then she said, "I have a lovely pair of sneakers in the cupboard, size thirty-eight. Would one of you be so kind as to go and get them for me?"

And finally, in her most charming voice: "I would like to thank you all for this lovely celebration, but I'm afraid I'll have to go now."

SIRI WAS ALONE in the kitchen at Mailund, just about to dial Jon's number on her cell. She turned down the volume on the baby monitor. It was complicated to have to listen to her mother's ramblings on the monitor while at the same time trying to have a conversation on the phone. *Fucking baby monitor. Fucking everything.* When it came to babbling and rambling she wasn't sure who was worse, her mother or her husband.

Siri rose and took a half-empty bottle of cheap red wine from the fridge. She would have to have a word with Irma about allowing Jenny, who quite clearly could not handle alcohol, copious amounts of red wine with her daily omelet. Not only had Jenny been a drunk for the greater part of her adult life (apart from those years when she had been a non-drinker) but mixing red wine with strong medication in the middle of the day had to be positively lethal. No wonder Jenny was confused. No wonder she was babbling. And once Siri had broached the subject of the red wine maybe she could also mention the omelets. An omelet every day. No vegetables. No meat. No fish. No mushrooms or cheese or anything. Just ketchup. And lashings of red wine. Siri had attempted to discuss the omelet with Irma before, but Irma simply would not listen, had planted her enormous frame in front of Siri and said, "The doctor says Jenny needs protein. Eggs are packed with protein. I'm only following doctor's orders." And then she added, "And I think the doctor knows a little more about this than you do, don't you?"

"Oh, no doubt," Siri said, "but an omelet and red wine every day, it's very monotonous…"

Irma listened with her arms folded and Siri pushed on.

"And I do know a bit about food, about nutrition, I mean… I could get you some good recipes for dishes that are full of protein…"

Irma cocked her head to one side.

"I realize it's hard for you to accept," she said. "You're her daughter. But I've been living with her for twenty years and I know her. She trusts me. We're—"

"What are you," Siri interrupted. "What exactly are you?"

Irma raised her hand, turned on her heel, and tossed her head to indicate that the conversation was over.

All of this was going through Siri's mind as she sat at the kitchen table, drinking ice-cold red wine. In one hand her cell phone and in the other hand the baby monitor. She mustn't forget to call Jon and hoped Irma would be out for a while yet—she was doing errands and had left Siri in charge.

Irma loved the baby monitor.

"It's important to listen in to Jenny's sounds," she said before she left. "She might stop breathing. Might call for help. Might hurt herself in some way."

Siri nodded.

"But if all you hear are normal sounds, just leave her alone. Don't keep popping in and out to check on her. It upsets her."

Siri nodded again.

She wanted to ask Irma what she meant by *normal sounds*, but she refrained. Don't spoil the good mood and don't say anything that could be construed as sarcastic.

It was the beginning of September. Jenny was more or less bedridden now, apart from when Irma washed and changed her, carried her down the stairs like a little peacock, and wheeled her into the kitchen for her one o'clock omelet.

Siri stared at the baby monitor. When you switched it off there was silence, except for the hum of the fridge. She poured herself another glass of red wine. She had also been meaning to talk to Irma about the baby monitor. Wasn't it a violation of Jenny's privacy to have that thing sitting on her bedside table? Shouldn't Jenny be allowed to keep her dying sounds to herself? And wasn't this kind of surveillance an infantilization of a person who had, after all, always been very protective of her independence? Siri drained the glass and punched Jon's number. She was not looking forward to this. He didn't answer so she sent him a text, asking how things were at home and this he replied to straightaway.

Shit, shit, shit.

Siri read the message and called Jon's number again. He didn't answer. She sent a text: *Pick up yr phone.*

Seconds later her phone rang. It was Jon. She could tell right away that he had been drinking.

"What's going on?" she said.

"Hah, do you really, really want to know?"

"Jon. Stop it. What's going on?"

"Okay. Here it comes. Alma hit a girl in her class. It was a regular fistfight, apparently. I don't know why. According to witnesses, Alma started it. The other girl, the little blonde, you know the one, Mona Haugen, had a bloody nose. There was blood everywhere, I'm told—"

"How's Alma?" Siri interrupted.

"Oh, Alma—she's fine. Suspended, of course. When are you coming home?"

Siri eyed the wine bottle. She'd had two glasses.

"I'll drive home this evening. I'll be home as soon as I can. How's Liv?"

"Liv's okay. She went home with one of her friends today. Laura. Laura's mother sent a text to ask if she could pick up Liv along with Laura, she said they play well together, that they have a great time."

"Well, that's nice." She closed her eyes. "Anything else?"

She heard him wavering.

"Well…"

She heard him attempting to pour himself a drink (whiskey? wine?), trying not to make any noise.

"Jon, what is it?"

"Oh, it's just that for some months now I've been getting texts from Amanda Browne."

"What? Milla's mother?"

"Yes."

Siri's voice rose. "Have you slept with Milla's mother?"

"No, Siri, I haven't. Stop it." Jon sighed. "I said I've been getting texts from her. She texts me and she calls. Sometimes she calls and then hangs up right away. Sometimes she calls and doesn't say anything."

"We should have written that letter," Siri said, emptying her glass.

"The thing is that I think she thinks we're mixed up in it."

"Mixed up in what?"

"I don't know! *Mixed up in it.* How the hell am I supposed to know what it means? She's crazy. I suppose she believes that we're somehow to blame for what happened."

"*I* don't know what happened!" Siri said. "Do *you* know what happened?"

"No. You know I don't know." He hesitated. "It has to be that boy that did it, that K.B. But as long as she remains un-found...I mean, as long as there's no body—"

"Were you in the annex that night?" she asked, interrupting.

"No, I told you. I wasn't in the annex! Jesus...are *you* accusing *me* now? Is that all you can do? Shouldn't we try, just once, to stick together? Sort this out together?"

"Okay," Siri said. "Did you fuck Milla?"

Jon screamed. He screamed so loud that she began to cry. "I did not fuck Milla, okay? I was not in the annex, okay?"

"Okay."

Siri held her breath. She couldn't sit here and cry, not now. What if Irma walked in? She switched on the baby monitor. Just heavy breathing. Jenny was sleeping. She eyed the empty wine bottle.

"Okay. I'll leave here in a couple of hours. Is there anything about Milla that you haven't told me? If you and I are going to stick together, as you put it, you absolutely have to tell me everything."

"There is *one* thing," Jon said.

Siri laughed. "Ah yes, I thought as much."

"It's nothing really," Jon went on. "But I just think you ought to know. Milla's mother, Amanda Browne, hasn't mentioned this in any of her texts, but it might come up. Although I don't think it will. It's really not important."

"Okay?"

"Do you remember the photograph that all the papers were running in their reports of the case? Do you remember we talked about it? She looked different than the way we knew her. Blue denim dress. Ponytail." He paused. She heard him take a drink. Then he went on: "We talked about it, you and I. We talked about the picture. You talked about it a lot. It's pretty blurred, a close-up. I remember you saying that Milla looked prettier in the picture than in real life. Not quite so moonish, you said. There's no way of telling, not really, where the picture was taken. It could have been taken anywhere, by anyone. It's a perfectly ordinary cell-phone snap of a perfectly ordinary girl. The only thing is this black speck in the bottom left-hand corner. Something bushy. Do you remember?"

"No...or, yes. Maybe," Siri murmured, thinking of that black smudge.

"It's not something you'd notice," Jon said. "You're looking at the girl, right? But, the thing is, that black, bushy speck is a bit of Leopold's tail."

"What?" Siri straightened up.

"What I'm trying to say is that I took a picture of Milla that summer and then she posted it on her Facebook page before she disappeared."

Siri didn't answer, and Jon went on: "She came up to my study to ask about something or other. Probably something to do with the kids. And for some reason she told me that she didn't have any pictures of herself, as a grown-up girl I mean, so I took a snap of her with her cell. *That's it.* That's all. And just as I took it, Leopold must have gotten up and walked past."

Siri said nothing.

"Are you there, Siri?"

"Yes."

"It was just a picture."

"Yes."

"Will you be home this evening?"

Siri switched off the baby monitor then switched it on again. Click click click.

"Yes, I'll drive home later this evening. We can talk more about it then."

She had never liked driving at night, the dusty warmth of the car, the headlight beams sweeping across the countryside that she knew so well, but with which she never became particularly familiar. This evening she didn't seem able to keep her eyes on the road, her hands on the wheel, she felt like calling Jon and screaming, *Why did you take that picture*, but that wouldn't serve any purpose. It was all just a pack of lies anyway.

The thing was, she didn't want to go home and she didn't want to turn back and she couldn't just stop in the middle of the road either, could she?

FIRST SHE RANG the bell. When Irma didn't open the door she let herself in and shouted hello.

"Irma, you there?"

She went out again and walked around to the other side of the house, where Irma had her own entrance to the basement flat.

"Irma, you there?"

Her cell phone rang. She pulled it out of her handbag. Unknown number. She pressed the TALK button and held the phone to her ear.

"Hello?"

Nothing.

"Hello? Why don't you say something?"

Then the line went dead.

It was more than a week since Siri had been to Mailund—and her plan for today was simply to sit for a little while at her mother's bedside. Not long. Siri had to get back to Oslo that same evening. She walked all the way back around and sat down in the kitchen. She stared at the baby monitor. Jenny was up in her room, calling for Siri's father, Bo Anders Wallin. Although *calling* was hardly the word. There was almost no strength left in her mother's voice.

She spoke her own language.

"Bo! Why don't you come!"

If you didn't know the language it sounded like this: "O! Ay doan oo ccc omm!"

Siri had heard somewhere that when the dying start calling for the dead, as if they were actually right there beside them, it wouldn't be long before the dying person was dead themselves.

"Syver!"

Or rather: "–yyyver!"

She went upstairs, knocked gently on Jenny's bedroom door, looked back more than once to check whether Irma was nearby. Siri opened the door a little way and peeked through the crack. Her mother was in bed, a tiny white strip of flesh and heart and sound.

"Is that Syver?" she said.

"No, Mama, it's me, it's Siri."

"Who's Siri?"

Siri crossed to the bed and sat down on it. She ran a hand over her mother's cheek and said, "Sometimes I have the feeling that this is all an act, that you're actually pretending to be mad, and that you know very well that you are you and that I am me and that Syver is dead."

Jenny laughed, and then she said, "Maybe you could fetch my shoes. They're in the cupboard. I'd like to go now."

"Oh, where are you going?"

"To the palace," Jenny whispered.

"See, Mama, that's exactly what I'm talking about, when you say things like that I can't help thinking that you're pretending to be mad. Like Hamlet."

Her mother squeezed her eyes shut, then she opened the left one and peered at Siri.

Siri placed a hand on one of her mother's breasts where it lay limply on her chest. Siri put her ear to her mother's heart and heard it beat.

"I know this house," Jenny whispered, "I know these rooms, but I don't know who lives here. Do you know who lives here?"

"*You* live here," Siri said.

"With Syver," Jenny replied.

"No," Siri said, "Syver's dead. He died thirty-six years ago. But I used to live here with you. And when I grew up and became a wife and mother I used to spend my summers here with Jon and Alma and Liv."

"And Alma? Where's she?"

"Alma's at home in Oslo. I'm glad you remember Alma. You didn't the last time we talked."

"Alma, yes," said Jenny, nodding.

Or maybe she said something else. Siri wasn't sure. It sounded something like: "A mm iss."

Siri said, "Is there any message you'd like me to give to Alma?"

Jenny shook her head.

"Alma misses you. I can bring her with me another time. She's having a bit of a tough time—"

"The car broke her." Jenny nodded.

"What?" Siri said.

"The car broke her," she said again.

"What are you saying?" Siri asked.

"The car broke her," Jenny said and looked at Siri. "Alma and I were in the car and the car broke the girl on the road."

"What girl?" Siri said.

"Give me water," Jenny said.

"What are you talking about?" Siri said. "Who?"

Jenny shook her head and lapsed into her own thoughts, but then she whispered, "Who really lives in this house?"

Siri placed her hands on her mother's shoulders as though she were about to put her arms around her and whisper, *You, you live in this house*, but instead she tightened her grip and began to shake, she shook the skinny body that looked as if it might snap in two, shook the big, lolling head, shook the long, withered hair (that had once wrapped itself around them both), shook the old deflated breasts and the beating heart, shook the wasted vocal cords that pressed out fresh, incomprehensible sounds every day. Two wasted cords that coiled from Jenny's lips to Siri's ear.

"What girl?" Siri asked again, louder this time.

"Don't," whispered Jenny.

"What girl?"

"No!" said Jenny. "Don't! You're hurting me!"

And Siri might have gone on shaking her mother until there was nothing left to shake, if a third voice had not interposed.

"Stop it right now!"

Siri turned. Irma filled the whole doorway.

"Get out," she hissed.

But Siri would not stop.

"What girl?" she shouted at Irma. "Does she mean Milla?" She looked at her mother again. "Are you talking about Milla?"

"Get out," Irma said.

Siri released her grip on Jenny's shoulders and her mother curled in on herself in the bed.

Irma didn't move.

Siri went on shouting. "Did you see Milla that night, when you were out drunk driving with Alma? Did you? Did you see her and say nothing? Did you see her?"

This time Irma took three strides across the room and lunged at her.

"Get out!" she screamed. "Get out!"

And then she dragged Siri away, hauled her over the doorstep, and slammed the door shut.

HALFTONES

IT HAD BEGUN to snow as they were driving out of Oslo and the snow had followed them all the way to Mailund; there had been snow on the roads, on the windshield, on the children when they ran to and from the shop at the gas station to buy candy, on the trees, on the roofs, on the fields and barns and farmhouses, on the jetties, and on the long road that wound from the old bakery all the way up to the house; they had been here for two days now and it just kept on drifting down.

Christmas was coming and would be celebrated at Mailund.

"Couldn't we just go and stay for a little while?" Siri had said.

She couldn't decide what to do with her mother's house. It had been in the family since just after the war and she didn't want to sell it.

"We need the money," she said, "but I just can't imagine strangers living here."

"No," Jon said.

He looked at her. He was sitting on the sofa, she was standing with her back to him, looking out the window at the garden, the maple tree, the white flower bed, which was whiter now than it had ever been, covered by new-fallen snow. He longed to touch her.

Jon had recently applied for and gotten a temporary job as the editor for a new book club. He would be starting after Christmas, which was perfect. A proper job.

"But," Siri said, "it would probably cost far too much for us to keep it." She flung out her arms, as if to embrace the whole house. "I mean it's completely run-down and I don't know how you and I would ever be able to maintain it. We can't afford to do it up and we can't afford to maintain it, we can't even afford to replace the boiler, never mind all the rewiring, I think the fuse box is from the fifties, and it would be horrible just to sit here and watch it all fall apart."

"I could clean the gutters," Jon said.

Siri turned and smiled. The light from the window fell on her face and he felt like telling her that she was so beautiful standing there in the light, but he didn't, he knew that if he said *you are beautiful standing there in the light* she would shrug and turn away. Jon would have to invent an entirely new language, one that didn't include the word *light*, if he was to get through to Siri.

Every morning over the past few months Jon and Leopold had taken a walk down to the butcher in Torshov to get Leopold his fresh meats; there weren't too many butchers left in Oslo, but in Torshov there was a butcher, and a pretty little park where Jon could sit with a coffee while Leopold wandered about. Leopold no longer ran away like before and could be allowed to run loose.

It had started with the trip to the butcher, but Jon had found that he liked being in this part of town, he knew no one, no one knew him, and gradually he discovered that on these early-morning walks he acquired what Strindberg once described as an *impersonal circle of acquaintance.* These were people whom he saw every single day but never spoke to. They all recognized one another, they nodded to one another, and that was that. An elderly man with a big, playful golden retriever. A pretty young mother of two on her way to nursery school with a four-year-old and a five-year-old. The four-year-old almost always lay down at the same spot in the road and howled that she was tired of walking. She wanted to be carried now. She would lie there on the pavement, all rigged out in a pink snowsuit, pink boots, and a pink woolen hat with rabbit ears. And her mother and five-year-older sister would turn to look at the tot and wait patiently until she couldn't be bothered to lie there screaming on the pavement any longer. Reluctantly, then, the little girl would get up and join them.

Jon recognized a writer couple on their way to have breakfast. Each morning this husband and wife had breakfast together in the same coffee shop. Sometimes they held hands and he wondered what their lives were like, were they happy. Yes, he recognized them and they recognized him. But they respected each other's reticence, it would never have occurred to any of them to stop and say *Hello,* or *How are you,* or, worse still, *How funny, seeing you here every day, do you live around here?* That would ruin everything. The writer couple would find somewhere else to have their morning coffee and Jon would find somewhere else to take his walks. A nod. A friendly, but not too friendly, smile. The impersonal circle of acquaintance, which had become Jon's preferred (and only) circle of acquaintance, had its own unwritten rules. And rule number one was that you did not attempt, by look or word, to make anything that could be construed as an approach, that you stayed within the bounds of the completely impersonal. For the most part this worked well, although some dog owners might cross the line by asking, "Is that a male or female you've got there?"

And not only does this leave Jon at a loss for words, he isn't even sure what the correct answer is. Obviously he knows the sex of his dog. But he's not sure whether Leopold being male is *good* (the other dog, according to its owner, is impossible around bitches) or *bad* (the other dog, regardless of sex, feels threatened by males). There are, Jon thought, a lot of situations in which it would be preferable for dogs (male or female) not to meet and sniff each other, as dogs do. Either dog A would want to mate dog B against dog B's will, or dog C would develop an immediate antipathy toward dog D and this antipathy would be expressed by dog C attacking dog D; either that or dogs A, B, C, and D would get so excited and/or confused at running into one another that their leashes would get all snarled up and their owners would have a hard time disentangling them.

Jon much preferred to avoid the small talk that comes as a natural consequence of having a dog, so he suggested to Leopold that he should also retreat to a kind of canine version of the *impersonal circle of acquaintance.* Which was to say: No snuffling. No sniffing. Merely a little friendly tail-wagging from afar—and then move on.

Jon thought only good of all the new people he encountered every day on the way to the butcher and the park, and it was a great relief to him that he had not endangered his own self-containment by trying, for example, to stare the gorgeous young mother of two to him. That he didn't want to. That he didn't have to.

His cell chirruped. He dug it out of his trouser pocket.

The worst thing is not knowing what happened, what became of her. The second worst is that today is a new day and tomorrow is another new day. A.

Jon had taken one bench for his own and here he would sit in the autumn sunshine, making notes for his novel. (He always had his notebook with him, no longer trusting himself to remember what he wanted to remember; more than once he had found himself seeing something or overhearing something or even thinking something that seemed important, a flash of insight maybe, only, when he sat down at the computer later, to find that it was gone. He could recall the sense of elation that this flash of insight had engendered in him, but the *insight* itself was gone. And so, because he forgot things, even important things, he always carried a notebook in his pocket, and he wrote in this as often as he could.)

At home in his study he had gone through old work documents and found his notes about a woman with a kinked waist.

He thought of his wife.

"Do you think that's how it is?" Siri had whispered, turning to him. He had pretended to be asleep, they had kept each other awake all night that summer in Gloucester, many years ago. First he had told stories to help her fall asleep and then, if she was still awake, she had told stories. He remembered her whispering, "Do you tell stories in order to become someone else, Jon? Do you think it's possible to put yourself in someone else's place, to suffer, breathe, feel as they do?"

As October passed into November Jon had to take his walks to Torshov (to the butcher, the coffee bar, and the park) without Leopold. His walks with the dog became steadily briefer, amounting eventually to just a couple of turns around the block. Leopold no longer strained at the leash. Jon remembered the power of that big body. The fights he and Leopold had had over what sort of dog Leopold ought to be. But Leopold wasn't interested in fighting anymore, and whenever they went for a walk he stuck close to Jon's side, grateful and finally conquered.

Jon bought chicken giblets, hearts, liver, kidneys, and other offal at the butcher's, but it got to the point where Leopold only sniffed at his food before lying down in a corner of the living room and going back to sleep. The last time the vet had examined him, he had scratched Leopold's belly and said, "There's not an awful lot we can do here, he's not in any pain, although that can change from day to day, it's already spread quite far," and then he had looked at Siri and Jon and said, "The important thing now is for you to have a good Christmas together, hold him, massage his paws, and prepare yourselves for making some difficult decisions come the new year."

Jon had gotten into the habit of waking early. He was up before six, showered, had breakfast and took a cup of coffee standing at the kitchen counter, whistled for Leopold, and off they went. When Leopold fell ill, he made a change in their routine. First he took Leopold for a little walk around the house, then he took his own long walk to Torshov, and when he got back he sat down at his desk to write.

It was December now, and he was back at Mailund, and here too he woke early. He opened his eyes and for a brief moment everything was blank. He was no one. None. None thought. None flesh. None sleep. None waking. Before everything came flooding back to him. Before he remembered everything. The bright expanse between being and not being.

The first thing he did on waking was reach out his hand and touch Siri, she didn't push him away, they were sharing a bed again, but more often than not she would roll over and carry on sleeping. She had started dreaming. Dreadful dreams that woke her in the middle of the night, and sometimes she told him about them and sometimes not. The dreams had started when Jenny died. *I should have done more*, she said, sitting up in bed. Jon took her hand and squeezed it in the way that she recognized, the way he had squeezed it when they were living in Gloucester and she couldn't sleep, when they lay side by side in the dark and told each other stories. Siri lay down again, but didn't settle. She should have been more alert! She should have taken better care! There was so much she should have said. But now her mother was dead and all that was said, was said and there was no way now to go back and start over. And then there was Alma.

We have to talk about Alma.

Jenny died only days before the three boys found Milla in the woods. The young man known as K.B. was immediately brought in for new questioning, his status was altered from witness to accused, he had been charged and remanded to custody.

But no one, except Jon, knew what Jenny had told Siri just days before she died, namely that she had seen Milla on the road that night.

"I know what I heard, Jon," Siri told her husband. "I know what she was talking about. My mother wasn't *that* mad. Sometimes I think she was only pretending."

"Pretending what?"

"To be mad."

"But why—it doesn't make sense. Jenny was many things, but not a pretender."

"You know why?" Siri said. "You know why she pretended to be crazy? So that she could escape, so she could opt out. *What a relief. I'm a looney and can't be held responsible for anything whatsoever. I'm no longer a member of normal human society.*"

"No, I don't think that's how it was, Siri" Jon said. "I think she was old and sad and very tired. I think her brain...I think her spirit was worn out."

"She had, like, five bottles of wine and took Alma with her in the car for God's sake..." Siri almost shouted. "She could have killed her, she could have crashed into a tree and killed her...she could have killed Alma!"

Jon nodded.

"So it was very convenient to start acting crazy after that. And then she tells me before she goes and dies that she and Alma might have been the last people to see Milla alive. Was she raving? Or was she actually speaking the truth and just pretending to rave? I don't know! And what about Alma? What did Alma see? What are *we* to do with this information? Do you think Alma saw anything that night and hasn't told us? What do we tell the police? And Milla's mother? What do we tell Amanda? She calls, sends text messages, and we say nothing. Oh, no. She's a bit of a nuisance, isn't she? With her grief and her texts and her telephone calls. Well, I mean, what can we do, except express our sympathy. What good is that? So we don't even express sympathy. Amanda says, *You two know something about my daughter that you're not telling.* And we say *No, we don't* and then we tell each other that she too has been driven mad by suspicion and anger and grief. She sends text messages and calls and hangs up and we put up with it because she lost a daughter. But the fact is that she's right! She's right. We *do* know something and we're not telling it and I don't know what we should do."

"Well, anyway," Jon said quietly, "it wouldn't have made any difference one way or the other. What we know, I mean. She'd still be dead."

"That's not true, Jon," Siri said, "it's not true what you say, that it doesn't make any difference one way or the other. It's not true!"

"What I mean," Jon said quietly, "is that no one could have imagined what this K.B. character was capable of. He raped her, followed her in his car, killed her, and buried her in the woods. This is what we know. He's the one who did it. And we don't know anything about him ... nothing except that until that evening he was just this ordinary kid living in this town among us."

Siri and Jon had been having this conversation, or variations on this conversation, ever since Jenny's admission during her last days. Maybe, Jon said to Siri, Jenny had been talking about something else entirely. Well, they would never know now. But Siri mustn't forget that toward the end it had been impossible to understand what Jenny said, she wasn't in her right mind, and the craziness wasn't an act, Jon insisted, she *was* crazy, and maybe Siri had conjured up this whole story about her mother and Alma seeing Milla there on the road, allowing her own fear and anxiety to weave themselves into disastrous events.

"And that's exactly why," Jon said, "we mustn't start pestering Alma with all sorts of questions. Bringing up the past. Asking what she might or might not have seen more than two years ago when she was out driving with her grandmother."

"I don't know," Siri said. "I don't know if she was raving."

"She could have been talking about anything," Jon said. "You said it yourself—it was almost impossible to understand her. She had her own language at the end, you said. We gave our statements to the police at the time. Remember? So did Alma. No one had seen Milla. Do we really have to drag Alma through all this again?"

Irma had construed this last encounter between Siri and Jenny in her own way. The day after the scene in the bedroom she had called Jon to say that now Siri had crossed the line.

"What line is that?" Jon asked.

Siri had shouted, according to Irma. Siri had shaken. Siri had actually been in danger of killing her own mother.

And while they were on the subject, Irma begged to remind him of the agreement between herself and Siri's mother, which was that Irma was to care for Jenny as she thought best *when the day came that Jenny could not care for herself*, and that day had now come, she said, and she would kindly request that Jon and Siri respect a sick woman's last wish and stay the hell away from Mailund. Irma considered it her duty to care for Jenny for whatever time she had left, so she had in fact decided to *forbid* Siri from visiting Jenny from now on.

"You can't *forbid* Siri to do anything," Jon said. "You can't! And your accusations against Siri are ridiculous. Downright spiteful. You are a very mean woman, Irma."

"I was there, I saw what I saw," Irma said.

"Well, no matter what, you can't *forbid* Siri to visit her mother."

"You just watch me!" retorted Irma and slammed down the phone.

Jenny died the next day. Irma sent Jon a text, informing him of this and asking him to pass the message on to his wife. She left it to the family to make the funeral arrangements. And then she had written: *My work here is done.*

After the funeral, Irma had packed her suitcase, fed the ducks in the overgrown garden pond one last time, and departed, never to be seen again. Jon seemed to remember hearing someone say that she had a place in the mountains at Hemsedal, but on reflection he came to the conclusion that he must have heard wrongly or misunderstood. He checked his notes. He remembered writing it down. *Irma in the skiing mecca of Hemsedal?* Yep. That's what he had written. Could he have dreamed it? Irma the giantess, Irma with the angel face, Irma with the long curly hair, swishing down the ski slopes. He pressed DELETE just to be rid of her, wherever she was.

Christmas was celebrated quietly with the children, and the snow kept on falling. Early in the morning on Christmas Eve, Jon and Alma and Liv went off to the woods to chop down a tree. They walked through the woodland and every time Jon said, "Look, that pine there, that could be our Christmas tree," Liv said, "No, it can't, that's not a proper Christmas tree." And Jon and Alma and Liv walked on, past snow-covered glades, past the green lake, which wasn't green but white like everything else.

And Jon scanned the ice and said, "Maybe we could go skating here someday."

"No," said Alma.

He turned to the girls. They were well wrapped up in jackets, hats, and mittens. Alma shook her head and clasped Liv's hand.

Jon's phone warbled. He groped in his jacket pocket, pulled it out, and looked at the screen.

"No," Liv echoed.

Christmas Eve is the hardest day of the year. As you can imagine, I'm sure. A.

Jon slipped the phone back into his pocket. He looked at Alma, he looked at Liv. They were standing in the snow, shouting at him.

"No, we won't," Liv said. "Papa, are you listening?"

"What won't we?" Jon asked.

"We won't go skating here," Liv said, rolling her eyes. That was so typical of Papa, not to listen. Typical Papa, to be the only one who didn't know what was so obvious to everybody else—that there could be no talk of skating on this lake.

Jon and Alma and Liv walked on. At last they came to a clearing and in this clearing was a tree, and it was here that Liv stopped and pointed.

"There," she said. "That's our Christmas tree." And Alma and Jon nodded and Jon set to work and chopped down the tree while his daughters looked on.

Siri cooked up good, traditional Christmas fare: mutton ribs (dried and salted, steamed over birch twigs), mashed turnip, special Christmas sausages, and almond potatoes, and Leopold had his favorite, kidneys, but merely sniffed at his bowl, went back to the fireplace, and lay down on his old blanket. The big head between his paws. The long, scrawny body. The dull coat with the white patch on his chest. Jon felt a sudden urge to weep. He looked out the window, at the snow falling through the darkness, and remembered the summer two and a half years ago when Siri was flitting about out there in the sea of mist, drifting between the tables with all the white tablecloths swirling around her.

Christmas night was quiet. The children slept. Siri slept. And in the morning Jon woke early, got dressed in the dark, and tiptoed out of the bedroom. The broad stairway wound from the attic to the basement apartment. Not all that long ago Leopold would have been standing at the foot of the stairs waiting for him. Now he was asleep on his blanket in the living room. Jon went over to him, bent down and stroked his head, whispered, "Hey, boy. Want to go for a walk? Come on, Leo, come on!"

Leopold opened his eyes and looked at him.

"Let's go out," Jon continued. "Come on. Up you get."

Slowly, Leopold got to his feet, staggered a little, and wagged his tail, as if to assure both Jon and himself that all was well. It was still dark when Jon opened the front gate and stepped out onto the road with Leopold by his side.

Jenny's funeral had played out pretty much according to Jenny's instructions. She was dressed in a red silk dress and nectarine-colored sandals, with the black handbag she was so fond of on her chest.

Before the funeral, Jon had accompanied Siri when she went to meet the vicar who would be conducting the service for her mother. The vicar, whose name was Beth, said she was looking forward to learning more about *Jenny*.

He noticed how she stressed people's names—as if she were speaking in italics—presumably to show how much she cared. And why were they all on a first-name basis? They had just met. She was a vicar, for God's sake. Someone one goes to in a moment of seriousness and need, not a pal.

"*Siri*, hello," said Beth, holding out her arms. Siri had flinched and Jon had had to pinch her hand to stop her from storming straight back out of there.

They took their seats on spindle-backed chairs set around a brown Formica table in the vicar's office, Siri and Jon said yes to coffee, poured into paper cups from a red-and-white thermos. Beth was new to the town, had spent most of her life in Trondheim, was in her mid-thirties, and had long, dark, curly hair that she pinned up with a big flower clasp. She wore a little too much lipstick and glasses with brightly colored striped frames. Siri had read an interview with her in *Aftenposten* on the day of their meeting, and after reading it, all she had really wanted to do was cancel the whole thing.

"We can't have this vicar burying my mother," she exclaimed.

The newspaper interview had been part of the coverage of the discovery of Milla's body and the remanding to custody of K.B., charged with an almost indescribably heinous crime (rape and first-degree murder, the police would not comment on reports that Milla had been buried alive).

And how, the interviewer asked, did a small community deal with a tragedy of such magnitude, especially now that it was known that a perfectly ordinary young man, not a stranger, was behind the murder of Milla?

Beth the vicar had talked about evil. *It's all around us, but if we stand together we can fight it.* She had talked about goodness. She had talked about *our times* and how they were very difficult. She had talked about an emerging new Norway and an emerging new Europe. She had talked about social media. *What's the good of being able to communicate with the whole world if we forget to communicate with each other and with God.* She had talked about grief. She had talked about forgiveness. And she had talked about empathy. But first and foremost she had talked about herself and her own difficult role in situations like this... and how it was a burden she could not refuse to shoulder...*It is my duty to support this shocked and grief-stricken small community.*

She had posed for pictures in front of the church, grave-eyed behind the stripy glasses, with the same flower clasp in her hair.

And now here they were, Siri, Jon, and Beth, and Beth said, "I know, of course, that *Jenny* was an important figure in the local community, what with her running the bookshop. I've heard that she built up a fabulous selection of foreign literature in translation. That's right, isn't it?"

Siri pressed her lips together and nodded.

Beth leaned across the Formica table and smiled at Jon. "*Jon.*"

Jon jumped when he heard her say his name.

"*Jon,*" she repeated. "You're a writer, aren't you?"

Jon glanced at Siri, her nose and cheeks were pink.

"I am a writer," Jon said.

"I read one of your books," Beth said. "I thought it was *wonderful*. It was that one with the title that has something to do with hair...?...*Your hair?*...*My hair?*...Something to do with hair." She smiled apologetically. "You know the one I mean, don't you?"

"No," Jon said, shaking his head. "I've never written a book with hair in the title."

"Oh," said Beth. "Really? Oops. Then it must be me who's getting mixed up."

"Maybe," said Jon and turned to Siri. "Maybe we could talk a bit about Jenny now, and about what you're going to say at the funeral."

"Yes, let's do that," said Beth. "And I'd like it if we could talk a bit about her grandchildren. You do have children, don't you?"

"Their names are Alma and Liv," Siri said flatly.

"*Alma* and *Liv*," Beth said and smiled. "Perhaps you could tell me a little bit about them and what their grandma meant to them? I bet there are some *wonderful* memories."

And so, a few days later in an almost full church, Jon and Siri held each other's hands very tightly, and tighter still during Beth's sermon. Jon didn't dare to look at Siri, but he could feel her fury and her grief. And her fear too. Felt it like a vibration just under her skin. When his turn came to speak he had to extricate his hand from hers. When he rose and made his way up to the altar, he was sure he could feel Siri's eyes on him. He stood for a moment beside the coffin before stepping up to the lectern and clearing his throat.

"I found this passage in a book that I was reading," he said, "and I thought of... well, I thought of all of us. Strindberg ought to be read in Swedish, but I tried to translate it, so here it goes." He looked up at the mourners and then at Siri and his children sitting in the first pew. "It's from Strindberg's novella *Alone*," he added, "and I'm going to begin in the middle of a sentence, I think Jenny would have liked that."

He smiled. And then he read:

"I had, however, noted that we were not so quick to smile as before and that we observed a certain care in our speech. We had discovered the weight and the worth of the spoken word. Life had certainly not mellowed our judgment, but wisdom had eventually taught us that all one's words come back to one; furthermore we had come to see that men cannot be described in full tones, but that one must also use halftones in order to express as accurately as possible one's opinion of a person."

After the funeral, Siri invited all of the mourners to a simple repast in the old bakery, and when Jon and Siri and the children were walking back to Mailund that October evening, up the long road to the house, Jon said, "If we could hear Jenny now, what do you think she would say?"

"I think she's saying: Who lives in this house?" said Siri, looking up at the old white mansion at the top of the road.

A few weeks later it was Milla's turn to be buried. Siri and Jon talked about going, they really ought to, but what would they say? What good would they do there? It might even cause offense.

"It was all a mistake, right from the start," Siri said. "The whole thing. And we should have done more."

The day after the funeral Jon received a text.

They found her in the ground and now we've buried her again. She was nineteen when we lost her and you are as mute as ever. A.

Jon and Leopold had reached the foot of the road, they had met no one. There was just him and Leopold and the road and the snow and nothing else was left in the world. But then, as it began to brighten up ever so slightly, a small figure appeared before him. It took Jon a minute to recognize it. The figure. And then, in a flash he realized who it was and what his name was. The only thing missing was the bike.

"Hi," said Simen.

"Hi," said Jon. "What have you done with your bike? I hardly recognized you without it."

Simen rolled his eyes and spread his arms.

"Yeah, well—it just goes on snowing and snowing."

"Merry Christmas," said Jon.

"Merry Christmas to you too," said Simen.

"Did you get some good presents?" Jon asked.

"Yes," said Simen.

"So what did you get?"

Simen began to walk toward the jetties and signaled with a jerk of his head for Jon and Leopold to join him.

"I don't want to talk about what I got for Christmas," Simen said. "That's not important...Did you know, by the way, that it was me who found Milla a few months ago? Me and my two friends?"

Jon looked away.

"Ah yes, of course...it was you, it—"

"He buried her alive," Simen said, coming to a halt. "Did you know that?"

"Well, that hasn't actually been confirmed," Jon said.

"It was K.B. that did it. He buried her. He was living right here in town and he buried her, while she was still breathing."

"Yes," said Jon.

Simen looked at him.

"She was buried deep in the ground all along. She shouldn't have been."

"No," said Jon.

"We were hunting for treasure," Simen said.

"Yes, I read something about that in the paper," Jon said.

"The thing is," said Simen, "that last summer Gunnar and Christian and I buried a milk pail in the woods—"

"A milk pail?" Jon repeated, puzzled.

"Yes, a milk pail," Simen replied. "That was like our treasure chest. And the idea was for all three of us to put something in the pail. Something really valuable and irreplaceable. You had to feel, you know, that you were *parting* with it. For example, Gunnar had an autograph book with the autographs of Steven Gerrard, Fernando Torres, and Jamie Carragher. That was his contribution."

"And what was your contribution?" Jon asked.

Simen didn't answer. He bent down, made a big snowball, and sent it flying down toward one of the jetties.

"What was your contribution?" Jon asked again.

"A necklace," Simen said. "One of those crucifix things."

"Was it your necklace?" Jon asked.

"No, it was my mother's," Simen said and looked at Jon. "And she's still really sad about losing it."

"Well, couldn't you just dig the treasure up," Jon said. "I mean...couldn't you just dig up that milk pail and give your mother her necklace back? You could say that you'd found it, you don't need to say that you had...how shall we put it... borrowed it for a while."

Simen looked at Jon and smiled.

"You mean lie about it, right?"

"A white lie," Jon said. "If you did it would be a white lie."

"Yeah, well anyway, I can't."

"Why can't you?"

"Well, for one thing the whole point of treasure is never to unearth it. That's what makes it treasure."

"Yes, but..." Jon wasn't sure how to answer that.

"And for another," Simen went on, "I've no idea where it is. That's the problem, you see. Gunnar and Christian, my friends, they were the ones who wanted to dig up the treasure, and that was what we were digging for when we found Milla." Simen shook his head. "I *knew* we were digging in the wrong place. I *knew* we were cycling in the wrong direction. And now I've no idea where to start looking."

Simen stopped, he eyed Jon, then Leopold, who was lying flat in the snow, panting hard.

"Is your dog sick or something? He looks sick."

"Yes," Jon said.

"And Alma's grandma is dead, right?"

"Yes," Jon said.

"And Irma's gone?"

"That's right," Jon said.

"She wasn't very nice," Simen said. "My mother says she was a lovely person, even though she was big and glowed in the dark, but she wasn't lovely at all."

"No, she wasn't," Jon said.

"Definitely not," Simen said, and then he turned and ran off.

Leopold was still lying in the snow, a black patch in all the white, Jon tugged gently on the leash and said, "Come on,

Leopold, come on, boy," and Leopold raised his big head and looked at him, and Jon wished he could lie down in the snow beside him, close to him, feel the warmth from his body, the thickness of his coat, and not get up again.

"Come on, let's go," Jon said, and Leopold got up, whining faintly, he was in pain now, although he tried not to show it. Jon wanted to pick him up and carry him home, but he was too big and too heavy.

They plodded slowly up the road. Snow and silence. No matter how slowly Jon walked it was a struggle for Leopold to keep up, and isn't it odd, Jon said out loud, as if to console him, that this road's called the Bend and not the Bends? Jon looked at Leopold.

"It's always a lot farther than you think," he added. "But we'll soon be home."

Jon and Siri and the children celebrated New Year's Eve quietly at Mailund. At midnight a text message flashed on Jon's mobile.

There's nothing to believe in. A.

Liv had been given a sparkler, she darted out into the snow with it. Alma stood alongside her parents, watching Liv from the window. No one said a word. Jon noticed that Alma had grown taller, her soft chubbiness was gradually disappearing, allowing another girl to reveal herself. Another Alma. Her eyes were heavily made-up, her face dusted white with powder—it looked quite dramatic. Like a boy playing a girl in some medieval pageant. She would be sixteen this year. They still called her Lull, but it didn't really fit anymore.

They stood quietly side by side, all three of them, watching Liv outside in the snow with her sparkler. The sky was black.

Alma took a deep breath.

"Did you know I went to Milla's funeral?" she said. "I went. You two didn't go, but I did."

Jon and Siri turned to look at their daughter. Her eyes were fixed on the window.

"And by the way," she continued, turning slowly to her father, "I saw her that night."

Siri shut her eyes and shook her head.

"Alma," she said, "are you sure, I mean —"

"I was with Grandma in the car," Alma went on. "And we were racing up the road and then I said *Stop* and Grandma stopped and we looked back and I said something like *That's Milla sitting there, all funny-looking, by the side of the road, shouldn't we take her with us* and Grandma said *Who* and I thought that maybe Milla wouldn't like us to see her like that, sitting at the side of the road, that she wanted to be alone, that it would only embarrass her if she realized that we'd seen her, it was only a few yards up to the house, and Grandma said *Who's sitting at the side of the road* and I said *Nobody, just drive on, there's nobody there, forget it*, and she drove on."

And Siri and Jon turned to Alma and Alma burst into tears and then Liv ran in, for the thousandth time crying: "Happy New Year, everybody!"

The next morning Siri packed backpacks and bags, stripped the beds, emptied the fridge, emptied the larder, emptied the drawers, put all the food into paper bags to take back to Oslo—there wasn't that much left, but Siri never threw away food. Then she vacuumed and washed the floors, swept the stairs, every single step, and wiped down the banister with a cloth.

Jon had gone out to the garage to check that everything was as it should be, he had straightened the tarpaulin covering the Opel, then he had gone up to the attic, cleared away notebooks in which he had written very little, and glanced through the collection of CDs, which were his, and the record collection, which must have been Jenny's, and after that he stood for a moment, looking out of the window at the meadow white with snow. He remembered standing here watching Alma and Liv and Milla, remembered Alma doing a wild dance, as if she knew he was watching her.

They had told her that she couldn't have done anything one way or the other. *What had happened to Milla had nothing to do with Jenny not stopping the car.* There was no connection between these two things. The house had been only yards away. Milla could have gotten up from the side of the road and walked home, of course she could. Alma must never, never, never blame herself.

Alma had stared long and hard at them both and at last she had said, "It's not true what you're saying. You're lying! There's plenty of connection. There's lots we could have done!"

And now they were leaving. Jon drew a finger over his CDs and turned, hearing something down in the hall. The vacuum cleaner. Its drone had stopped.

"Jon," Siri called softly, "we have visitors. You better come down."

He walked slowly down the stairs. He counted every step, hoping that this time they might actually swallow him up. Siri turned and looked at him, Liv and Alma beside her. They too turned. Liv was wearing the invisibility cloak that Siri had given her, and that Siri had once been given by her father. Liv put a finger to her lips, looked at Jon, and breathed *shh*. Also standing there were a man and a woman. Jon knew who they were. Siri didn't need to introduce them, but she did anyway.

"You know Milla's mother and father," she said. "Jon, you remember Amanda and Mikkel."

"Hello," Jon said.

"Hello," said the woman, who was carrying a large brown leather bag over her shoulder.

Jon regarded Amanda, that slim, taut woman with her dancer's body and her hair drawn severely back from her face. He wondered whether he should ask her about her text messages. Whether she didn't think it had gone far enough now. He wondered whether he should ask what they were doing here, what did they mean by showing up here like this, breaking in on him and his wife and children? It was a goddamned invasion. That's what it felt like. He looked at Alma. She stared at the floor. He looked at Siri and at Liv in her invisibility cloak and at the two strangers here in their house. He thought of Leopold, lying asleep beside the hearth. Next week Siri was going to take him to the vet to be put down. Why weren't Amanda and Mikkel in their own house? Why were they here? It wouldn't have made any difference: The scrapbook that he had stolen from the annex that night and read and torn up and thrown in the lake. The picture he had taken of Milla, the one she had liked so much. The car with Jenny and Alma in it, hurtling past her as she lay there in the ditch. K.B. was the guilty party. K.B. and nobody else. An ordinary young man called K.B. He conjured up the image of the big slug under Milla's duvet. He looked at Milla's mother and wanted to shout, he didn't know quite what, but he wanted to shout that she and her husband had to go now and leave them in peace, but instead he walked over to them and shook their hands, and Siri said, "Why don't I fix us something to eat." She said, "It's not much. But you have to eat, right? Sometimes you forget to eat and things become awfully hard, and I have bread and I have cheese and I have some nice ham and a really good jam that I got from Liv for Christmas."

She chivied them all into the kitchen and unpacked the bags of food. She found a tablecloth, put it on the table, pulled out the chairs, and said, "Sit down, sit down, now you'll have something to eat," and Amanda and Mikkel and Jon and Alma and Liv sat down, and then Amanda opened her mouth and blurted out: "I wanted to ask you about that summer with Milla—"

Her husband interrupted her. "It's just that...it's just that I wake up every morning and it takes about a tenth of a second before I remember that she's actually gone, and I wish it were longer...that tenth of a second, I mean." He stared at the table. "I wish it were longer," he repeated.

Amanda lifted the big brown leather bag onto her lap, opened it, and took out a book. She placed it on the table. On the cover was a black-and-white photograph of a little girl with brown curly hair and dark eyes, wearing a pair of dotted underpants that were a little too big for her. Amanda spoke slowly.

"This is a book I put together years ago to tie in with an exhibition. I thought you might like to have a look at it."

The photograph must have been taken in the summer, Jon thought, as he leafed through the book, not knowing what else to do while Milla's parents struggled to compose themselves. The little girl in the grass was wearing nothing but dotted underpants and her skin was all tanned. You could sense the color of her even though the photo was in black and white. The skinny little torso, with the shading of the ribs. The long arms and the long legs. The tiny nipples where her breasts would one day develop.

The little girl stared straight into the camera lens unsmiling.

"Why is the book called *Amanda's?*" asked Liv, who had just learned to read and had now taken off her invisibility cloak.

Amanda looked at her and shook her head.

"Because," she said, "because it was me who...my name's Amanda...this was something Milla and I did when she was just a little bit younger than you are now." Amanda nodded to Liv. "One summer a long time ago."

"I really liked her," said Alma, who had taken the book from her father and was now flicking through it. "But these pictures don't look like her at all—I mean even if she is a child here and I only knew her as an adult. She looked so different when she was with us." She put down the book and looked at Amanda and Mikkel. "She was nice. She taught me to do my makeup, she taught me to do smoky eyes." Alma fluttered her eyelids.

"And I remember us dancing together. And she told me that she believed in God, and she told me that she used to play rock, paper, scissors with you."

Alma nodded to Mikkel and Mikkel nodded back.

"Yes," Siri said, "we need to talk. But first," she said, with a wave of her hand, "won't you have something to eat? Look. It's all laid out. Help yourselves."

And Jon surveyed the table that Siri had set while he and the others had been looking at the book. The little girl stared up at him from the page. He grabbed a slice of bread, took a bite and swallowed. It was good. He said, "We only knew Milla for that one summer." He turned to Amanda and Mikkel. "But maybe you could tell us a little bit about her. There's so much we've wondered about. So much we don't know."

"But we've wondered too," Amanda said. "We have questions too. That's why we're here. We never heard from you, so I sent you messages. Although it's not like me to send messages like that. It's not who I am. It's just that everything was so...nothing was any good. And I have so many questions. And Mikkel has so many questions. And we can't seem to work this out. We can't move on."

Siri looked at Alma, she looked at Jon and Liv, and she looked at the two who had just arrived, and she saw that they too had helped themselves to food, and then she said, "Couldn't we just sit here for a while and have something to eat and talk about Milla? Why don't we do that? Yes," she said, placing both hands on the table. "Yes," she said again. "I think that's what we should do now."

LINN ULLMANN is an award-winning author, journalist, and literary critic. Her four novels have been published in more than fifteen languages, all of them critically acclaimed international best sellers: *Before You Sleep*, *Stella Descending*, *Grace*, and *A Blessed Child*. She lives in Oslo with her husband and children.

BARBARA J. HAVELAND is a translator of fiction, poetry, and drama by leading Danish and Norwegian writers such as Peter Høeg, Jens Christian Grøndahl, Pia Juul, Morten Søndergaard, Øystein Lønn, Jan Kjærstad, and Merete Morken Andersen. She lives in Denmark.